TOKYO TANGO

TOKYO TANGO

Rika Yokomori
translated by Tom Gill

Duckworth Overlook
London • New York • Woodstock

First published in Japan by Bungei Shunju-sha
First published in the UK in 2006 by
Duckworth Overlook

LONDON
90-93 Cowcross Street, London EC1M 6BF
inquiries@duckworth-publishers.co.uk
www.ducknet.co.uk

NEW YORK
The Overlook Press
141 Wooster Street, New York, NY 10012

WOODSTOCK
The Overlook Press
One Overlook Drive, Woodstock, NY 12498
www.overlookpress.com
[for individual orders and bulk sales in the United States,
please contact our Woodstock office]

This book has been selected by the Japanese Literature Publishing
Project (JLPP), which is run by the Japanese Literature Publishing
and Promotion Center (J-Lit Center) on behalf of the
Agency for Cultural Affairs of Japan.

A catalogue record for this book is available
from the British Library

ISBN 0 7156 3543 3 (Pbk)
ISBN 1 58567 814 7 (Hbk)

Typeset by Ray Davies
Printed and bound in Great Britain by
Creative Print and Design, Ebbw Vale, Wales

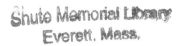

ONE

'Whatever you do, never go with a gambler. A gambler may have one big win, but he'll use up a lifetime's luck on it. Life is long. People don't die that easily. An ordinary life but a long one – that's what I call winning.'

This was what my mother said to me when I first started going out with Bogey.

'Bogey' was the nickname that emerged on our first date. Sitting across the table from me in the dim, candle-lit bar, he suddenly took it into his head to pretend he was Humphrey Bogart in *Casablanca*.

'"Last night? That's so long ago, I don't remember."'

So saying, he leaned back and blew two long, slow streams of smoke through his flared nostrils.

Look at the size of those nostrils, I thought. They reminded me of an old Japanese saying: 'People with big nostrils spend money like water.'

Hmm ... some truth in those old proverbs.

Still, he looked kind of interesting and pleasant in an everyday sort of way.

'Just call me Bogey,' he said.

Right then he looked more like Yogi Bear than Humphrey Bogart, but I decided to humour him. So 'Bogey' it was.

Somehow Bogey and I hit it off right from the word go. Or as he put it, in his weird Japanese English, we were a 'just-meet feeling couple'.

Eventually, Bogey got to be like Linus's blanket in *Peanuts* for me. He was my favourite possession, and I didn't feel right if I couldn't get hold of him. He was warm, hard to do without, and I wanted to drag him around with me everywhere I went. The most comfortable blanket in the world, right next to my skin, that was Bogey. There was something about that pet name that seemed to say it all about my love for him in the early days.

Of course, I didn't know then what a wet blanket he could be.

I was nineteen; he was going on forty. And he was one hell of a gambler.

☆

My mother knew all about gamblers. Her family had run a small construction company in one of Tokyo's rougher districts. It thrived, but it was also a line of business with a fair amount of *yakuza*-style involvement. My granddad was a pretty straight, hard-working guy, and he got the company off the ground, but the next generation – my uncles – well, they were a bunch of wasters. They were brats to the bone. There wasn't a way of burning money they didn't try, not a lemon they didn't suck dry.

They grew up in an era when Japan hadn't yet got properly rich, when people still used to mouth the old wartime slogan, 'Luxury is the enemy'. No one had told my uncles about the slogan, apparently. Playing around with geishas, concealing bastard offspring, gambling for high stakes, wearing designer threads, gourmet dining, Harley-Davidsons (at a time when there were only three of them in the whole of Japan), booze, drugs, the clap, failed love affairs ending in attempted murder – between them my uncles mastered just about every mode of behaviour frowned upon by respectable society.

Granddad died. Uncle Keizo, a man with a magnificent tattoo all over his back, inherited the business and proceeded to ruin my mother's family. She reckoned his gambling was the cause of all the trouble.

'Keizo's creditors took every single thing we had: the factory, the house, the lot. Things were going from bad to worse when I was your age; they even carted off the decorative rocks and trees in the garden, and your grandma's kimonos went to the pawnshop one by one. When I was twenty years old, I phoned my folks one day and a stranger answered. At first I thought I'd got the wrong number, but it was the same thing each time I dialled. Can you believe it? They'd actually sold the telephone line.'

Having grown up in the wreckage of a household of wasters, my mother was determined that she, at least, would lead a decent, respectable life, and that whatever happened she'd always walk the road of independence. Even if somebody's life were at stake, she wouldn't allow herself to get into money trouble. This was in the days when women weren't supposed to go out to work, and she hadn't been to university, so there weren't too many jobs she could hope to land.

'I wanted to become a lawyer. But when I told Uncle Keizo I wanted to go to university, he told me a woman's place was in the kitchen, washing potatoes.'

Ma somehow swallowed her pride and went looking for a job. A middling sort of insurance company took her on, selling policies door to door. Her own policy was to lead an upright, civilised life, staying out of debt and avoiding trouble with the police.

And that's how I, with all that bad blood in me, came to be brought up as good as gold – like it or not.

She made me do piano, English conversation, oil painting, stuff I was never going to keep up for long, and she made me quite incapable of doing the things I'd probably have been better at – shoplifting, smoking, booze, boyfriends, sniffing glue, riding motorbikes … those little rites of passage that make youth so exciting.

I couldn't lie, I couldn't cheat. If I'd ever stepped out of line – well, my indulgent dad might have let me off, but Ma would have had me gated and whipped. She was that tough.

On top of it all, when I was in middle school, my indulgent father suddenly got up and left.

Dad was a third-rate suit in some company. Ma got better and better at selling insurance, and the richer she got, the more pathetic Dad became. Caught between a super-tough wife and a cheeky daughter who took after her, he had no place to turn at home. So he developed a serious attachment to the *mama-san* who ran one of the hostess bars he used to hang out at. Only this *mama-san* was being kept by some *yakuza*, and there was a whole load of trouble. In the end the pair of them did a runner. It would have been glamorous if they'd gone to South America or somewhere like that, but we heard through the grapevine that they'd holed up just a few prefectures away, in Kochi. Ma didn't bother to chase after him.

'Who needs a guy like that? Good riddance to bad rubbish! Let's you and me live together – just the two of us.'

My mother sounded so bold and decisive you'd have thought she was a man in woman's clothing. As for me, I was still too much of a kid, and didn't really understand what was going on.

In character I took after my mother, but I looked just like my dad, so he doted on me when I was small. But as I got bigger my insolent nature asserted itself, and I guess it was hard for him to take since he'd already lost the respect of his wife.

He got to look more pathetic with every passing year. I don't have a lot of memories of my father, but I do recall him coming home drunk one evening and sitting on the table in the kitchen, going on and on about how his career was shot to pieces because his boss was mean to him or something, how his wife and his kid didn't respect him, how unfair and unsatisfactory everything was in the whole wide world. He was sniggering in a twisted sort of way, *heh-heh, heh*, and had a feeble grin on his face. I felt physically sick.

Dad had an unrelenting bitterness in his eyes, and a sneer that had nowhere to go played around his mouth. Through his laughter he may have been trying to show that he was big enough to laugh at his own situation. Or maybe he realised that his troubles were all of his own making and he was jeering at his own weakness. Either way, I hated that weird laugh of his.

That's just about the only memory I have of him. I guess it's the closest he ever got to self-expression. They say some people 'cast a thin shadow', a turn of phrase that fitted my father like a glove. Too weak, too kind, he couldn't even say goodbye to my mother and me when he left. Weak and pathetic, pathetic and sad – that was Dad.

After he disappeared, my mother's one remaining hope was to get me into university. To her, missing out on university had been the greatest mess-up of her own life, and she said to me, 'Just get yourself into a good school and after that I'll let you do whatever you like.' She had decided that her responsibilities as a mother would be fulfilled if she brought me up properly and gave me a decent education.

Alas, however, I didn't grow up to be the intellectual my mother had in mind. I was a feather-brained girl with hardly a thought in my head. I did have a certain low cunning, I suppose, but mastering the techniques of passing university entrance exams had nothing to do with true intelligence.

Mind you, such fine distinctions didn't bother Ma one bit. Along with a natural wish to see her child happy, she was consumed by a powerful desire to prove that she could raise a child all by herself. My mother's life was spent in perpetual competition with other people. If she couldn't get me into a good school, she would never make up for the points she'd lost from her husband's disappearance. She made me painfully aware of her feelings on the matter: 'If you can't get into university you won't get any money from me.'

With that threat hanging over my head, I got her to send me to a night school to cram for the exams. I liked it better that way. Taking lessons till late in a noisy, overcrowded classroom was marginally better than studying at home under my mother's obsessive gaze.

Eventually I managed to get into Sakura Women's University. It was the nearest women-only college to my house, and all my mother's friends called it 'a good school'. Anywhere would do for me, so long as it agreed with her idea of a good university. When I heard that I'd passed the exam, I heaved a sigh of relief. Now, at last, she would leave me in peace.

I entered university without any particular dreams or aspirations. I hadn't got the slightest interest in all that stuff about 'warm, friendly campus life among hard-working fellow students'. The moment I walked through the gates, free at last from parental control, the bad blood in me came bubbling and boiling to the surface.

As soon as I'd finished the entrance exams, I chucked away my virginity on a passing boyfriend I didn't like that much, then promptly ditched him, mainly because I was fed up with his scruffy, poor-boy lifestyle. He was in a student new-wave band and was kind of good-looking because he had some foreign blood, but my friends called him 'Mister Ten by Twenty' because they reckoned his long, thin face measured ten centimetres by twenty.

Too poor to afford manners or pride, he'd always want to make love at my place because he couldn't afford a hotel, or he'd bring me an overripe melon as a present because it was going cheap at the store. We'd have furtive sex before my mother came home from work, or when she was away on business. When we got hungry we'd eat any leftovers lying around the house. That was good enough for him.

'Man, I'm hungry!'

'There's nothing here – shall we go out to eat?'

'Eh? Whatever's in the fridge will do fine.'

'All we've got is some cod's roe and salmon roe in soy sauce that somebody gave us, and a few pickles.'

'That'll do nicely! Sounds yummy. Salmon roe in soy sauce? You guys live off the fat of the land!'

There was no answer to that. He didn't have a shred of masculine pride.

On top of that he was always late for dates. The last time – well, it didn't help that it was a very wet, sticky day in the rainy season, 120 per cent on the discomfort scale – he kept me waiting for a solid half hour in front of the statue of Hachiko the Faithful Dog at Shibuya Station. When he finally showed up, grinning sheepishly and making some pathetic excuse about his band practice running late, I completely lost it.

'You stupid bastard! Leaving me standing around waiting for you again and again and again! You and the sweet words you say only when you want a fuck! You don't love me, you bastard! I'm through with you!'

'Hey, stop it! Ow! That hurts!'

Through my tears I noticed that I was hitting and stabbing him with my rolled umbrella.

After that I always made sure that I had more than one boyfriend on call, and I embarked on a period of devotion to the three supreme pleasures of boozing, partying and shopping.

I just wanted to go somewhere with someone. Any person and any place would do, so long as they were trendy. I didn't know anything about booze, so I'd order cocktails, starting from the top of the menu and working my way down until I was legless. Following a night of dedicated debauchery, I'd struggle home after dawn. Quite often I'd have embarrassing encounters with Ma in the street when she was taking the garbage out in the morning.

On such occasions she'd look at me as if I were subhuman.

'You're putrescent,' she'd say.

It was a strange word; at the time it sounded like some kind of VD symptom, but looking back I now understand it well enough. There was definitely a spiritual corruption about me in those days.

Without a clear objective before me, such as exams that needed passing, I couldn't stand being alone in the house. I'd feel its loneliness seeping through my body. The memory of my dad, always sitting with hunched shoulders, still clung to the walls. Although I'd treated him coldly when he was around, now that he was gone the place felt more miserable than ever. These days my mother didn't come back at any fixed time, and without her around the house was sunk in deep silence.

Worse was to follow. Ma found herself a new boyfriend, and the old geezer started coming and going as he pleased. This guy was married with kids, so they couldn't see each other whenever they wanted. When they were not in contact, Ma would rely on me for company, but when he showed up she'd make it perfectly clear that I was in the way.

I was not loved. I was just an encumbrance. That thought made me feel wilder still. Yet at home I had to act the role of a cheerful young lady to keep mother sweet. If I annoyed her she might cut off the money, and that would be the end. I had no intention of slaving away at part-time jobs and working my way through university – that wasn't my style. So I wound up drawing a very sharp line between home and the rest of my life. I learned to behave in a very adult way for a kid my age.

Better to have fun when you have the chance than not to. So long as I kept up appearances at home, Ma's boyfriend would slip me some pocket money now and again and occasionally take us out to a restaurant. Still a teenager, I strove to be as calculating as possible; that was my method of self-defence.

I no longer felt at ease at home. Home was a crucible of restlessness, loathing, alienation and loneliness. Ma's boyfriend was allergic to cats, so she even got rid of the beloved tabby we'd had for years. My life was becoming an unending procession of miseries, and I was ashamed of my inability to do anything about this.

The only time I felt a bit better was when some guy would chat me up over a drink, or when we were having sex – because then I felt I was worth something. Only then could I feel happy because somebody wanted something I had. To fill the emptiness in my soul I filled the hole between my legs. In the first six months after I dumped my first boyfriend I must have had well over twenty guys – if you count the one-night stands.

I was wearing myself out, body and soul, looking for that special someone who could heal my loneliness. Someone reliable and warm, someone who would love me passionately and no one else, someone who'd never neglect or abandon me.

But it was no good expecting that kind of service from the young men I hung out with. They were as empty-headed as I was and incapable of loving anyone except themselves. They only wanted one thing and they wanted it all the time. The more I gave them what they wanted, the more the emptiness piled up inside me.

✲

This was all going on in the early 1980s. At that time Japan was poised to enter the 'bubble era', when the economy heated up to boiling point and finally became totally out of control. People craved money and material possessions, and the city was full of beautiful goods and elegant spaces such as had never been seen before. Above all, everything was expensive. Kids are idiots and slaves to desire. We didn't know what we really wanted, so we wanted everything.

I myself was young. I wanted everything I saw and everything I heard about, and if there was somewhere where fun could be had, I wanted to go there. I would tire of things the moment I had them, and I was never, ever satisfied. My pet phrases were 'This sucks' and 'Isn't there something better?' What I particularly craved was money.

There's not a lot to a teenager's life. Dancing at fashionable discos; going to gigs at trendy venues; shopping for designer clothes at sales; going on dates to nice little cafés or bars. You soon get bored with that stuff, and then what you want to do is to have the kind of fun you can't afford, or go to places where kids can't get in on their own.

My image of such places was drawn from the hotels my mother took me to on my birthday: the elegant restaurants where the customers weren't all students and teenagers, and those cool, uncrowded boutiques that sold designer fashions at non-discount prices. But going to places like that without Ma required cash.

Everybody wants money in a capitalist society, and that desire doesn't necessarily mean you're spiritually sick. You're sick when your desire for money has no limit, and when you'll stop at nothing to get it.

Most of my friends had little part-time jobs as waitresses in coffee shops or as private tutors. When I heard about the wages that they were getting, and the hassle they went through to get them, I thought, *No way!* I had an inflated sense of pride; I didn't want to bow and scrape to anyone. Besides, my lust for money was now completely out of control and could not be quenched with what my friends were making working at part-time jobs. It would be like chucking a glass of water at a forest fire. Motivated by the desire for cash to buy clothes and go partying, I got a friend to introduce me to a hostess club, surreptitiously donned a long wig, and started working there without breathing a word to my mother. At first I was pleased with the 10,000 yen I was paid for a four-hour shift, but that started to look pretty pathetic once my lecherous *nouveau riche* patrons took to slipping 10,000-yen notes into my pocket, along with a phone number and a whispered invitation to give them a call and join them for dinner one evening.

At places like that, customers pay through the nose, and a lot of them think that that entitles them to try it on with the hostesses – a warped notion of 'free love'. That's why they came on to you like this. They liked to give the girls a whiff of the big money – money that can be got so much more easily than by sitting around for hours straining to keep a polite smile in place.

Seeing that it was in my nature to gravitate toward easy money, had I stayed on at that club I would probably have become a hostess in name but a common prostitute in practice. Indeed, for every honest hostess there are several prostitutes using that job title as a gossamer-thin veneer of respectability. Rot like that spreads fast, and pretty soon I was flirting with trouble.

Once you break one taboo, others soon come tumbling down. Once you start rolling downhill, you carry on rolling until you reach the lowest point. For someone with no aim in life and who has never known love, leading a respectable life seems utterly pointless and unbearable. But if you get the money and time to allow you freedom, feelings just run that much wilder. I fell into a pit of loneliness deeper than I'd ever known.

Three nights a week I would sneak out from beneath my mother's gaze, do my bit of hostessing in the Ginza, act like a prostitute with any horny old geezer who'd pay, then blow the proceeds on having all sorts of expensive fun that wasn't really fun at all. During the university's spring vacation, I was at more of a loose end than usual. It was then that Hajime, one of my casual, doesn't-really-matter boyfriends, came up with a suggestion.

'Hey, Saya, why don't we go for this temporary job? You haven't got anything to do in the vacation anyway, right? Why don't we work for a month and spend the money on a trip somewhere?'

I couldn't think of any particular reason to say no.

It was quite a good idea, actually. Spend the day at some undemanding part-time job, run over to the Ginza for hostessing in the evening, then skip off on a journey somewhere. There'd be no time to think – it'd be very relaxing!

What I didn't know was that the company that was advertising for temps and part-timers was none other than Kabutocho Journal, an investment consultancy firm shortly to achieve notoriety in a massive fraud scandal.

'It seems to be a risky company,' said Hajime, 'but that needn't bother us since we'll only be temping. It says here that men can earn over 200,000 yen a month in sales, and women can make 700 yen an hour answering the phone. We'll just work there for a month, pick up our pay, and quit.'

'Er, well, all right.'

Our first day there it snowed – unseasonably and surprisingly heavily. It was settling fast. 'Oh, look!' I squealed to Hajime as we came out of Kyobashi Station and frolicked in the drifts, 'Everything's white all over!'

We emerged from the station and Hajime took me crunching through the crisp snow toward the Kabutocho Journal offices. Tall and thin as a beanpole, and clad from tip to toe in designer clothing by the likes of Y's and Comme des Garçons, Hajime resembled nothing so much as a walking boutique clothes hanger. In those days he was one of my more presentable boyfriends. Thinking back now, though, he was a bit like Wally in *Where's Wally?*. It was really difficult to spot the guy beneath all the smart clothing. Certainly there wasn't a glimmer of sex appeal about his skeletal frame. On the other hand, his dad was head of a small company and let Hajime have his own gold credit card, which he could hit for several hundred thousand yen a month, and now and again he'd buy me stuff. I wouldn't say that that was the only reason I went out with him, but since I didn't like anyone in particular, I felt I might as well go with a rich kid. It made life that much more pleasant.

Alas, when his father's firm went bankrupt, Hajime's most appealing feature just faded away. He'd had his gold card taken off him, which was why he was looking for part-time work. And since he didn't want me dating another guy while he was at work, he'd had the idea of taking me along so he could keep an eye on me.

'What's this Kabutocho Journal, anyway?' I asked. 'Does it publish business magazines or something?'

Though we sensed that there was something fishy about the company, Hajime and I were horribly ignorant. We didn't know that Kabutocho, where the company was based, was globally famous for being the Tokyo equivalent of Wall Street. We didn't even know that there were these grown-up folk trying to get rich by buying and selling shares in companies and stuff. We were babes in arms. The only things on our minds were the cool musicians we saw on MTV, or the new café-bar in Nishi-Azabu, or some product we fancied – that sort of thing.

'Maybe we should have changed trains and got off at Kayabacho, after all. Careful you don't slip, Saya.'

The snow was piling up. On either side of the snow-covered road we started to notice heaps of posh cars.

'What's this? Ferrari? Lamborghini Countach? Mercedes Benz? MR2? This place looks like a supercar fair!'

Hajime's eyes were as round as soup plates.

'It's incredible! This company must be raking it in. The ad said men get paid according to ability, so maybe if I really made an effort...'

Like a donkey with a carrot dangling in front of it, Hajime was suddenly ablaze with enthusiasm for the work, whatever it was.

'"Kabutocho Journal". There it is!'

We saw the name emblazoned on a cheap plastic signboard on top of a small rental office building. We went in and took the lift up to the floor indicated, to a room full of grey metal desks, each with a shady-looking character hunched over a telephone. The room was thick with cigarette smoke. Each desk had a small, fat volume on it entitled *Quarterly Corporate Reports*.

From a window seat at the back of the room, a tubby little man emerged smiling. He appeared to be the personnel manager.

'Hi! Thanks for coming. All right, the girl can sit over there and answer the phone. If somebody calls, say nicely, "Good morning, this is Kabutocho Journal, how may I help you?" If the caller asks for someone by name, ask them to hold and pass the call on. The seating layout and telephone extensions are all on this piece of paper. Some of the guys have two names. We change the seating order every week according to sales results, but you'll get the updated list. Now, see the names on this other memo? If you get a call for one of these names, you say, "I'm sorry, he's not at his desk right now." If they ask when he's coming back, you say, "Sorry, I'm only temping here and I don't know." OK?' He rattled on like this for a while.

Well! This was *really* shady. Hajime and I exchanged meaningful glances.

'Er, what about the interview?'

'Oh, that! No need. I'm sure you'll both do fine. I mean, you're college students, right? We don't pay much attention to age or qualifications here, but we're glad to get bright young people working for us. We get quite a few student part-timers as a matter of fact. These days students are always planning "events", you know. And they work hard to raise the funds for them. Oh yes. Umm, I'll take the boy to another building.' He turned to Hajime. 'You can come back here once you've learned the ropes and started to make a few sales.'

Hajime and I exchanged glances again. The room had virtually emptied, leaving only a vaguely irritable-looking guy aged forty or so and a young lad with bad-boy looks and big, round yellow-tinted glasses like Akira out of Finger Five.

Bad Boy looked extremely young. He glared at Hajime and me and hissed 'Punks!' in a low, half-strangled voice. Hajime and I looked at each other nervously. We'd never met people like this before. We felt under pressure, but at the same time I have to admit it was exciting.

'OK, I'll give you a call later on,' murmured Hajime, and with that he followed the absurdly cheerful roly-poly personnel manager out of the room. From that moment on I had to sit behind a dull grey desk in a room that stank of stale cigarette smoke.

Good morning, this is Kabutocho Journal. Good morning, this is Kabutocho Journal. Please wait a moment. He's not at his desk right now.

I kept practising my lines in my mind, but the telephone never rang.

What is this weird company? If only I'd brought a paperback along...

My idle thoughts were interrupted by feeling a piercing gaze directed at me from behind my right cheek. Bad Boy was talking to me in his insolent bad-boy drawl.

'Hmm, not too much of a dog on closer inspection. What's your name, then?'

'Saya Takagishi.'

'Oh yeah. And that guy who was here just now – he's your bit of stuff, is he?'

'Er, well, sort of, I suppose.'

'*Er, well, sort of, I suppose*? Good grief! Heh-heh-heh. Oh well, it doesn't matter. Look, sorry about just now. I can see that you don't look like a punk at all. I used to get into lots of fights with punks a long time ago, down in Harajuku, you know? Even now, when I see guys dressed in black I always think they must be punks. Can't seem to help it.'

Bad Boy proceeded to clue me in on what the company did and what went on in the room.

The job involved working your way through a list of clients' telephone numbers and persuading the clients to buy stocks that had been selected by someone higher up. From the client's point of view, it was a matter of sending cash to the company, which theoretically would use it to buy promising stocks on the client's behalf. In fact, however, the company used the money as operating capital to buy much larger parcels of other stocks – ones that it really did fancy – and never actually bought the stocks it had been recommending.

'The point is we use their money to buy other, more profitable shares, make a wad for ourselves, and then give the clients back their original investment, saying we're terribly sorry but the stocks didn't go up this time, or something like that.'

I didn't completely understand what he was on about, but I did gather that the key was to sweet-talk the client into believing that he was going to make a packet so that he would send his money to the company. Apparently Bad Boy was particularly good at this.

'The better your sales record, the closer they move your desk to the window on the sunny side of the room. The guy nearest the door – in the darkest seat with the foulest air – he's bottom of the league. Naturally, I'm top of the league in this room, which is why I'm sitting here, with the best view of the cute little girl on the telephone. And let me tell you that this seat is mine for keeps, 'coz the rest of them have got shit for brains. The world's full of idiots, but the guys in this place are really the pits. You saw that old geezer sitting in the middle of the room just now? He's always going on about his student days at Waseda University because most of us never went to college. Anyway, his sales record ain't going nowhere. In fact, it's worse than that. He's got a load of fancy theories about how to predict share prices from data and uses them to buy stuff on his own account – but he's always losing, the stupid wally. He came here to pay off his debts, and all he's done is sink deeper and deeper in debt. He'll never get out, never!'

Once Bad Boy started talking, you couldn't stop him – just as you'd expect from a master of sales spiel. Apparently the irritable old guy used to run his own publishing production company, which went bust, leaving him up to his neck in debt. He'd come here hoping to make enough to clear his losses.

'So that's why he seemed so bad-tempered. By the way, why is no one here now?'

'You really don't know much, do you, Saya? The stock exchange closes at three. They won't be back till evening 'coz they've been here since seven this morning. And then they'll be around till ten o'clock tonight. It's all right for me, I'm young, but the rest of 'em are tired old guys. They need a rest, yeah? They'll be back in the early evening, ready to start calling up office workers at their homes.'

Amazingly, Bad Boy was only eighteen. He'd quit senior high school after three months, lied about his age to get hired by the company, and had recently purchased the red Ferrari buried in the snow below.

For a moment I wondered what sort of a world this was, how much Ferraris cost, and so on. But then I thought, *Oh well, it's got nothing to do with me. It seems kind of fun here, and in a month I'll get my salary and quit.*

21

From that day on my life became very busy. The moment I finished my stint on the telephone I was ready to put on my night-work face. I didn't have time to think too deeply about the things happening around me.

✫

I'd sit in the club from eight till midnight, then head for the station with my girlfriends from work to catch the last train at half-past, scoffing hot rice-cakes bought at roadside stalls and swapping rude comments about the evening's customers as we rushed to the subway platform. With a mixture of pleasure and embarrassment, I realised that these hostesses were far tougher and livelier than the affected girls I knew in school.

The bar where I worked, the Cocteau, was probably one of the more respectable bars in the district. The *mama-san* who ran it was supposed to be an artist of some sort. I have no idea if there was any truth in the story – certainly the interior was decked out in the most hideous rococo you ever saw. There were only two professional hostesses there; the rest were college girls like myself, working a few nights a week for pocket money.

A friend called Minako introduced me to the Cocteau. We'd met at the crammer school when we were sweating for our entrance exams. Minako was the daughter of a director of a large pharmaceutical company. He had made a half-hearted attempt to control her lifestyle by skimping on her allowance, so the moment she got into university she'd landed the night job without telling her parents.

'It's easy to think up excuses for your folks when it's only two or three nights a week. You just tell your mother that campus life has changed since her day and that students stay out late a lot more than they used to. Parents know about all the hassle we went through with the entrance exams, so usually they'll let you do what you like, so long as it doesn't make trouble for them.'

Of course sitting around in a bar full of boring middle-aged men isn't exactly fun, so girls who take on jobs like this often try to find a friend to get hired with them so they have someone to talk to. It's part of the scene, really.

Minako was looking for some wealthy patron to sink her hooks into, a doctor ideally, but I think intended victims noticed the predatory gleam in her hawklike eyes, and so far they'd all escaped.

I guess everyone carries the weight of their parents' frustrations through life. Minako's father had wanted to become a doctor, but he wasn't good enough so he had to settle for a job in pharmaceuticals. Minako, however, was a lazy girl – typical friend of mine – who would respond to any challenge with: 'What a drag. I really can't be bothered.' She had no interest in studying like crazy to become a high-powered medic. Her ultimate aim was not to *become* a doctor but to *marry* one.

Minako often used to complain that life was so tedious and hard that she'd be dead before she turned thirty. This was hard to imagine, since she was the picture of robust health. Anyway, the two of us loved to go out on the town with the money we'd made at the Cocteau and blow it as fast as we could on smart clothes and partying. Minako was one of the best of my bad friends.

☆

The house style called for long hair, but I wore my hair in an art deco bob cropped short at the back. So I borrowed the wig Minako had used (she had been growing her hair since the summer and it was already down to her shoulders) and learned from the *mama-san* the gentle art of applying make-up thick enough to show up in the dim lights of the club. The *mama-san* also lent me some flashy suits and dresses she'd worn in her youth, and with that I was ready to hold the stage at the Cocteau.

When the club closed for the night I'd get changed at the speed of light and dash for the train. I didn't even have time to take off my wig.

The last subway train would be jam-packed with drunken old men. They were totally out of it, asleep on their feet, and sometimes they'd even chuck up on themselves, right there in the train. *Why on earth do they do it? Why not just have a quiet drink at home?* Enduring the last train was understandable for someone like myself who was doing it for money, but these guys had actually paid for this misery. It was a perennial mystery to me.

Once I'd got off the last train with its stinking cargo of booze-soaked wretches, for me things were even tougher. In the few minutes it took me to walk home from the station, I had to get the wig off under cover of darkness, conceal it in my bag, and rub off the worst of the eye-liner with a cotton swab I'd earlier soaked in cleansing oil.

If my mother was still up when I got home, the encounter would be more awkward than when I came home after dawn. This was because the *mama-san* who ran off with Dad had been a typical hostess, with dyed, reddish hair and super-thick eye shadow. When Ma had lifted the ban on me going out and partying, she'd imposed a couple of conditions: 'Don't work in a bar and don't dye your hair, OK?'

In order to bring me up properly, she'd worked like a slave for years, resolutely ignoring the loss of her figure and her whitening hair. She was both jealous and contemptuous of women who dyed their hair, beautified themselves, and made a business out of the blunt fact of being a woman.

✳

A week into my new job at Kabutocho Journal, Hajime and I compared notes. Hajime was burning with enthusiasm and very busy. His eyes shone with excitement – he was a man transformed.

'It's an incredible world, really! In the morning we have this ceremony where we all stand at attention, like a bunch of *yakuza*, yeah? We get a pep talk from this real fat guy with a beard who talks with an Osaka accent – he's the chairman or something. He does crazy stuff, like cracking a boiled egg on his head right there in front of everybody – it's straight out of the comics! He has these two beautiful girls, one on each side of him. They're like fashion models and they're supposed to be his secretaries or something, but of course he's sleeping with them. They're with him all day long, and he just gets them to run off a few photocopies for him now and then.'

'And what are you doing, Hajime?'

'Telephone sales. If you sell a lot you get enormous bonuses. I seem to be pretty good at it, so I think I can do OK. I'll be able to start buying clothes for you again. Like that Bigi summer outfit – remember? – The one in the sailor style. You liked that, didn't you?'

Is he some kind of an idiot? Is there nothing else he'd rather be doing?

That's what I thought. What I said was, 'Wow! Fantastic!'

Somehow I'd got into a state where all I could do was respond mechanically to each new situation as it came along. All those years of keeping my mother sweet by conforming to her expectations had turned me into a robot, programmed to accept the suggestions of others cheerfully.

'And what about you, Saya?'

'For some reason I was moved to another place today.'

25

'Really?'

'Yeah, a single room in a newish condo, a bit nearer Kayabacho. There are only three guys working there. Me and this other girl, who reckons she's very cute; we handle the telephone and make tea.'

'I see. Oh, and one other thing – you know what the guys at work call you and me? "Romeo and Juliet!" Ha-ha-ha. Amazing! Anyway, how come you got moved?'

'Well, there was this greasy old geezer who strolled into the office and started chatting and sniggering with the personnel manager. Next thing it's all been decided. The personnel guy just said I'd get much better treatment there and took me straight over.'

'And how was it?'

'Well, the room's nice and cozy, and everyone's really friendly. They also seem a lot freer with the cash than the guys in the other room. They treated me to a sushi lunch today.'

'Wow, lucky!'

'I guess you could say that. Abalone and beer for lunch can't be too bad, eh?'

'Abalone? Hey, not fair!'

What a fool I was! I should have sensed that something fishy was going on right away. One day at the end of the week, the greasy guy who'd arranged for my transfer to the new room – apparently he was the boss of this particular office – came over and asked if I was free for lunch.

'It's like this, you see. I've got to go with the president to a French restaurant, the Crescent, in Shiba. Know it? He's taking his girlfriend on a date, but he doesn't want it to be just the two of them in case he runs into one of his wife's friends or something. So he's asked me to come along with a female companion to make a foursome. Well, it wouldn't be too smart if I took the wife, and although I did ask one of the hostesses at a club I go to she's cancelled at the last minute.'

'All right. I've been thinking it would be nice to check out the Crescent.'

'Really? That would be a great help.'

So the fact was that my tea-making day job was really just another type of hostessing. Hostess by day, hostess by night – such was my working life.

Still, I had to admit it was nice to go to a posh French restaurant I'd never been to before, at no cost or trouble to myself. Very nice!

✢

There were some real tight bastards among the customers at the Cocteau. Their only concern was to get laid, cheap. They would slip me the minimum face-saving amount of cash and pay for the love hotel. Some of them clearly thought it was a waste of money to feed a woman good food just for a quick bang, so they'd take me to some god-awful sushi chain. It had to be sushi, of course, nothing common. I think I was supposed to be impressed.

Speaking of mass-market sushi, Ma's boyfriend actually ran a chain of family sushi restaurants and he'd often bring us a jumbo pack of Osaka sushi, which he had the nerve to describe as a present.

A present? You cheapskate! Those are leftovers! Such would be my unvoiced scream of protest. Worse still, he would take us to Mansei, this cheap chain restaurant in Kandabashi that served a boiled beef and vegetable dish called *shabu-shabu*, and tell me to lie to my friends and say that we'd been to Serina, a really posh restaurant in Roppongi that did the best *shabu-shabu* in town. He made me totally sick. I just can't bear these one-track businessmen. How can you go through life calculating profit and loss in every single thing you do?

Mind you, I was spending plenty of time in the company of just

27

such types at the Cocteau. Guys running speciality food stores, owners of little art galleries, jewellers, kimono sellers. Whether there was a limit on how much money they could blow without the company or the wife noticing, or whether they were just business-men to the core, they all used to count every penny spent on their naughty out-of-hours activities.

Even when they were in bed with me, I sometimes noticed that calculating look cross their faces, as if their whole bodies were suffused with thoughts of maximising profit and minimising risk. Just because I was a college student didn't mean they knew where I'd been, and they weren't going to take a chance on catching the clap or being confronted with an unwanted child someday, so they always took good care to wear a condom. With all these considera-tions weighing on them, I used to wonder why they bothered with the whole shabby business in the first place. *Why didn't they just do it with their wives?* It wasn't as if they were trying out any particu-larly exotic moves.

Different girls attracted different customers. For some reason Minako seemed to get all the perverts.

'Oh boy, you should have seen the guy I was with last night! It was incredible! He had a snake! He suddenly pulled it out and plopped it on my belly. I didn't know what to do! Oh boy!'

Regular fetishists – guys with leather gear and whips who wanted her to dress up like an SM queen – were a piece of cake. Minako was quite used to that kind of thing, and she even per-suaded the guys to let her keep some of her favourite bondage clothing, which she then wore to discos. There was this red vinyl studded bodysuit, for instance – she would get up and do her thing with that on at some disco and blow the rest of the girls right off the stage.

Luckily I didn't seem to get those customers. With me it was just regular sex with regular horny guys. The most adventurous they ever got was renting a room with a mirror ceiling and a pommel horse, like a kid going to an amusement park, or taking me to a love hotel with traditional Japanese decor so they could pretend they were with their young mistress on a trip to a secluded rural hot spring. After they were through with their simple, run-of-the-mill sex, they all said the same thing: 'Wow, that was great! Fancy me making love with a young girl like you. You know what? I've got a daughter about your age.'

They said it with feeling, and it was actually sweet to observe them putting all their effort into this pathetic little moment of pleasure – while taking all the necessary precautions, of course.

But sympathy was quite out of place. I wasn't a professional but a student at a top-flight women's university. Not only was I young, but I was also rather proud of my looks. My partner, on the other hand, would have his belly hanging out, or be bald as a coot, or stink of that vile hair oil you always find by the washbowl in love hotels: 'Eroica', or whatever. So this was certainly not the world of true love; it was the world of fleshly pleasure purchased at market rates by men with an eye for a bargain.

I had no sense of wrongdoing. When it was nearly time to go home, I would sit on the bed, watching the guy hand over the cash and smiling vaguely for some reason, wondering how much he had spent on me in the course of the evening and calculating my worth in cash terms.

For a year, now, sex had meant nothing to me, no matter who I slept with. I didn't like any of my partners – in fact, I despised them. Even when we were hard at it, I'd find myself scorning their blind commitment to the job in hand, wondering whether it wasn't extremely silly to get so totally absorbed in something like this.

✫

When I first met Bogey at the Kabutocho Journal offices, I finally began to feel ashamed of myself. Until then I'd never given it a thought, but now it came to me with a sudden flash: *I am unclean.*

I'd never felt that way before. For the first time in my life I'd encountered something warm and pure. Was this to do with something inside me? Or was it Bogey? Either way, from the moment I met him I stopped showing up for the night job, never bothering to give notice, causing no end of trouble and embarrassment for Minako who had introduced me to the Cocteau.

I would never go back to that life. Of course, the big spenders who worked at Kabutocho Journal were hardly likely to patronise a dive like the Cocteau, but the fact was that they were out on the town every night – Ginza, Akasaka, or Roppongi – and you never knew when or where you might run into one of them. What if Bogey himself were to stroll into the club and see me dolled up like a cheap tart? What if he happened to be passing at the very moment I emerged from some shabby love hotel in the company of some disgusting old punter? That would be the end of the world, or so it seemed to me.

☆

Bogey made his first appearance in my life when he turned up at my new workplace early in the week after I'd been moved there.

He wore a Burberry trench coat wrapped around a plump, teddy-bear body. His hair was soft and wavy, some of it having turned prematurely white; his drooping eyes were framed by long, fine lashes, half-hidden beneath smooth, oriental eyelids. He had a small nose and full, slightly pouting, lips. His complexion was olive-coloured and his face looked boyish. Unusually for someone middle-aged, his skin was smooth and dry, not greasy at all.

Bogey was the picture of my ideal man. You couldn't have painted a better one.

The first time I laid eyes on him was when he walked into the office just after lunchtime, brow furrowed, shamelessly picking his nose, flicking cigarette ash in all directions while he read through a crumpled mess of financial and sports papers. Taeko, the other tea girl, cheerfully chided him: 'Honestly, Mr Hotta, how am I going to get the room clean with you messing it up like this?'

'Oh, yeah, you're right … Ha-ha-ha … *excuzee moi!*'

When he was not talking, Bogey had a detached and serious air about him, but the moment he opened his mouth the laughter and witticisms would start to flow. The first thought that came into my mind was: *He's middle-aged, but he doesn't act it. There's something youthful about him.*

Just then there was a telephone call for Bogey and he left the room.

'Who's that?' I asked Taeko. She blushed a little.

'Oh, Saya, don't you know? Of course you don't. He was away last week on a business trip so you haven't seen him before. Not that he shows up much at the office, even when he isn't away on business! His name's Hotta, and, well, he's pretty scrumptious, isn't he? He's the only reason I don't quit, if you want to know!'

'Really?'

'And he's single! Apparently his wife died. They say it was suicide.'

Taeko lowered her voice but carried on in the same gossipy tone.

'These days he's shacked up with a Ginza *mama-san*, but apparently he wants to dump her. She's always calling him up at work, the cow! "This is someone from Mr Hotta's house" – that's how she introduces herself. I don't think he goes home much. He always looks cross when she calls. I hear she even shows up at the company sometimes, begging for money and all. Bitch! He should

31

ditch her right away! Then maybe I ... but ... oh, I don't know! They say he's bad news, a real lady-killer!'

Taeko was getting all worked up. She started cleaning Mr Hotta's desk with gusto.

'I see.'

I started to think about him. And the more I thought of him, the more I liked him.

There was a dark side to his life, but he still had a sense of humour. He never tried to chat up the young girls around him – on the contrary, he seemed thoroughly tired of the game of love. A thought occurred to me: *At first glance he seems cold, but if he really fell for someone, he'd love them deeper than the deep blue sea.*

With a certain animal instinct, I sensed a capacity for deep love in him. What I was searching for, he had. I wanted someone who would care for me, come what may. Someone who would genuinely love me, no conditions attached. Someone who would risk his life to protect me. Bogey had what it took to do all that.

But as I thought about it, I gradually realised how unlikely it was that I might be the recipient of all that love, and sank into despair. After all, he was living with a Ginza club *mama-san*. Having observed my boss at the Cocteau, I knew that women like that are not easily defeated in battles of the heart. They are not ordinary, respectable folk. They need to love men to stay alive. They are professional love machines.

I didn't see how I could hope to beat such a formidable opponent. OK, so I'd played around a bit this past year, but I was still barely out of kindergarten compared with her. And you could tell at a glance that Bogey was adult in every sense, a true man of the world.

Maybe sensing my gaze on him, he said to me one day, 'Could you give me a five-minute shoulder massage? There's a thousand yen in it for you.'

It was just after three o'clock. The stock market had closed and as usual everyone had disappeared: to coffee shops, saunas, massage parlours, or wherever. The room was deserted except for the two of us.

I don't suppose I will ever forget that moment, that feeling when I first laid hands on Bogey's broad back and thickset shoulders. For the first time in my life I touched a man's body with reverence and love. I had given my body to any man who wanted it, yet my heart was still virgin.

I had never felt such comfort from contact with a male body – not from Hajime and the other soft, pliant boys of my acquaintance, and certainly not from the greasy, middle-aged bodies I'd encountered at the Cocteau. With those men I had just lain there like a slab of tuna on a chopping-board, wishing that they'd get it over with quickly. But this was different. I was only giving him a massage, for heaven's sake, yet as I kneaded his shoulders an inexpressible happiness seemed to flood from the tips of my fingers through my entire body.

I'd heard from Taeko that Bogey's mood rose and fell in sync with the stocks he was handling. Today had been a bull market, and sure enough he was in excellent spirits. He cracked joke after joke, laughing out loud at his own wit.

'Saya, do you go out all night, every night? I hear that college girls these days have a pretty wild time.'

'Not really. I used to go home after dawn sometimes, but these days I'm taking my studies seriously.'

'Really?'

'Really!'

And whose fault do you think it is that partying has lost its thrill? It's all because of you!

Perhaps he sensed my unspoken thought, for he suddenly came out with, 'Saya, what would it take for you to go out all night with me?'

His tone was humorous, not at all lecherous, and I chose to accept the comment as a lighthearted, grown-up joke.

'Oh, I don't know – a first-class restaurant, a traditional Japanese restaurant, maybe. I haven't been to many. And then maybe a really exclusive bar for adults, no kids. And then a top-class hotel that isn't a love hotel. Yeah, that might be enough to get you a date.'

I hated to be taken for a naive little girl in an obvious panic. A seasoned dandy like him couldn't possibly think of going out with a kid like me. I was trying to conceal my lack of confidence by carrying the attack to him. He took it calmly enough.

'So which hotel do the young ladies like to go to these days?'

'Well, a lot of people are talking about the new wing at the Akasaka Prince.'

'The Akasaka Prince, you say? All the princesses love the Prince, eh? If you see what I mean!'

'Very funny. Ha-ha.'

I guess there may also have been a hard, calculating part of me that wanted to see if Bogey was the real thing, whether he was truly different from the mean, pathetic losers that I knew from the Cocteau. Bogey was clever enough to sense that curiosity. And like a professional gambler, he made his move.

'All right then! How about this Saturday? I'll see you at seven o'clock, in front of the Almond coffee shop in Roppongi.'

TWO

It had snowed a lot that winter.

I used to go slithering through the snowdrifts down the Usen-zaka slope from Roppongi Station to Bogey's pad in Azabu Juban. It took me thirty minutes to get to Roppongi on the Hibiya line, and after that it was a fifteen-minute walk. Azabu Juban had the same kind of raffish, easygoing atmosphere as Minowa, the district in Tokyo where I'd been born and bred, but it also had a certain vigour that Minowa could never match, and you could smell money in the air.

In the old days, Azabu Juban had been known as one of Tokyo's leading pleasure quarters. And nowadays, apart from the local shopkeepers, just about everyone who lived there had something to do with the night world. Either that or they were wheeling and dealing in the financial or property markets. I guess there wasn't much difference between these people and the night birds who hung out near my home at Asakusa, but those living in Azabu Juban were in a higher league – hostesses from the glittering Ginza, Japan's Number One Nightspot, and their menfolk. The amount of money floating around was different, too. This was where the hostesses chilled out when they came off duty, so the place had something of the air of a backstage changing room for butterflies of the night. It had a buzz to it.

In the middle of Azabu Juban stood Bogey's regular coffee shop, the Edinburgh. During the daylight hours, the Ginza and Rop-pongi hostesses would hang out there, unmade-up, brunching in sunglasses and shiny spats, each with her yapping little dog, of course. Their men would be sporting frizzy gangster perms and baggy bomber jackets and be clanking with thick 18-carat gold bracelets and Rolexes, devouring the sports papers and working the phones at the back of the coffee shop.

No doubt Bogey chose to make his base there because he liked the commonness and the *nouveau riche* atmosphere, together with the rough humanity that rubbed off from its *demi-monde* associations. There were no ordinary folk here, no regular guys squeezing into overcrowded trains to get to their companies or government offices, earning the bread to support their suburban families. But that didn't mean Azabu Juban had lost out in the great game of life – far from it. The only people living there were people who weren't regular but were nevertheless successful. They rented expensive condominiums and lived gaudy, glittering lives of leisure. Of course, the slightly off-colour tone of the place didn't bother Bogey one little bit. He took to it like a duck to water.

Bogey was a graduate of Hitotsubashi University, an elite school. This fact created a little space in his heart, in which he fondly imagined that he was different from the other people in his profession. He used to go on about how circumstances had forced him into this 'shadowy world' against his will. The truth was that he liked the simple, desire-driven humanity of the place.

Bogey had come to Tokyo three years previously. He'd been running a travel agency in Kobe but it went bust, so he decided to make a fresh start in the big city. At thirty-five, he was flat broke. He started by crashing at a friend's place on the outskirts of Azabu Juban. This friend was an unsuccessful writer I called 'the Old Man'. Actually, he was only a year younger than Bogey, but he seemed really old – he had this totally worn-out air about him.

Bogey and the Old Man had first met up years ago, when the Old Man had borrowed some money off Bogey after being introduced by a mutual acquaintance. Not the most promising start to a friendship perhaps, but Bogey was a romantic at heart and would have liked to have been a novelist, or something like that, himself. So although he'd drifted into the world of finance, he still tended to look on guys like this unpopular novelist as his true friends.

By night Bogey was sleeping on the couch at the Old Man's house and by day he was job-hunting. Mind you, no respectable employer was going to take on a guy of his age and background, so what he really had in mind was sniffing out some niche in which to start his own business. He checked out all the possibilities – selling study aids, flower wholesaling, supplying portable toilets to construction sites, and so on.

'I was just hanging around town, wondering what I could do,' he said. 'I used to wander around the Almond coffee shop with my hands in my pockets kicking pebbles. Makes you want to laugh, eh? Once I was having a coffee there and I suddenly realised I didn't have enough small change to pay for it. I slipped out when the waiter wasn't looking and legged it. Hiding in the shadows, you know. Ha-ha-ha.'

Bogey was always good for a laugh. I never tired of listening to his stories.

The food at the Old Man's place was so bad that the Old Man's wife was virtually suffering from malnutrition. Naturally that didn't suit Bogey, who always yearned for the best food he could get, so he quickly acquired a girlfriend and moved in with her. This was the Ginza *mama-san* who was now plaguing him with phone calls at work. He wanted to dump her, but it was a bit awkward considering she'd taken him in and looked after him when he was down and out. He couldn't bring himself to leave her just like that. On the other hand he couldn't bear possessive women, so as a compromise he'd rented himself a little hideaway in Azabu Juban.

Bogey's pad was smack in the middle of the shopping district, in a very fancy cream-white condominium that had *nouveau riche* written all over it. The first floor featured a sushi restaurant and an elegant French bistro, and the people who lived there were mostly women of the not entirely respectable variety – Ginza or Roppongi hostesses, prostitutes, or someone-or-other's kept woman. The boyfriends and patrons would come and go, so at first glance you'd think the condo was full of married couples, but in fact most of the residents were single women with visitors. And although you're not supposed to keep animals in these rented condominiums, the management turned a blind eye to the pets that most of these women kept.

The top floor of the building was a single massive penthouse, inhabited by a porno video actress who was a particularly keen animal-lover. I heard the following story from one of the sushi chefs on the first floor.

'I went there one day to make a delivery, and it was amazing! You'll never guess what she had – a bear! No kidding! A goddamn bear. I've seen a few pets in my time, but I have to admit that it was a first for me, that bear. I mean, what's she going to do with it when it grows up?'

I often bumped into that girl in the elevator. She used to wear fishnet tights and new-wave clothes that looked like they'd come straight out of Madonna's wardrobe. She never had the bear with her, though. I used to wonder about that. Didn't bears have to be taken for walks? Did the bear get to appear in videos with her? If so, would that make it a bare bear? My imagination raced. Anyway, just about all the people living in that condo were of that sort.

Bogey was keeping a pair of pedigree Persian kittens in his hideaway. There was a white male, born of grand championship American stock, and a blue-cream female.

'Actually, I wanted something bigger,' he said, 'like a giraffe, you know? But when it grew up it would have to stick its neck through the window, and then the landlord might notice that I was breaking the no-pets rule.'

Bogey was a kid when it came to animals. His favourite TV programme was 'Happy Happy Animal Land'.

'I hear they've come up with a new breed of Persian,' he said. 'The kittens weigh eight kilos and they look like chow-chows. But apparently the breed hasn't stabilised, so they can't sell them yet.'

Bogey loved talking about animals.

As he attempted to get rid of the Ginza *mama-san*, she was steadily becoming more hysterical. He didn't want to walk out on her suddenly in case she did something weird, like sticking a knife in him, so instead he came up with the cunning idea of renting a second home on the sly and gradually spending more nights in the new apartment and fewer with her. The woman was getting to be a pain. On the other hand, Bogey easily got lonely, so he bought the kittens to keep him company.

He was barely capable of looking after himself, let alone a pair of champion Persian longhairs. So I became a kind of housekeeper for Bogey and a baby-sitter for his kittens, and started to make regular visits to the cream-coloured condo in Azabu Juban.

✶

That night Bogey had taken me to a restaurant that specialised in fish and vegetable cuisine, with an unpretentious atmosphere but first-class food and prices to match. Then we went to a very grown-up jazz club with headquarters in Osaka, followed by the new wing at the Akasaka Prince Hotel – all exactly as requested.

At the jazz club, Bogey's favourite hostesses had shown us a new drink called a Nikolaschka – neat brandy served with a slice of lemon covering the mouth of the glass and a conical pile of sugar resting on the lemon. You were supposed to fold the lemon and sugar into your mouth and drink the brandy through it in one gulp. We knocked back an awful lot of Nikolaschkas and got stinking drunk. We swapped bad jokes, and somewhere along the line the 'Bogey' nickname emerged.

Bogey was a different man after a few drinks. He became high as a kite. He kept joking about how unfair life was, how he kept shelling out so much money to entertain girls in clubs and then ended up going home alone, and so on. I'm also a different person when I'm drunk; somehow his drunken good humour hit me right on the funny bone and I made a few jokes of my own. After a while we were both laughing away, railing against society's injustices and bouncing jokes off each other like a couple of clowns.

'Well, you two sure seem in tune with each other. Anyone would think you were his daughter!'

'Is this really your first date?'

'No hanky-panky, Mr Hotta. Let this young lady go home, OK?'

That's what all the hostesses said when they heard I was just nineteen. Actually, I had not the slightest intention of going home, nor he of letting me. We tumbled into a cab, virtually legless, and since we were heading for the Akasaka Prince rather than some seedy love hotel, it really did feel more like a father and daughter thing than a date. It was as if we'd just been to some friendly social gathering that had turned us into parent and child.

*

I awoke the next morning with Bogey's huge belly right in front of my eyes. I'd gone to sleep with my head stuck under his armpit. His chest muscles were running to flab and I gave one of them a playful rub.

'Nice tits!'

I felt surrounded by warmth and contentment. There's a Japanese saying that some people are so naturally suited to each other that 'their skins match'. For the first time in my life I knew what that meant. It was the first time I'd come across a man who made me feel nostalgic, as though it wasn't the first time, as though I had come home.

Of course I didn't know yet whether Bogey loved me, but I reckoned he probably would eventually. True, anyone would have taken us for father and daughter: I looked younger than my age, while with his white hair he looked older than his. And we lived in different worlds. Even so, deep down, Bogey and I belonged to the same species.

I got fired from Kabutocho Journal right after that. Bogey was no good at dissembling and the roly-poly manager spotted what was going on with one glance at Bogey's moonstruck face. So instead of going to work at the company, I took to going to Bogey's apartment instead.

'You like cats, right? Well, come and play with my cats.'

The key he gave me was just as it had come from the estate agent, with that little paper tag giving the address of the property attached to it by a twist of wire. It was only two weeks since Bogey had decided he'd had enough of women and had rented this pad for himself, and here he was handing the key over to a girl half his age.

'When I phone, I'll call once, hang up, then call again. That's the code, OK? Don't pick up the phone otherwise. Got it?'

'Got it.'

He'd told the Ginza *mama-san* that he was living on his own, and he'd given her the phone number, but not the address.

I checked the place out right away, with a guilty thrill as if I were visiting a secret amusement park open only to me.

The condo was still brand-new. It had a fancy awning over the entrance and one of those lifts with windows, which were still considered smart in those days.

But when I opened the glossy white door and entered the apartment – oh dear! The whole place stank of cat piss, sour milk and stale cigarette smoke. And there, amidst the cat hair drifting through the room like tumbleweed, I spied a couple of larger balls of hair, rolling toward me and mewing for milk.

'Oh, you poor things! What an insult to your pedigree!'

They were still kittens and hadn't learned to be suspicious of people. They must have felt lonely, having being left on their own so much, and they came nuzzling up to me as if I were their mother. Their faces were encrusted with milky scum, and their bottoms were filthy with bits of shit sticking to the fur.

'Ugh, this is just awful!'

With the kittens in my arms, I spoke out loud. Lazy as I was, I found myself surprised by a sense of purpose and excitement, unfamiliar feelings indeed.

I found a crystal ashtray piled high with a fortnight's worth of cigarette butts and surrounded with ash. The sofa cover, too, was littered with ash, as well as cat-droppings and hair. There was a pile of old sports newspapers stained with cat piss, some weekly magazines, and a pile of hard-boiled crime novels, all by Kenzo Kitakata. There were stacks of glasses that had once held whisky and water, and quite a few glasses and cigarette ends with lipstick on them, along with the business cards of hostesses and call girls. Some of them had personal telephone numbers written on the back and messages such as 'Call me', always in that rounded, childish handwriting that women like to affect. It was horrible – a typically filthy bachelor apartment.

Worse still, the whole place was furnished in the worst taste imaginable, with furniture that Bogey had bought from Yoshizuya, a pricey but unfashionable local store. Features included a rose-pink velvet sofa with matching plump frilly cushions. The sideboard was vaguely Japanese in style, reddish brown and designed to look as heavy and clunky as possible, its shelves and cabinets all empty. Strewn around were a couple of bottles of Chivas Regal and Hennessy, cut-glass whisky tumblers and brandy balloons, an ice bucket and a packet of beef jerky, somewhat chewed at the corner by a hungry kitten.

The bedroom was in no better shape. The closet proved to contain several crumpled, dark suits, covered with cat hair. The bed and sideboard were huge, bulky things from Karimoku, a company specialising in furniture designed to look expensive. The burgundy velvet bedcover was on the verge of turning white with its dusting of cat hair.

The television was exactly the kind of gigantic monster you'd expect an old guy at an appliance store to recommend, and near it lay a Mayumi Itsuwa video that must have been suggested by someone with a taste for outdated folk songs. The area around the glass door of the TV cabinet was strewn with crumpled envelopes – the sort that banks provide for your cash withdrawals – and torn paper bands that had once encircled wads of bank notes.

There were no curtains.

What a mess! What a lifestyle! Got to do something about this! I felt suffused with a strange determination.

How can he do this to such a great room? What a waste! Running to seed it may have been, but it was still a white condo in the centre of town, very different from the twenty-year-old wooden house in the working-class part of town where I lived.

Bogey's work at Kabutocho Journal continued until about nine or ten in the evening. He'd then go straight out on the town for another night's boozing and wouldn't get back home until the small hours. Weekends he still spent with the hard-to-ditch Ginza *mama-san*. Sometimes he'd be out playing mah-jong the whole night and wouldn't come home until the following day. It wasn't right to neglect the poor kittens like that, and if I didn't do some-

43

thing about these rooms, nobody would. Having spent all those empty years shrugging my shoulders and saying 'Whatever', the feeling of suddenly being needed lit up my days and made them sparkle like new.

✵

I had to keep the kittens properly fed, so I would go to Azabu Juban at least every other day. I was seldom able to see Bogey himself. Just occasionally the double-ring phone call would come from the Edinburgh and he'd take me to the pet store to buy stuff for the kittens. He would buy whatever the store clerk recommended, even if it happened to be a gigantic artificial tree, costing 150,000 yen, for use as a scratching post.

There was something special about the way Bogey used money. It was so graceful and charming that you hardly had time to notice the slightly suspicious, not-quite-on-the-level, aspect of his spending behaviour. Never before had I met or even seen a grown-up who used money as if it were litter or toilet paper.

'Money's just money,' he used to say, 'so there's no point getting too attached to it. Lots of guys do and wind up in the gutter. Greedy guys get together with other greedy guys in greedy places, take money off each other, get money taken off each other, and that's it. That's not my style. There's plenty of money around, stacks of the stuff, if you know where to look. Whichever way you earn a ten-thousand-yen note, it's still worth ten thousand yen. And I don't want to mess around doing fiddly little jobs for some guy until I drop dead. All I do is take money from where there's plenty of it and spend it on stuff I like doing. Where's the harm in that?'

Such were Bogey's thoughts on money. But when it came to me, he stubbornly insisted that I should stick to a more orthodox scale of values.

'You're a student, right? So you've got to be sensible about money. I'm only giving you this much, OK? If you're ever short, just let me know.'

So saying, he would hand over no more than 50,000 yen as pocket money. This was the first time I'd ever been spoken to in the way a father should speak to his child, instilling a little discipline, and I loved it. At last someone I could rely on. I promptly dumped Hajime and my other boyfriends, and my bad girlfriends such as Minako, and began living like a housekeeper. I'd go to the apartment, clean it up, play with the kittens, and be satisfied.

As for Bogey, he was far from satisfied with me as a woman. But he'd indulge me, as if I really were his daughter. He enjoyed casting a critical eye over me as I struggled to please him, and he'd look for ways to improve me as a woman.

'It's about time you started dressing like an adult. Are those baby clothes all you've got? How about if I get you a new rig-out? You know – shoes, clothes, bag, the works!'

As far as Bogey was concerned, the Tokyo designer brands I wore were just kids' stuff, and my fashionable art deco bob looked like 'the bell-end of some guy's cock', as he charmingly put it.

'Guys prefer girls who look a bit more regular, a bit more ordinary. If a girl looks too trendy, we feel we can't keep up, know what I mean? And you should also grow your hair longer. Definitely.'

I gladly grew my hair and adopted a more 'ordinary' style. I just wanted him to like me more. I wanted Bogey to be satisfied with me. And with that, I set out to become the kind of woman that appealed to his tastes.

Whenever we met, Bogey would ask 'You OK for cash?', and he'd hand me 50,000 yen. I'd use the money to buy cat food and cat litter, replenish the booze supply, and generally keep the apartment in good order, enjoying a taste of newly-wedded life. If I had money left over, I'd use it to buy things that weren't so necessary – such as fancy pot-plants, indirect lighting units, and other stuff. Little by little, I decorated Bogey's pad to express my feelings for him.

I was content. Every day I went to the place of the man I loved, used my own ideas to make it more cozy, and played with the kittens who seemed ever more charming. After all, I had time on my hands, and at home I wasn't allowed to keep a cat. Seeing the kittens every day strengthened my affection for them, even though they weren't actually mine. I told myself that it was a shame to leave them unattended for such long periods, and used that as an excuse to spend as much time as possible at Bogey's.

'You came over to my place again today, right?'

'Yeah.'

'Thought so. The room was so clean.'

In the early days, Bogey often called me up in the middle of the night (Ma had fortunately stayed sound asleep). He'd ramble on for a couple of hours about some pointless topic, but nevertheless I'd eagerly await his calls. Generally they'd come after he'd had a few drinks and was in a good mood. He'd just have got back to his room and would have started drinking again.

'I'm drinking a "Hennesui",' he'd inform me. That was one of his little jokes. He liked to drink Hennessy cognac with water – *sui* in Japanese – hence 'Hennesui'. Or it might be: 'I've just made myself some Charumera instant noodles and I'm eating them now. They're the best, don't you think? They taste just like instant noodles should taste.'

Apparently he had to tell me all the details of what he was doing or he'd feel lonely. I would listen like a mother and talk a bit about what was going on in my own life, and sometimes he'd drift off to sleep still holding the telephone. On other occasions, he'd suddenly say, 'Want to come over? I'll pay for the cab. Come on, get going!'

And so, like some sleazy call girl, I'd smarten myself up and head over to his place. At three or four in the morning the roads were empty, and the cab ride from home to Azabu Juban only took about fifteen minutes.

Since Bogey's spirits rose and fell with the Nikkei stock average, his mood would swing drastically from day to day, so much so that you'd have to describe him as a manic-depressive. When he was down he'd call up and say, 'Don't bother coming around any more. It's all over between us.'

From Bogey's point of view, when he lacked confidence in himself, a naïve young thing like me was just surplus baggage.

'You're still young,' he'd say, 'and you shouldn't be messing around with someone like me. I'm a guy whose life has already ended once. Go back to your old life.'

That's the kind of thing he would say. But, truth to tell, my 'old life' wasn't worth returning to. OK, it looked good – living with my mother and attending a supposedly high-class university. But the reality was rather different: Ma's boyfriend showing up at the house whenever he felt like it, myself part-timing at a crummy club in the Ginza for money to mess around, occasionally sleeping for pin money with bald old bar-flies I didn't even fancy, going out with boys who had nothing to say. It was just too boring and I was sick to death of the whole scene.

I knew that Bogey was still carrying on with the Ginza *mama-san*, and I was aware that even though he could have me for free he would still send for call girls now and then. I knew, too, that he was out to get his paws on every hostess he met. I'd sometimes find little gift-wrapped fashion accessories lying around the apartment. They weren't for me.

I didn't have any sexual techniques to match those of the professional women he'd knock around with. I'd just lie there like tuna on a sushi chef's chopping board and let him get on with it.

47

This drew comments from him that weren't very gentlemanly, such as: 'Shit, you just haven't got a clue what to do!'

He was dreadful, Bogey was. Even so, it was fun to talk to him when he was drunk and in a good mood, and although I only went out with him a couple of times a month, those dates with Bogey were the most fun I'd ever had.

I took him to a Nishi-Azabu café-bar in a street of little bistros that was trendy at the time, but it wasn't Bogey's style. He enjoyed mimicking the po-faced waiter who took our order, though. Sometimes he'd take me to a real high-class club in Roppongi to observe the various types of professional hostesses there, and he'd provide little social commentaries: 'What do you reckon about that couple? I'd say he's a financier and she's a Ginza *mama-san*, eh?' 'They say that guy's the president of a property company, but I reckon he's got some other business on the side,' and so on. Once the club closed, he'd take me to an after-hours bar in Akasaka or Roppongi, where the nightclub professionals would go for their own R&R. Again we'd check out the couples and engage in a little playful social observation. It was a whole lot of fun.

Though I'd done a few naughty things in my time, I was still only a college girl. I knew a few places where kids like me liked to hang out, and I had a rough idea of life as a third-rate hostess. But Bogey was a veteran of Tokyo nightlife. His territory was expansive and his history long. I loved listening to him talk about it.

Apparently Bogey had been so brainy in his youth that he'd been called a child prodigy. School had been boring for him and he'd devoted all his time to baseball and card games. 'I was just too good at cards. I cleaned out all the neighborhood kids and they would go crying to their mothers, who'd give me a helluva scolding.'

When he got to high school, Bogey learned the joys of horse-race betting from the older boys, and at university he graduated to bicycle races and mah-jong. A pattern developed: he'd make money on mah-jong and gamble it away on bicycle races. Things were still like that when I met him.

At college, Bogey first checked out all the mah-jong clubs around the Hitotsubashi campus, then moved on to larger establishments in Shinjuku. Eventually he found that even the Shinjuku stakes weren't high enough to give him a buzz, so he moved on to a special club for high rollers in nearby Higashi-Nakano. That became his regular haunt, and he said he made nearly all his nightlife money at the mah-jong table.

Bogey graduated and got a job in the marketing department of a big advertising agency. The salary was nowhere near enough to keep him in the style to which he'd become accustomed, so he started a small printing company on the side, using his position in the agency to quietly channel a bit of business his company's way. By this time he'd taken to clubbing around the Ginza, and after a while he married the agency's cutest part-time girl, a former campus beauty queen. They moved into an apartment in Shinjuku where the rent was almost the same as Bogey's monthly salary. Then, at the age of twenty-nine, he was suddenly transferred to the Osaka office, where he didn't get on with his boss and soon ran into trouble.

'He was such a cheapskate, Saya. He'd take the boys from the office to a bar and expect everybody to pay for their own drinks. Really! It was like "OK, you had a highball, right," and he'd figure out exactly how much each of us owed. I just couldn't stand it, you know. And he kept picking on me – "Blah blah blah", on and on and on, all day long. I took to going out at night to this club in Shinchi, and after six months I was five million yen in debt, a lot of money in those days. I tried to get it back by playing the commodities market.'

'Commodities market?'

'Good grief, Saya, don't you know what the commodities market is? What innocence! It's like being with a nun or something! It's a market where they deal in beans, rubber and stuff. It's a very dangerous market to play, nevertheless I reckoned I'd be OK because I was naturally lucky. But I blew it – boy, did I blow it! There were *yakuza* banging on the door, demanding their money. I sent the wife and kids to her folks' house for safekeeping. With debt-collectors on my back and in-laws out for my blood, I had nowhere to turn to. What a mess!'

Bogey told the story like it was one big joke, as he always did, but I knew better. That was probably the time when Bogey tried to end his life. Being kicked about by *yakuza* thugs and not being able to do a thing about it must have been a terrible blow to his pride.

He often used to say to me, 'Saya, it may be a hassle and all that, but no matter what you do, don't drop out of college. Whatever kind of life you lead later on, so long as you've graduated from a good school, you'll know you're not the worst of human beings. Look at me. It was because I'd been to Hitotsubashi University that I was able to believe I was different from other guys.'

Bogey had eight scars on his wrists – four on the left and four on the right. The years had left them only faintly visible, but they spoke clearly enough to me of the intensity, the unutterable loneliness and suffering, of Bogey's way of life.

For some reason I had become involved with this man. Maybe it was precisely because he was the kind of guy he was that I felt attracted to him. The moment I saw those scars, I made up my mind that there was no way I could abandon him. Bogey's heart had been ripped to shreds at the time he had made those awful gashes in his wrists. He was still terribly wounded, caught in a tragedy beyond words. Something would have to be done about it – by me.

His need for me was also my great solace. At last I had found a haven – the one and only haven – for my restless soul.

So, yes, when summoned I would go flying to his side, even in the middle of the night. Of course you don't get too many young women all dolled up at three or four in the morning climbing into a cab and asking to be taken to a place with a dubious reputation like Azabu Juban. Cab drivers drew the obvious conclusion, and sometimes they'd make persistent efforts to hire me for a quickie.

Anyway, I'd get out of the taxi in front of the Azabu Juban condo and take the elevator up to Bogey's place. I always felt sad when I went there. Despite the way he treated women, Bogey was a really lonely guy. He generally bought his daily necessities at all-night convenience stores, and there'd be two of everything: two boring towels, two toothbrushes, two plastic cups, two nylon flannels, even two bottles each of shampoo and conditioner. Each pair was colour-coded 'his 'n' hers'. One would be pink and the other blue, or one would be red and the other green.

'Guys are selfish animals,' he'd explain. 'We want women around, but only when it suits us. The rest of the time they're a nuisance. We want to be pampered, but only when we're in the mood. That's why I'm through living with someone else. I've made the decision to live on my own.'

He used to say this – but of course he wasn't really comfortable living alone. His nightly phone calls, his habit of always shopping for two, and the business cards of the call girls all testified to that.

One night I got the usual summons and heard him singing in the bathroom when I arrived.

'Lover of mine, be close to me. Embrace me, I am numb with cold...'

It was one of those sentimental ballads by Mayumi Itsuwa. Usually I'd have laughed, but there was something about Bogey sitting in the bath and singing this sad song so seriously that pierced me to the core. I found myself in tears. The bathroom door was open a little, and I could just see Bogey's face in profile. He was crying, too, for heaven's sake.

'Bogey?'

'Saya, is that you? Want to join me in the bath?'

I got in with him. I'm not a big girl, and I fitted snugly between Bogey's thighs. Hugged like that, I sank into the warm water.

'Ah, lovely!'

I soaped his broad back and shampooed his hair. And like a masseuse working in a seedy sauna, I washed him all over. I liked washing Bogey's body.

Once we'd emerged from the bath and started on the usual Hennesui, Bogey began to talk.

'Today's the anniversary of my wife's death, as it happens.'

I couldn't manage a response.

'You could say that I killed her. After the travel agency in Kobe went bust, you see, we and the two kids were staying with her folks, just temporarily until I got sorted out. Her family ran a trading company in Kobe. They put us up in the director's office. Can you believe that? Day after boring day I had to bear her relatives' nagging, until finally I just couldn't take any more. I came to Tokyo and told my wife I'd be back for her once I'd got back on my feet. Well, as you know, pretty soon I wound up living with that *mama-san.*'

I had once taken a peek at the photo of Bogey's late wife that he kept in his business card case. As you'd expect of a former campus beauty queen, she was very pretty. She could have been an actress. Apparently it was credit card bankruptcy that drove her to suicide.

'I ruined her,' he continued. 'Thanks to me, she couldn't lead an ordinary life any more. The debt collectors caught up with her, and she couldn't send them on to me because she didn't know where I was. So she went crying to her dad, but the old skinflint refused to help her out. That same evening she was killed in a car crash –

apparently she was drunk at the wheel. Even if it wasn't strictly suicide, it was pretty much the same damn thing.'

Bogey was weeping. It was only two years since his wife had died, which helped to explain his air of melancholy and occasional forced gaiety.

'I really loved her, you know. Then this had to happen. They wouldn't let me come to the funeral. They wouldn't even let me see the kids. And I had been thinking that I would soon be able to go and get them...'

It was hard to see the man I loved crying openly for another woman, but the sight made me all the more determined to be the one to rescue him from his misery.

That night, just to be on the safe side, I stayed awake and kept a bedside vigil over Bogey as he slept.

'Kimiko... Oh, Kimiko...'

It must have been her name that he was moaning in his sleep.

When he woke up the next morning, Bogey was a man transformed. He dressed briskly and prepared for work, and as he was knotting his tie he turned to me and said, with a very straight face, 'Saya, would you be kind enough to let me have one of your pubic hairs?'

'All right,' I said blearily, 'but what for?'

'It's good luck to have a woman's pubic hair in your breast pocket,' he said. 'Today I'm going to do battle to avenge her death!'

My mouth fell open and I forgot to close it.

Whatever afflicted Bogey, he always tried to solve the problem by doing what he liked doing. I admired his guts. Once again the living room was littered with torn bands that had held bundles of bank notes. Reassured, I fell asleep alongside the kittens.

I awoke at dusk. Bogey came back looking disheartened.

'Lost two million yen,' he said. 'It's the curse of my late wife, that's what it is.'

✷

Come the summer vacation, Bogey and I were virtually living together. My mother had told me that so long as I got into a good university I could do whatever I liked after that. True to her word, she never criticised my lifestyle so long as I kept on attending lectures. Actually, it looked better to the neighbours if I lived away from home and showed up occasionally at a respectable time of day rather than at dawn every morning.

Around then I told her about Bogey. Of course she wasn't too pleased that I was having an affair with a big-time gambler twice my age. She knew there was no chance she could stop a love-struck child like me, but in any event she gave me a lecture.

'You should never have anything to do with a gambler. A gambler may have one big win, but he'll use a lifetime's luck on it.'

'No need to worry, Mother,' I said. 'I've never known Bogey win at gambling.'

It was true, basically. OK, maybe he did have a biggish win, now and again, but I felt sure he was losing far, far more than he won. All that cash he chucked around came from the big bonuses they were paying him at Kabutocho Journal. Bogey was a walking, talking illustration of the Japanese proverb: 'Ill-gotten gains are never kept for long.'

Almost every night Bogey would stop off at a club in Roppongi on his way home from work. There are all sorts of clubs in Roppongi, but the ones Bogey favoured would set you back at least 50,000 yen a visit. The rent on his Azabu Juban pad was 300,000 yen a month. And he would always dine at some classy restaurant – Japanese one night, Korean or Chinese the next, plenty of gourmet sushi. That was his lifestyle.

Essentially, he was living in a way that was only fleetingly possible on the cusp of the bubble economy. Bogey had lovely manners and was incapable of doing or saying anything vulgar, but his associates *were* vulgar. Once Bogey took me out drinking with them, and I will never forget their disgusting behaviour.

It must have been one evening after they'd made a killing. I suppose that when people are engaged in high-risk work the stress is bound to explode when they've had a big day. I didn't know much about the work they were doing, and even if they'd told me I wouldn't have understood, so I never bothered to ask. But Bogey often described it like this: 'What I'm doing is barely legal. But everyone does it if they really want to hit it big, and the guys who get caught are the idiots. It's just a big bunch of greedy guys congregating in greedy places trying to take money off one another. So who's to say who's in the wrong?'

It might have been all right if Bogey had been able to save some of what he made when he'd hit the jackpot and put it toward a more respectable business that would eventually enable him to get out of this life – something he often talked about. But in the end he just pissed it all away on nightclubs and gambling. I knew the score – my own brief career in hostessing had shown me that when money is flowing like water, not a drop would be left in the bucket. It's a rule of the night world.

I had a glimpse of the mad, sad ways Bogey's workmates had with money one night at a cabaret-bar in Roppongi, where they used the power of cash to make monkeys out of the waiters.

The waiters, all of them smartly turned out in suit and black tie, were young guys about my age. Some of them were in fact moonlighting university students. Probably they were working in a place like this to support the expensive tastes of some stuck-up girl such as I used to be: they were all tanned and looked the type. Bogey and his pals kept on handing the waiters enormous tips, which were driving them into a feeding frenzy.

They swarmed around Bogey's party like ants that had found something sweet.

'All right then!' said Kenjo – known to Bogey and company as 'Ken-ken' 'I'm going to put some cash and some brandy in this ice bucket, and whoever drinks all the brandy in one go can have the cash.'

So saying, Ken-ken slowly emptied a nearly full bottle of Remy Martin into the bucket. Then he tossed in a handful of crumpled 10,000-yen notes.

'Oooooh!' The waiters were close to orgasm.

'I'll do it!'

'No, I will! Me! Me!'

They were fighting for the ice bucket.

'Hmm,' said Bogey. 'Up for it, eh? OK, let's spice it up a bit.'

With that, he lobbed a few more 10,000-yen notes into the bucket.

The waiters' eyes were ablaze. I suppose it was a case of drunken horseplay carried a little too far, but I was still astonished that they showed no shame as they battled to drain the ice bucket right in front of a girl their own age. I guess, however, that I wasn't in their field of vision right then.

There they were, on duty, in their black suits provided by their employer, swilling brandy from a customer's ice bucket with filthy bank notes – touched by who knows how many grubby hands – bobbing in it. All this amidst gales of drunken laughter from some very dubious customers. I understood only too well their desire to make money fast any way they could, but surely even taking cash to sleep with a bald old punter who fancied you was better than this!

At the same time I felt a sudden wave of sadness as I realised that Bogey himself was a member of this world. However much money they made, Bogey's pals still acted in the cheapest possible way. Ken-ken's behaviour with money was particularly vile. And when Bogey was with these guys he instantly became vulgar and coarse. Maybe this was partly to avoid spoiling the fun, but even so I found the transformation disturbing.

One of the waiters finally polished off the last of the Remy Martin and collapsed on the floor. Taking advantage of the confusion, the others stuffed the 10,000-yen notes into their pockets and started clearing up. I suddenly sobered up. *Bogey should not be getting mixed up in this sort of thing*, I thought.

He had no idea how to use money. If he were going to throw it around like waste paper, it would be much better if I spent it for him. It's a fact that this same Bogey was often unable to pay his household bills. The electricity would be cut off for non-payment, as would the gas, the telephone, and even the water. At the weekend he'd gamble away all the cash he had on him and be left flat broke. The apartment still had the same horrible furniture he'd bought when he first moved in, and nothing other than that.

One day, not for the first time, I happened to notice a couple of bundles of cash on the sideboard, next to the TV. Each bundle consisted of a million yen. *Now's my chance!* I thought, and I confronted Bogey.

'Bogey, since you've got all this cash lying around, how about buying a slightly better sofa?'

Bogey was taken aback. 'A better sofa? So you reckon this one isn't smart enough, or it's in bad taste, or something?'

'Well, you can't deny it.'

'Hmm … I suppose you may have a point. I bought it because the guy in the furniture store recommended it.'

'I thought as much.'

'But, Saya darling, I'm not the worst. You know Ota – the guy in charge of that room where you used to work?'

'The pudgy old guy who took a fancy to me and got me transferred to the room where you were working?'

'The same. Well, you should see his place. He's got this fantastic apartment over in Iikura-Katamachi with a gigantic living room, about 500 square feet of parquet flooring, but he didn't know what to do with all that space. So you know what? He partitioned off one corner of it and put in a *kotatsu*.'

A *kotatsu* – a short-legged table with an electric filament underneath to keep you warm in winter. What you'd use in a poky little room in an old wooden house. It was kind of out of place in a centrally heated luxury penthouse. Ota had built himself a little peasant's hovel in the middle of a palace.

'Really?'

''Fraid so.'

For a moment I was lost for words. The guys at that company didn't have a clue how to spend money. That was why they ended up playing silly games with it, using bank notes like toilet paper. Guys like that could make all the money in the world and it wouldn't do them any good. Bogey had no fashion sense, but, as he said, he was not the worst.

Come to think of it, Ken-ken's residence was also a monument to bad taste. He lived with this Roppongi hostess who'd pretty much decked out the pad in the style she liked: that is, nautical. The walls were festooned with crappy blow-ups of Hawaiian islands and sailboats. Even the toilet had a seaside motif, with bits of fishing net and glass buoys hanging on the wall.

'Anyway, Bogey, please let's get a sofa?'

I felt myself turning slightly pale. I couldn't bear the thought of him belonging to the same category as those guys.

Bogey was won over. 'All right,' he said, resolve written all over his face, 'go and pick a nice one and bring me the brochure.'

I went skipping off to the Roppongi Forum Building to a store I'd had my eye on for quite a while. It sold high-class imported furniture, and among the many lovely items available I'd noticed an Italian leather sofa that was even more lovely than the others. On inspection, the price proved to be a shade under two million yen. Perfect! Clearly, Bogey and I were fated to buy this sofa. It was elegant, not obviously designed for either young people or old, and it was very comfortable. No cat hairs would stick to its smooth surface and it was just the right size for the room. What a find!

I returned to base, clutching the glossy brochure with photos and specifications. Bogey took one look at it and was not pleased.

'*One million, eight hundred thousand yen*? You must be joking! You can't spend that kind of money on a piece of furniture!' Suddenly he sounded like one of those dodgy tipsters that hang out at off-course betting shops.

'But, Bogey, you blow that kind of money in a single day at the bicycle races!'

'Oh, for goodness sake – you just don't get it, do you? However much money you spend on stocks or bicycle races, there's always a chance you'll get back ten times more than you spent, right? Now tell me: how are you going to get money out of a sofa?'

'All right, you can't get money out of it, but also you can't just lose it, not unless the house burns down. And it's *a nice* item.'

My answer made no impact. Bogey pulled a face that clearly stated, 'I can't bear any more stupidity from this little idiot', scooped up the two million yen, went straight to the bicycle track, and lost the lot that same afternoon.

Bogey wouldn't spend the whole day at the races. He'd show up for the afternoon session and stay just long enough to enjoy the excitement of the final race. So he'd be there for only about three hours. Three hours, two million yen – gone in a puff of smoke!

'Now, listen, Saya. The time to buy posh furniture is when you've got your own house, one that you really like. There's no point buying furniture for a rented apartment like this, because sooner or later you're going to have to move. For a place like this, furniture from Yoshizuya is fine.'

'But it's so ugly.'

'Saya, one of these days I'm going to build you a nice house, fashionable, the way you like it.'

'Really?'

Ah, the innocence of youth!

'Well, I grew up near Shonan Beach, so I'd probably want a house somewhere by the sea. Odawara might be nice. There's a bicycle racetrack there, and it has hot springs, of course. You can get to Tokyo in no time on the highway. Eventually I'd do everything from home – you know, play the market on the computer, just like that Ginzo Korekawa. Have you heard of Ginzo Korekawa? The guy they call "the last of the great speculators"?'

'Sounds pretty cool.'

In those days Bogey and I used to suck on our dreams the way you suck on candy. Making those dreams come true would, of course, involve patience, endurance and hard work over a long period, but in our minds there was no place for such obvious, unappealing thoughts.

'Once I've hit it big, we'll buy a house by the sea. I'll do my trading on the computer, so we'll have an easy time earning a living. Once we're settled, I'll write a novel. But I'm not so hung up on the idea that I'd make my wife and kids suffer for it, like that Shigeo (the Old Man). I'm only going to indulge myself when the financial foundations are firmly in place. I'm going to write a real classic one of these days. Eh, Saya?'

Bogey was a big fan of the author Kenzo Kitakata. He bought all his hard-boiled crime stories the moment they hit the bookstores. He also loved to go on about 'dandyism' and 'the male aesthetic', and he had an intense loathing of respectable, everyday lifestyles.

His burgundy-coloured wallet always had at least half a million yen in it, sometimes a million. He wasn't allowed a credit card as he'd been blacklisted because of all the debts he'd welshed on when he messed up in the commodities market. You can always spot guys like Bogey by the chunky wallet sticking out of their back pocket, like a big fat bar of chocolate. It is their pride and glory and their main distinguishing feature.

Oddly enough, though, however much he despised the respectable lifestyle, Bogey always wanted *me* to be the model of respectability. He liked me to wear my hair long and look like the daughter of an impeccable middle-class family. Though he tended toward foxy women who looked like his favourite actress, Kiwako Taichi, he always told me to look decent 'because you're different from those bar girls'. I liked it, actually, for behind those words I could sense that slightly warped sense of pride and principle that distinguishes casual dalliance from True Love.

In matters of the heart, Bogey was an old-fashioned Japanese: he wanted a saint for a wife and a whore for a lover.

'You know, when I first met you I thought *This girl's kind of dumb,*' he said. 'I can tell you that now 'coz you don't mind, right? And then someone said you were going to Sakura Women's University and I thought, *Well, well, you really can't judge by appearances.*' And with that he burst out laughing. Just as he was proud that he'd gone to a good university himself, he felt good about the fact that I was 'a proper student at one of the better schools'. I was glad it pleased him. *I'm glad I'm going to Sakura Women's University,* I thought. It was the first time that particular thought had ever struck me.

✻

I was happy. At the time I had no idea how dangerous it would be to get mixed up in Bogey's life. I was just happy to be with the man

I loved, happy to feel him gradually coming to trust me and becoming gentler and kinder towards me. I thought very little about anything else.

The summer holidays came around again, and I took to living almost full-time in Bogey's apartment. I grew my hair even longer and went on a diet. I knew that Bogey liked slim, long-haired women with an orthodox beauty.

Around this time he suddenly quit his job at Kabutocho Journal. All the work-related stress disappeared and he became altogether nicer and sweeter-tempered the whole time. When he wasn't playing mah-jong we'd go out for dinner and spend the night bar-hopping. I was happier still. It wasn't right for Bogey to be working for a weird company, knocking about with weird guys. He'd been right to quit. It had done him good. I was quite sure of that.

Since Bogey liked the sea, we used to go sea-fishing together. Once we ran into a great shoal of mackerel and caught about twenty tiny tiddlers with hardly a scrap of fat on them. They weren't good enough to eat, so we gave the whole lot to the Old Man, who was as usual struggling to maintain an adequate nutritional intake. The Old Man had finally managed to publish his first novel, but he was still only just on the right side of the breadline.

I was happy. Now that Bogey and I had so much time together, he would talk more truthfully and intimately. Sex was also getting better. I was becoming too excited to preserve the dead tuna pose.

'Saya, did you know that human bodies adapt to their sexual partners?' he said once. 'Your body's getting more used to mine, and sex is going to get better still. Soon you won't be able to sleep with anyone else.'

He was right. I had just passed one of life's little milestones – my first orgasm.

People talk a lot of nonsense about sex. They go on about the length and width of the male organ, the shape of the bell-end, whether it's straight or curved, the colour, the sheen, all that structural stuff. Or they blather on about how long people can keep it up, and all the various techniques. In fact, all you need for great sex is love – and effort. I had lots and lots of sex with my beloved Bogey, and after six months I had finally managed to come.

When it happened I was so moved that I burst into tears. I asked myself, quite seriously, what on earth I'd been doing all this time. All those sex sessions with no orgasm seemed such a waste. So when Bogey went on about how I wouldn't be able to sleep with any other man, I couldn't laugh, even though it was such a corny line. Because, in emotional terms, maybe it was true.

✿

'Saya, I'm not going to tell you what Kabutocho Journal does, because you wouldn't understand, but take it from me, that company is headed for trouble. The cops are going to arrest the president one of these days. I could see it coming before I quit, and that's why I refused to join the board of directors. I was happy just to make some quick money while I had the chance. Ever heard of Tomita Trading?'

'Nope. What is it?'

'It's where I worked before Kabutocho Journal. They're both pretty dodgy companies. There aren't too many guys around who've worked for both.'

'Hmm … Amazing.'

'You're pretty hard to impress.'

'All right then, what am I supposed to say?'

Actually, I'd never thought of Bogey as a man with a shady side to his working life. Work was work, money was money, men were men, and women were women – that was all.

'Well, you could show a little concern! Like that Taeko who used to work in the office. "Mr Ho-Ho-Hotta could be in terrible danger!" He mimicked Taeko's flustered stammer.

'All right then: Bo-Bo-Bogey could be in terrible danger! Will that do?'

'Honestly, Saya. Are you really a college girl?'

'At a better school than Taeko ever went to.'

'Posh girls like you don't usually come anywhere near *yakuza* types like me.'

'That's got nothing to do with it. You are what you are.'

'I see. So it's not that you fancied a *yakuza*. You just fancied a guy who happened to be a *yakuza*, right?'

'I didn't fancy a *yakuza*. The guy I fancied just happened to be a bit of a gambler.'

Having quit even the shady companies that would hire someone like him, Bogey was now making a living as a roaming professional mah-jong hustler.

Living fancy-free with a professional gambler – I was enjoying it, but there was just one problem. Now that Bogey had quit his job, the Ginza *mama-san* he was trying to get rid of had no phone number for him except the one at the apartment, and she took to calling the number all day long. The only respite came when she was asleep or running her bar. The rest of the time the phone just kept on ringing. Ring ring ring, ring ring ring. The bitch! The goddamn bitch!

Just when I was starting to think that I couldn't bear it any more, Bogey came home one evening in a panic.

'We're in the shit. She's got hold of the address. Today's Saturday, so the bar will be closed. I bet you she'll come here. Bound to. We've got to get out of here!'

'Where to?'

'To some hotel, of course.'

And that was the start of our life on the run. We rang up a hotel, made a reservation, grabbed a few things and hopped in a cab.

'Hotel New Otani, please.'

'Er, Bogey, how exactly did she get hold of the address?'

'She tracked me down at a mah-jong club last night.'

'That wouldn't give her the address of the apartment.'

'After the game finished, we went to her place. I was finally going to tell her we were through, but, you know, one thing led to another. And then I fell asleep, and while I was sleeping she found the apartment key in my jacket pocket with the address on the tag.'

'So you *weren't* playing mah-jong all night...'

It was just the beginning. I had set out on the long and winding road to becoming Bogey's woman, and the road wound uphill all the way.

THREE

'Takashi! Open the door, Takashi!'

BANGBANGBANGBANGBANG.

'It's me, Keiko!'

BANGBANGBANGBANGBANG.

The *mama-san* from the Ginza bar was launching another attack. Since she'd discovered Bogey's address, the attacks had escalated from the telephone to the doorstep. Here we were in this ultra-fashionable white condominium in Azabu Juban, and she was banging on the door like an avenging harpy from hell.

BANGBANGBANGBANGBANG.

Her blows reverberated down the hallway as she hammered on the rococo door.

'Takashi! I know you're in there! Come out! I'm not going till you come out!'

The weekends were particularly dangerous. People who work in the night world have it tough at weekends, at New Year and during the midsummer vacation period. Why? Because at those times the old guys – their regular patrons and boyfriends – will be back with their families. The law of supply and demand dictates that most of the city nightspots will be closed, so the hostesses who work there are plunged into a sea of loneliness.

It's all right for the younger hostesses. They can get to enjoy some nightlife as customers for a change, or take a trip overseas. They can hang out with girlfriends in the trade or enjoy a fling with a male acquaintance. But for the tired older women who've been in the business too long, these times are tough. So it stands to reason that if they manage to find a decent-looking middle-aged man who is divorced and available for companionship, they're not going to let go of him that easily.

'Takashi! I love you! Open the door!'

She was frantic. Say what you like about Bogey, he had a powerful attraction for this kind of butterfly of the night. He didn't have the sultry looks of a gigolo or a film star, but he did exude a special charm that appealed to women who have a professional interest in men. Besides, he was generous with money, an interesting talker, affectionate, and never nasty or sarcastic. He appreciated good food and had been to a posh university. Guys like that don't come along too often.

Bogey's only faults were a weakness for women and an addiction to gambling. But a veteran hostess hardened by thousands of romantic encounters could easily deal with the former problem (or so she thought). As for the latter, a woman used to earning her money at night would be able to spare a few banknotes to finance the occasional flutter. As a matter of fact, probably the only kind of woman who could sustain a relationship with a gambler would be a woman in the nightclub business, and not just a regular hostess, either, but a *mama-san* with her own establishment. When such women gazed upon Bogey, they got the feeling that it was OK to lend him money, that they would get it back a hundred times over.

This *mama-san* was a formidable adversary. Since her countless phone calls were never returned, she must have figured out that Bogey and I had a special code, and one day the cunning old witch tried the trick of letting the phone ring once and then calling again. Brilliant! She got it first time. There I was, sitting nervously in the apartment waiting for Bogey to call, like one of the little goats waiting for its mummy to come home, when I heard the familiar code and dashed to the telephone.

'Saya Takagishi, I presume?'

Somehow, she'd got hold of my full name. I froze right away, while she launched straight into a powerful harangue.

'You're a student, right? Well then, act like a student and go to school! You're nothing but a nuisance to Hotta. You brazen little hussy! It's money you're after, is it? Or do you reckon you're going to bully him into marrying you? How much longer will you hang around where you're not wanted? It's high time you learned to behave yourself!'

Wow, this was one of those catfights I'd heard rumours about. But all I could think of was, 'You have no right to talk to me like that.'

I said it in a really cool, disdainful tone.

'You what? Now listen – do you have any idea how many years Hotta and I have been together?'

'Just a couple, right? I also happen to know he's been trying to dump you for the last six months or more.'

A palpable hit. She was lost for words, but not for long.

'Don't you worry about our relationship. Hotta and I are going to get *married*.'

And with that she hung up.

Well, close to age forty and with the future to think about, you could understand her wanting to buy herself a little security by getting married. Still, it wasn't something you could do on your own. Bogey knew how she felt and had taken steps to ensure that she could continue to support herself on her own. For instance, he'd bought the rights to the bar she ran and had signed them over to her. And he'd bought her a little dog to keep her company after he was gone. Until then she'd just been a hired *mama-san* who did not have her own bar or her own toy dog.

Despite that, her crazy talk about how she was going to marry Bogey had me worried. She seemed to be at the end of her tether. What would she do next? I was scared to death.

✢

'Uh-oh, I reckon she's going to come again tonight. Saya, call a hotel, quick.'

We were still spending weekends on the run, escaping by cab.

'Take us to the Tokyo Prince Hotel.'

'The Hotel New Otani, please.'

'The Akasaka Prince Hotel annex ... Ha-ha, that brings back memories.'

'The Capitol Tokyu, please. I like that hotel. It's got a very sophisticated ambiance, especially the Lipo Bar. Let's have cock-tails there!'

So you see we actually enjoyed our tour of Tokyo hotels. Bogey could turn any situation into a joke.

'I just adore hotels,' he'd say. 'The sheets are smooth and clean, the towels aren't covered in cat hairs, and they'll bring you any-thing you want, twenty-four hours a day.'

But one day something happened that could have cost me my life. It was a Saturday afternoon and Bogey was still not back, he having left the previous evening for an all-night mah-jong session. That was the moment the *mama-san* chose to launch her doorstep attack.

BANGBANGBANGBANGBANG.

'Takashi! Open the door! It's me!'

It was a typical nightlife voice – deep and husky from long years of drinking, smoking and talking, night after night. *It was kind of sexy*, I had to admit. What was I thinking of? This was no time to be admiring her voice! Every week she was coming over to bang on the door. It was intolerable.

Still, I couldn't resist peering through the peephole to see what she looked like. The peephole had a fisheye lens that made anyone look ridiculous, but for once I couldn't laugh. I just stood there, holding my breath.

There was something special about her. She reminded me of the time I noticed a madwoman on a street corner. Amidst all the hustle and bustle of hurrying people, she was standing there, stock-still. The air and the flow of time around her seemed different. She was looking up at the sky with an enigmatic smile on her face, suffused with a mysterious beauty not of this world. Peering through the fisheye lens at this woman gave me the same kind of feeling.

She looked much younger than I'd expected, and her complexion was strikingly fair. Her lightly permed brownish hair was tangled around her face in total disarray. She looked as if she hadn't slept the previous night. Her mascara was smudged in long, black tearstains across her cheeks. Despite everything, she was a beautiful woman. The years had taken away some of the sparkle, but you could still tell she was special, with her translucent skin and the fine-boned delicacy of her arms and legs.

Her long, white fingers were aglitter with ruby and emerald rings, set amidst clusters of little diamonds in gold and silver. And, of course, she had a gold necklace around her slender neck. I recognised her lacquered Caran d'Ache wristwatch, the one that matched Bogey's, because he had once brought it home to take to a local pawnshop. Obviously he'd managed to get it out of hock and return it to her elegant wrist.

She was wearing a lemon-yellow summer knit suit, which accentuated her slender figure and ample bust, and high-heel shoes with decorative stitching. Whichever way you looked at her she was clearly a lady of the night world, but a very classy one.

There was no way out for me, and just as I was wondering what to do, her terrifying voice came right at me through the door.

'Saya Takagishi. I know you're in there. Come on out!'

71

God! How had she guessed? Just then the telephone rang. It was Bogey's code, and this time it couldn't be a trap. Saved! I rushed to answer it.

'Bogey! What am I gonna do? It's the *mama-san*! She's here again, and she's calling for me to come out!'

'I see. That *is* tough. The trouble is I haven't finished my mah-jong game yet.'

'Mah-jong! I don't believe this! Don't you care what happens to me? She's rattling the doorknob, you know!'

I spoke in a furious, hissing whisper. That gave Bogey slight pause for thought, but he soon came up with a solution.

'I've got it! Call Ken-ken. He'll come right away. Here's the number.'

✲

It was always like that with Bogey. Gambling came first in his life, boozing second, and women were an afternoon snack between more important matters. I was reminded of that some time after this incident, when he got me pregnant.

'I see,' he remarked casually when I told him. 'Bad news. Get an abortion.'

'You bastard! You can't say it just like that!'

'But you're a sophomore, right? You can't have a baby now, can you?'

'But...'

'And while you're about it, have one of those rings put in. We don't want you getting knocked up again. A woman can't manage too many abortions.'

'A ring? You mean one of those IUDs they told us about in our health and hygiene lessons at high school?'

How could he talk about such things so casually to me – an

72

innocent girl who'd never had a baby and who'd been a virgin just a year previously?

Needless to say, Bogey would never have dreamed of taking the trouble to use a condom. I had to take care of contraception, and up until now I'd used Mylura, a ring-shaped spermicidal capsule that you popped in a few minutes before having sex. They were supposed to dissolve on contact, but they weren't totally reliable, as I discovered one night when Bogey's dick emerged from a job well done, wreathed with a Mylura ring.

I had to laugh at the time, but I believe that night was my undoing. Mylura only works once the ring has dissolved, and sure enough I got into trouble.

I had awful morning sickness. At first I thought I was just having bad hangovers, but Bogey and I were getting through a bottle of Hennessy a day and I had developed immunity to hangovers. The truth slowly dawned.

'Bogey, I think I'm throwing up because I'm pregnant.'

'Pregnant? How come? You said you were taking precautions!'

'Yeah, but remember that time when the Mylura got stuck on the end of your penis, right?'

'Mylura? What's that?'

'Oh, never mind!'

He looked so totally vacant that I couldn't be angry with him. I was much more bothered about the morning sickness. It was so horrible that I'd happily have had an abortion there and then if it'd meant an end to the nausea. I'm quite sure that any anti-abortion activists overhearing this conversation would have been foaming at the mouth.

'If you don't fancy the operation, ask the doc about taking some medicine to induce the abortion. I'm fairly sure some new stuff's been developed. The company that makes it is a hot stock right now. It's a drug that makes you go into labour and the thing just comes out by itself. If you do it in the first three months, the baby's still tiny, so it doesn't hurt much apparently.'

Another wave of nausea swept over me. 'Ugh, anything, anything! But fast!'

I did as Bogey had suggested and asked the doctor about the new abortion drug. He looked totally horrified.

'No, no, no. You don't want to be messing with that. You wouldn't even mention it if you had any idea how painful it is to go into labour. If you'd ever experienced childbirth it might be an option, but a young girl like you? No way! You just can't imagine the pain.'

He was a local gynaecologist – the sort to whom large hospitals referred women who wanted abortions. An abortionist from tip to toe, he was assisted by an elderly wife, who served as nurse and receptionist at the little clinic.

On the day of the operation, I went there alone. Bogey gave me the money for the abortion, but he wouldn't come with me. 'Today I'm going to do battle to avenge that child's death!' he said, and headed off to the bicycle track.

'All right, lie down here.'

Apparently the table that the doctor used for internal examinations also served as the operating table. He and his wife were very brisk and businesslike. Their air of experience was comforting and reassuring.

'Relax, there's nothing to worry about. It'll all be over before you know it. Now I want you to count slowly to a hundred.'

There was a shabby kindness about the old doctor that seemed to suit his not-so-respectable profession. I did as instructed while the anaesthesia took effect.

'One, two, three, four, five, six, sev, sev...'

Afterwards I couldn't remember getting past seven.

'There you are. All done. You can go home in an hour or so.'

When I came to, the old doctor was just taking off the cloth that had been wrapped around my nether regions, and he was talking away in the same matter-of-fact manner.

I couldn't move. My mind felt miles away as I slowly lifted my heavy eyelids. Somehow or other I had been carried upstairs and was lying in a Japanese-style room on the second floor. It was kind of snug, reminding me that the old-fashioned clinic was also home to the old abortionist and his wife.

✳

I telephoned Ken-ken as Bogey had suggested. He came right away – he lived in the same condo a couple of floors above us. I could hear him talking with the *mama-san* outside the door.

'Oh dear, oh dear, oh dear, Keiko, we can't have you squatting in a place like this. You'll catch your death of cold!'

'Ken-ken...'

'Be a good girl and come along with me.'

'But that woman's in there...'

The *mama-san* was sobbing as she spoke.

'No, she isn't. There's no one in. Let's go down to the sushi bar on the first floor and have a drink. And we'll call Hotta from there, all right?'

Ken-ken always had several girlfriends on the boil, and he was a real pro when it came to handling women. His gently coaxing voice worked wonders on the *mama-san*. She'd seemed so determined and implacable, yet she quietly allowed herself to be led to the sushi bar – from which I received a whispered phone call shortly after.

'Saya? Everything's under control. But it might be a good idea if you went home while I've got her in the sushi bar. Will you do that, please? I'll get Hotta to give you a call later.'

Ken-ken had a knack for putting people at ease. OK, so maybe he didn't have a heart as such, but his voice was so full of kindness and consideration it would soothe anyone. He had a natural talent for fraud, that man. Thinking about this, I headed for the sanctuary of home and my long-neglected mother. My legs were still trembling from the recent trauma.

✡

My mother was evidently out.

The dusty old house seemed more like a warehouse than a home. There were stacks of documents and books to do with my mother's work, piles of dry-cleaning in plastic bags, mounds of those midsummer gifts, still in their wrapping paper, that the Japanese customarily send to anyone who's done them a favour. So this was what became of the house when I was away! I heaved a deep sigh and started to tidy up.

In the old days, my dad used to do the housework. When he left I took over. There was a time when Ma earned five times as much as Dad, and she largely footed the bill for our increasingly luxurious lifestyle.

'Tsk! I earn all the money and I have to keep the stupid house clean as well. It's all wrong.'

That was her subtle signal to Dad that he ought to take a more active role in household chores. At work Dad was a waste of office space, so they just parked him by the window and gave him a few pointless tasks for the sake of appearances. No heavy overtime or drinking sessions with the boys for him – he'd be home on the dot and proceed to lounge around while Ma got angry with him, which she did constantly. He was useless, he was good for nothing, he was a parasite living off her earnings. Once she'd made that crystal clear she'd give him his orders and set him to work.

He'd do as he was told. He'd wash the dishes, take out the garbage, clean the toilet and the bathroom. And he'd whistle while he worked. Normally he never whistled, but when he was under a lot of stress, when he could hardly bear it, then he'd whistle. It was supposed to sound cheerful, but it sounded sad and slightly hysterical to me.

Was he whistling to make it sound as if he were happy doing this kind of work? Or was it an attempt to find some tiny enjoyment in the middle of his misery? Whenever I lingered for any time in that house of ours, his tragic figure would float before my eyes.

'I just don't understand why he doesn't get the hell out of here!' That's how Mother used to rant about him, loud enough to be sure he heard. 'No woman would put up with it! I wouldn't! He's disgusting!'

Dad did put up with it all. Why didn't he leave? Because he was terrified of being alone. But the moment he found someone to keep him company he was gone like a bat out of hell.

By the time I'd finished cleaning the house it was past midnight. I didn't know what time Bogey would call, so I put the telephone next to my pillow and went to sleep in my old bed. It stank of mould.

The phone rang some time later. Half asleep I picked up the receiver and glanced at the clock. It was three in the morning.

'You're gonna get killed, you know, Saya.'

'Wh-what?'

I was exhausted, and my voice was weak. I'd had a very stressful afternoon, followed by five hours of cleaning a house.

'That woman – Ken-ken says she had a carving knife this afternoon.'

'*A carving knife?*'

I sat up abruptly.

'If you'd opened the door, she'd have killed you.'

This was the kind of story that cropped up in Bogey's wild years in Osaka and Kobe. I'd never for a moment imagined I could get mixed up in something similar. He'd told me about some of the hairier moments in his past affairs, like the time a bar girl he'd broken up with had called him down to the docks and tried to stab him with a big pair of scissors. Then there was this other woman who'd faked her own suicide. I'd always assumed that these tales of desperate love had nothing to do with little me. But now I was right in the middle of one of them. My face went white as a sheet.

'It's better not to meet for a while.'

'Better not for who to meet?'

'You and me, of course.'

'Why?'

''Coz it's dangerous! You don't want to get stabbed, do you?'

'If only you'd make a clean break with her, everything would be OK! It's because you keep on popping back to her for a quick one now and again that she doesn't get the message! That's what's causing all the trouble, right?'

It was the truth. Every couple of weeks Bogey would pretend he was out playing mah-jong all night when in fact he'd be shacked up with the *mama-san*. It wasn't too tough to figure out, since he'd come home wearing different underwear and smelling of different shampoo. I supposed that a young, inexperienced girl like me could not keep him satisfied all the time, so I kept my mouth shut and turned a blind eye. But this time I had to speak out. I'd finally found some meaning and purpose to my life and that woman was trying to take it away.

'Saya, it's all very well saying that, but there's an order to things, you know. You've got to deal with people one at a time. First come, first served, sort of thing.'

I lost my temper. This guy spoke as though it had nothing to do with him, as though it was someone else's problem, as if he thought women just buzzed around him like flies.

'There's no first come, first fucking served in love!' I screamed into the phone.

Besides, I was younger than her, cuter than her, and I was still at college. I was worth much more to Bogey than that old witch – of course I was! You could tell that I meant something special to him from the expression on his face when he introduced me to his friends, an expression that said here was something more than just another girlfriend.

On this occasion, however, Bogey kept his cool.

'Even so, you know, there is a pecking order.'

'Just a goddamn minute – I'm coming over, right now.'

'Hang on, hang on! She might be waiting to ambush you again.'

'Huh! That old bitch? You could see she hadn't slept all night. She's bound to be asleep now.'

I piled out of bed, ran out of the house, found a cab, and shot straight over to Bogey's place. No way was I going to let that old harpy get her claws back into him!

Was I really so determined? Up till now I'd always been a don't-really-care, either-way, whatever, sort of person. I wasn't the type to grit my teeth and fight it out. I'd never seen the point of making a fuss over anything. Love changes a woman. Somehow I'd turned into the kind of woman I used to despise most – the scary type who's always hustling to get her way. You see them everywhere.

'I don't care if she's hiding in the shadows waiting to stab me. Let her stab away. She'll be the one who goes to prison. It might hurt a bit, but if it means getting her out of the way, who cares? I won't die. A little stab won't bother me. That bitch could never kill me. A few days in hospital, that's the worst that could happen. I AM NOT AFRAID!'

Muttering to myself like that, I braced myself against the night wind and crossed the road to Bogey's condo.

I rattled the key in the lock, opened the door with a bang and made a beeline for the bedroom. There was Bogey in characteristic pose, sprawled on the bed in his boxer shorts, his chubby tummy exposed and a glass of Hennessy and water in his hand. I went straight for his trousers, which lay crumpled on the floor where he'd tossed them, rifled through the pockets and pulled out a jingling bunch of keys. There was one key on the ring that I'd often wondered about, but now I reckoned I knew whose door it opened. I slid it off the ring, and – ignoring Bogey's cries of '*Stop it! What are you playing at? Don't!*' – ran to the veranda and hurled it out into the darkness with all the force I could muster. We were on the seventh floor and the little sliver of silver was instantly swallowed up by the night. There were a number of temples in Azabu Juban, and one of them was just opposite the apartment block. I guess the key landed somewhere in the temple's wooded grounds.

I turned on my heel and spoke to Bogey.

'That's better. No more visits to that woman. No more whimpering about not being able to dump her because you feel sorry for her. That's an insult – to her too! She's a good-looking woman, and once she's shot of you for good she'll find another man right away. As for you and me, let's leave this condo and move somewhere else!'

It occurred to me that this was the first time I'd ever got tough with Bogey. For the first time I had thought for myself and expressed my opinion. Bogey was dumbstruck.

We had to leave the condo in Azabu Jubanin any event, for economic reasons. Bogey had long since quit Kabutocho Journal. All the fat bonuses that had come jumping into his pocket from that job had jumped out again in the course of his nightly binges of wine, women and gambling.

You can get some idea of Bogey's finances from the fact that he'd had to hock the *mama-san*'s Caran d'Ache watch, together with his gold necklace and bracelet, to raise funds for his next mah-jong game, which, in turn, was a necessary step to raise funds for his next excursion to the bicycle races.

Despite the desperate straits he was in, Bogey couldn't stop going out on the town – he was a dyed-in-the-wool nightclubber.

'You know, Saya, ever since you started choosing my clothes, I've been a great hit with the club girls. They're all over me! You should hear the way they go on. "Look at that big fish! Isn't he cute?"'

As always, it took only a couple of drinks to put Bogey in a frolicsome mood. Since he'd quit Kabutocho Journal, he no longer needed to wear suits, so he took to dressing informally, or 'in civvies' as he put it, at all times. At first the outfits were selected by his Ginza *mama-san*, and they all had that slightly seedy, night-life look about them: casual linen jackets, linen trousers with razor-sharp creases, belts by Yves Saint Laurent or Hermes – clothes that made you wonder why the wearer would wish to stress so intensely the fact that he was middle-aged.

So I took it upon myself to choose Bogey's attire. Whenever he went clothes shopping he'd head for boring places – the local gents' tailors or an old-fashioned department store such as Takashimaya or Tokyu. But I managed to drag him, kicking and screaming, to the Seibu B store in Shibuya.

There I found him an elegant white summer sweater, a coarse cotton knit sporting a big fish motif. I found some white jeans to match and some slip-on shoes instead of the usual lace-ups, and lo and behold Bogey was transformed into a cutie-pie, as I'd predicted. Add a copper-toned short-sleeve cotton shirt with an open neck, and the picture was complete. The outfit complimented Bogey's smooth, dark skin and bull neck perfectly.

Men, like women, have different shapes and builds, so naturally the clothes that suit them also differ. Unfortunately men think of clothes as a kind of uniform: 'I'm middle-aged so I've got to wear this.' And they all end up looking dull and dowdy.

Bogey immediately noticed the difference when he went about town in the Saya Takagishi Collection. His mah-jong buddies would grumble about how he was showing off just because he'd got himself a young girlfriend. On the other hand, he was a hit with all the hostesses. 'Oooh, Mr Hotta. You've become so youthful all of a sudden!'

Of course he loved it when they made a fuss of him like that. He'd always thought that it didn't matter what he wore off-duty, but now he'd totally changed his thinking: he'd actually search in his wardrobe to find his favourites.

'Saya, where's my sonblue?'

'I keep telling you – the word's *"blouson"*.'

Now he would look at himself in the mirror even when he was wearing something casual. Up until then he'd only ever looked in the mirror when he was knotting his tie. He was learning the pleasure of dressing up.

Mind you, he still had a few things to discover about the gentle art of coordination. If I didn't help him out, he'd end up with the most dreadful mismatches.

'Hmm, I've got to hand it to you, Saya. You may not have much common sense but you certainly have dress sense.'

He gazed at me in fascination as I quickly picked out a few usable items from among the mountain of tasteless brand-name clothes he owned and put them on him.

'That's right, Bogey. Actually, I really wanted to be a fashion designer.'

'A fashion designer?'

'Yes. That was my dream since I was a small kid. In those days there wasn't much in the way of cute clothing in Japan, so my mother used to design clothes for herself and me and ask one of my aunts to make them for us. This aunt graduated from the Bunka Fashion College, a trendy design school in Shibuya, and I really wanted to go there. I had set my heart on making clothes you couldn't buy that I wanted to wear myself, or see somebody else wearing.'

'Why didn't you go to the fashion school?'

'Ma wouldn't have it. A vocational school wasn't good enough for her precious daughter. It had to be a proper university or she'd have cut off the money.'

'So you abandoned your dream?'

'I did.'

'You're hopeless, Saya! I thought people were supposed to try for their dreams at any cost.'

'Well, you're not exactly the type yourself, are you, Bogey?'

'Yeah ... you're right, of course.' And he guffawed.

That was indeed the truth. Bogey didn't have anything he wanted to do badly enough to endure hardship for the sake of it. His education, for instance. He'd had no burning ambition to go to a famous public university. It was just that in his high-school days, when he had nothing on his mind but mah-jong and horse-racing, his dad's company went bust and his mother told him they wouldn't have enough money to send him to a private university. It would have been ostentatious to have tried for Tokyo University (the snootiest in Tokyo), so he went for Hitotsubashi University (the second poshest). Much the same sort of cynical reasoning had led me to Sakura Women's University. We'd both managed to get into what our respective mothers considered to be 'a good school', and that was fine by us. We both liked to pour scorn on those poor saps who studied themselves into the ground to get into a school a notch or two above their level and then struggled frantically for a career to match.

At the same time as Bogey was revamping his wardrobe, I had

managed to grow my hair long enough to start getting him to buy
me designer clothes for elegant young ladies: dresses by Renoma
and Alpha Cubic and shoes with slender heels.

I had decided that I was going to become the kind of woman
Bogey liked – a sophisticated young lady, demure on the surface
but with a lot of careful grooming beneath the polished exterior. I
always went to extremes and now I redoubled my dieting efforts.
I will get so slim that my waist will snap I thought to myself.

☆

There was another reason we had to move. Things were heating
up at Kabutocho Journal and Bogey heard through the grapevine
that the police would soon be searching the residences of former
employees.

Bogey and Ken-ken were talking about finding some out-of-the-
way area where they could rent apartments. Ken-ken had quit at
about the same time as Bogey, and the two of them were equally
short of cash. Ken-ken didn't gamble; he was the type who prefers
to blow all his money on women.

We wanted a place for about one-third of our present rent,
which meant going out into the sticks. Ken-ken suggested
Kawasaki, the drab industrial city wedged between Tokyo and
Yokohama where one of his girlfriends lived, so Bogey and I
dutifully started looking for an apartment in Kawasaki.

However, the place we saw was in such a boring, nondescript
district that I couldn't stomach it. The building itself wasn't bad it
had plenty of sunlight, and Ken-ken wanted us to sign contracts
there and then, but I moaned and groaned, and kicked up a fuss
with Bogey to persuade him to look somewhere else.

I disliked Ken-ken. I couldn't trust him. Admittedly it was a gut
reaction, but I smelled something fishy about the guy. Of course,

Bogey had been doing exactly the same kind of business as Ken-ken, but he wasn't innately shady like Ken-ken. Some people are naturally shady: they're like mould and can only live by sucking the vitality out of others. Other people are naturally sunny: they emit light that can warm people. That was the fundamental difference between the two of them.

I could see it all. Bogey, with his intelligence and good nature, was being exploited by Ken-ken, with his low cunning. And Bogey was not even aware of this. I tried to talk to him about it, but he didn't want to know. He'd simply say: 'This is a friendship between men. Women should shut up about it.'

Whenever Ken-ken came to visit I would get cruel treatment. Bogey liked the idea of 'a man's world'. He judged women severely but was soft on men. It was the thought that he could place such trust in Ken-ken, of all men, that I found utterly infuriating.

'Bogey, I could never learn to like this place. Besides, it's just too far out from Tokyo. We'd rot if we lived here!'

'Hmm, perhaps you're right. It's a long way to the nearest mah-jong club, too, although there's a bicycle track nearby.'

'Look,' I said, 'how about Nezu? That's close to the centre of Tokyo, just a few stops on the Chiyoda Line. Rents are cheap there, it's near where I live, and there are lots of famous old buildings and sights so that we can enjoy going for walks now and then.'

It was September and school was about to start. I was still a student, sort of, and that meant having to do homework and stuff. So it would be really convenient to be within easy reach of my own house.

Another thing about Nezu was that it had such a working-class reputation that Roppongi and Ginza people would never go and live there, not even by accident. Besides, Bogey was out of cash, so surely we'd be shot of the *mama-san* for good?

I was bubbling with confidence. In those days I never felt the

85

slightest anxiety. I took Bogey to Nezu and got off the train in high spirits. There was an estate agents right in front of the station. In we went, and since Bogey didn't seem to care either way I was able to pick out an apartment on the spot. It was a 2LDK, meaning two bedrooms - one Western style and one Japanese style - plus a combined living room, dining room, and kitchen. The place was in a new block and rented at 130,000 yen a month including management fees. It was a steal.

You could pick up a bargain like this now and again in this part of town. Apparently, quite a few landlords had built these rental condominiums as a means of avoiding taxes. There was only one little snag: unlike the place in Azabu Juban, the ban on pets was strictly enforced. The cats would have to be hidden away, but I didn't view that as a big problem.

'Once we've rented the place we can do as we like.'

✡

If I was going to have Bogey all to myself, I would have to accept some womanly responsibilities. I would have to make sure that he was satisfied with the arrangement. So I threw myself with gusto into the role of newly wedded wife.

First I went out and bought one of Masaru Doi's books on traditional-style cuisine. Now that Bogey's days of living like a lord were over, he'd have to have more of his meals at home. I would have to graduate rapidly from the girlish cooking I was used to doing. Pasta and omelettes wouldn't persuade Bogey to pick up his chopsticks. He'd end up going to some other woman, or feeling sad and sentimental about his deceased wife. That would never do!

It was time for me to show some feminine determination. Every evening I'd come home from college and devote myself to preparing fish stock, peeling shrimps, and so on – all with the greatest care and dedication.

As with the college entrance exams, I proved to be just as good as the next guy at reading the manual and acquiring skills. I didn't have a long attention span, but it was long enough to pass a math test or prepare crispy deep-fried tempura. I was good at such short-term challenges.

At first Bogey turned up his nose at my cooking, but as it improved he took to spending more time at home, eating and drinking until the small hours.

Exactly as planned, I chuckled to myself.

It was tough at first. I made a thorough tour of the Nezu shopping street, taking good care to make friends with all the old men and women at the fishmongers, the food stores, the shellfish shops, the shops selling chicken and other meat, and even the sales staff at the Akafudado supermarket. I cultivated these people and got myself little discounts on stuff that was just in season, and I'd throw myself body and soul into preparing these carefully selected ingredients. Then I'd just as carefully deposit the cold and shrivelled results in the rubbish bin.

Bogey was conscientious about telephoning, and he'd often call to let me know he was on his way home. But it was difficult when he was out playing mah-jong. You never know when a game of mah-jong is going to end (if ever), and though he'd call to say he was 'about to be on his way', such calls never actually heralded his return. Even so, when he finally did arrive, wreathed in smiles and blathering on about what an interesting game mah-jong was because it gave you so many fascinating insights into human nature, and so on, I couldn't be hard on him.

Besides, although we were living a more restrained lifestyle , the fact was that we were now living off Bogey's mah-jong winnings. It was his business, and I couldn't very well criticise him for putting in a bit of overtime. I guess he sensed that, because he'd casually turn up his nose at my beautifully prepared dishes and have some beef jerky and a drink instead, saying something to the effect that 'it won't taste right now that it's not freshly made'.

Without a word I would slide the whole plateful into the bin, take the bin-liner bag out to the garbage disposal shed, and relieve my feelings by quietly smashing one of the cheap plates that we didn't really need.

When you're angry, smash a plate.

I coughed, wheezed and spluttered as I gabbled to myself in the privacy of the garbage shed. I was putting too much into the performance. Tears and slobber mingled on my face.

Day after day, I would tie my hair back and set to work looking after Bogey and the cats. Feeding and cleaning, that was all I did. My once-long nails were now clipped short; my fingertips were coarse from all the water and soapsuds; and, of course, I didn't have manicures any more. They weren't necessary as Bogey never took me anywhere – he no longer had the money for a night out.

As I stood in the garbage shed I heaved a deep sigh, blew my nose on my apron, and gazed up at the cold night sky of early winter.

This time last year I had felt like a queen among the cheap young lads of my acquaintance. Now here I was living like a shabby housewife. And Bogey wouldn't even eat the food I'd struggled so hard to prepare. Here I was, in the garbage shed, weeping amidst the rubbish bins with the remains of his uneaten dinner. I'd nearly been stabbed by a Ginza *mama-san*. I'd had an abortion. And although things had been good for while in Azabu Juban, my standard of living was threatening to fall below what it had been before.

Before Bogey, I used to go on dates with Hajime and other boyfriends. They would buy me things, and we would go to trendy bars and discos, and all that. I'd do some part-time job now and again, maybe sleep with an old geezer occasionally, and it had been fun in its own way, sort of. Or so it seemed to me now, looking back from my present situation.

These days I never saw my old friends I'd had a year ago, least of all Hajime. When he found out that I was seeing Bogey, he stood there gaping so long I thought his jaw was about to drop off. I never saw him again. He immediately quit Kabutocho Journal. Freed from the need for funds to take me out, he no longer needed to work.

You can say what you like about Hajime, but he was quite a presentable young guy with a certain amount of money. I had dropped out of the category of presentable young ladies that appealed to boys like him. For six months now I hadn't been to the movies, I hadn't been to a concert, and even if I happened to run into one of my old friends, we had nothing to say to each other. I couldn't even have a cup of tea in a café with one of my fellow students without being consumed by guilt and anxiety about the possibility that Bogey might come home while I was out, that he would start to feel lonely and end up running back to the mama-san.

At college I attended just enough classes to avoid getting thrown out. The only students I bothered to hang out with were the serious ones – girls I wouldn't have been seen dead with in my first year – who would lend me their lecture notes for classes I'd missed. Back in Nezu, I'd curl up with the cats and ploddingly copy those notes.

Ah, what a dull thing am I!

Even with all these dark thoughts scudding across my mind, I would tidy up the broken bits of plate, feel a little better, and return to the room with Bogey and the cats.

I had chosen this life, and I had made Bogey choose me, so I had nothing to complain about. That's what I told myself. Bogey rubbed it in, of course, with 'think how miserable you'd be if I found someone I *really* fancied'.

That was an issue I had to resolve before he would consider me a true woman. Somehow I had to make Bogey love me as much as I loved him. Otherwise my woman's pride would never forgive me. Sex, cooking, making him a cup of coffee – whatever the task, I would strive to produce a performance that would please him as far as was humanly possible.

At the end of the day, Bogey's skin was so inviting that the pleasure of having it next to me would dispel my anger at his selfishness. However furious I felt, I had only to snuggle into that warm embrace and drift off to sleep, cleansed of all dissatisfaction, breast brimful of happiness.

'Hey, it's getting cold. Too cold to sleep alone again, eh?' he'd say.

✧

We were heading into winter. Bogey's wallet was enduring a financial winter: he was finding it harder to raise funds for his mah-jong campaigns. He usually had to borrow his stake money before he could start a game.

He would go through his address book, call somebody up, dash out to meet them, and come back with 200,000 or 300,000 yen he'd managed to borrow. It seemed mysterious.

'Who are these people who'll lend you that kind of money?'

I was worried that he might have resumed relations with the *mama-san*, but Bogey simply said, 'It's money I lent them, so I'm just getting it back.'

I had no deep moral feelings about where other people obtained their money, so I was happy to shrug my shoulders and take

Bogey's word for it. He continued in his secretive ways. These days he had two telephones, each with a different number, and one of them I was not allowed to answer. All very suspect.

We could get by when he was winning at mah-jong, but recently he'd been on a losing streak. The utility bills had gone unpaid and we were facing the prospect of the telephone, electricity and water being disconnected. His watch and all his jewellery had long since gone to the pawnshop, and we had to pay interest on them to avoid them being forfeited. Eventually even the ring my mother had given me for my twentieth birthday went into hock.

'What the hell's happened to my luck?' he'd ask. 'It's hit rock bottom. You know, a long time ago I had my palm read by this fortuneteller who told me that guys with lines like mine would always have brilliant luck or terrible luck – nothing in between. He also said that the good times and bad times would come in two-year cycles. Hell, I could sure do with a change.'

'Let's have a look at your palm.'

Bogey did indeed have an unusual palm. He had big, fat lines that looked as if someone had drawn them in with a marker pen. He had hands like those of a cartoon character.

'Hey! You've got cartoon hands!'

'Saya, you're incredibly cheerful considering how broke we are. If I don't have a few ten-thousand-yen notes in my wallet I feel too scared to go out. But you happily go off to school with just three hundred yen on you, right?'

'Yep!'

'It really doesn't bother you?'

'Nope! I have my bus pass to get there, and three hundred yen's enough for a cup of coffee if I want one. If something crops up, I can always borrow some cash from a friend and pay her back next time I see her.'

'That's fantastic. Me, I just get depressed when I'm out of money; so, so depressed.'

Actually, the truth about my financial situation was rather different. I would go back to my own home now and again and do some cleaning for Ma, who would slip me some pocket money for my pains. Going to college does entail quite a lot of little expenses, and these small donations just about covered them. But I wasn't going to let Bogey put that money into his mah-jong war chest, so I remained discreetly silent on the subject.

After all, this was money that my revered mother had earned by the sweat of her brow, working hard at a proper job. It was fundamentally different from money given as a tip to a hostess, or won at the gambling table, or fiddled out of the stock market. But though I couldn't give Bogey money, I did sometimes help myself to one of those presents of food that were cluttering up my mother's apartment – a nice ham, maybe, or some tinned fruit, sometimes even a bag of rice or some green tea. Her business associates would give her these items during the summer and winter gift-giving seasons, and there were always plenty left over so there was no harm in doing what I did. I didn't tell Bogey about this habit of mine, either.

I didn't want to make Bogey any more depressed than he already was about money. You could read the decline in his fortunes by his drinking habits. From Hennessy he'd descended to Chivas Regal, then to Wild Turkey, to Four Roses, and then he descended further down to Canadian Club. From Canadian Club he'd finally given up whisky and bourbon altogether and had settled for Beni Otome – a brand of *shochu*, a cheap domestic spirit, although I guess Beni Otome, translating as 'Scarlet Virgin', is a fairly respectable brand.

We'd make the best of it. We'd mix the *shochu* with hot water and toss in some salted, pickled plums, a delicacy I'd brought over from mother's. I'd cook some fermented fish that happened to go very well with *shochu* and we'd be as happy as kings. The fish would stink rather (it was called *kusaya*, meaning 'smelly' in Japanese), and we got complaints from the neighbours, but we didn't care.

'You know the film star Yoshiko Sakuma? Apparently she has *kusaya* and *shochu* every evening. Says she's never happier than when she's having *kusaya* and *shochu*.'

Bogey was greatly cheered by that thought. In funny ways like this, he was no different from the next middle-aged guy. He liked the glitterati, especially the more glamorous actresses of his generation.

As for me, it was amazing how little I was bothered by poverty. I could understand Bogey finding this puzzling, for it was quite a puzzle to me, too. But I didn't need money. Apart from spending the bare minimum of time at the university, I was nearly always in the apartment with the cats. The apartment was much shabbier than the one in Azabu Juban: it had only one Japanese-style room, and the living-dining-kitchen area had awful plastic floor tiles. Even so, it was new and had a lot of sunlight.

Most of the furniture was the same old stuff we'd had in Azabu Juban, and since the apartment had no closet, at Bogey's suggestion we'd also bought a cheap plastic wardrobe for our clothes.

'Wow, I didn't know they still made this kind of thing!'

That was my reaction when I saw the plastic wardrobe in a furniture shop. Also, since the cats were still at an age when they loved to get up to mischief, we had to lay down a heavy carpet over the tatami mats in the Japanese-style room. You could imagine what a mess the cats would have made of the delicate tatami as they gleefully sharpened their claws on it.

'In that case, how about a grass-green carpet?' suggested Bogey. 'It'd give the room a nice warm feel.'

I winced and hung my head in dismay. Bogey's tastes were stuck in the 1970s. He liked styles that were in fashion when I was in elementary school. Come to think of it, he'd have been making the transition to adulthood at about that time. It's when your tastes are formed, and I guess you keep them with you forever after. Hence the grass-green carpet and the reddish brown furniture. There was something dull and oppressive about the whole scene.

Never mind; I was satisfied with the apartment. In the days when we still had money, we'd gone and bought ourselves a clothes drier at one of the big electrical stores in Akihabara, so I had no problem doing my homework and my housework there.

Best of all, I had Bogey with me nearly all the time. Having no job and no money meant he had to stay at home, apart from the occasional tête-à-tête with Ken-ken, plotting some fresh villainy, no doubt.

We used to go down to the video store and rent a stack of tapes to watch together. The less said about Bogey's taste in films the better (samurai sword-fights and cops-and-robbers says it all), but it was cozy to watch them together. Sometimes the two of us would go shopping and then cook together.

When his gourmet instincts surfaced, Bogey would do quite a bit of cooking, even chores such as washing vegetables and gutting fish. He'd complain about our poverty, of course, but he was capable of enjoying life without money. We had so much time on our hands that we would go for walks around the neighborhood.

There are a number of grand old houses in Nezu. Bogey would eye the properties and say, 'If only I'd been born into one of these houses, I'd be able to pursue a respectable profession without putting up with all this. Then again, I'd probably squander my fortune in six months.' And he'd have a laugh about it.

Gradually I was able to live without smashing plates. But Bogey was still plotting some new enterprise with Ken-ken, and it wasn't going well. He'd go out to attend a planning session and come home in a state of deep depression.

'It was looking at my dad that made me realise how miserable it is to be a man with no money,' he'd say at such times. 'My mother liked to put on airs, and I knew that she was even taking in work to help pay the bills and keep up appearances. Meanwhile Dad went through life while his wife and kids complained about how useless he was. No way was I going to end up like that. I was determined not to.

'Spending your whole life being shaken about in a packed commuter train, being bullied all day long by a mean boss, watching your wife pocket all your salary, barely giving you enough for cigarettes, going home and being pelted with complaints from the family, and never once going out on the town for a good night out.

'You know, Saya, there's a world out there where you can have fun just by spending money, but a lot of guys go to the grave never even knowing it. That wasn't going to be my way. I gave up all thought of a respectable life. I just wanted to grab as much money as I could. That was the decision I made.'

Clearly, Bogey and I came from the same stock. We'd both been brought up in households with a father who found no meaning in life and a mother who bullied him for it; and the two of us had the blood of that hopeless father and that bullying mother coursing through our veins. We both hated it.

Bogey had looked at his dad and had decided that whatever happened he would avoid becoming a man like him, and he'd looked at his mother and decided that no way would he ever live with a woman like her. Similarly, I was resolved never to live with someone like my dad and never to become a woman like my mother.

So what were we going to do about it? We adopted extreme methods. We were both versatile and smart, so that to some extent we could do whatever we turned our hand to. But we never really committed ourselves to anything, and we soon grew bored. We looked around for the easiest way to get what we wanted. We became wild and reckless, and when we found a like-minded partner in each other, we became wilder and still more reckless.

I was about to turn twenty and had no idea I was running out of control. When Bogey talked to me about these things, I listened to him like a young school kid listening to an old man going on about Life. The only thought in my tiny mind was that I wanted Bogey to be with me forever. These days he was eating the food I cooked, so there was no need to break any plates.

'Y'know, I really do forget about the world and its troubles when I'm with you,' he said to me once. 'Remember when we started living here and I wouldn't touch the food you cooked? It wasn't because the dishes didn't look tasty or anything. I may not seem it but I'm actually quite sensitive, and until you came along I'd never eaten anything except food prepared by restaurant chefs or by my wife. The fact that I can eat what you make is a sign that I'm starting to trust you.'

I was delighted. This was the fruit of my labours. Every minute, every second since we'd started living together in Nezu, I'd been working with total concentration towards winning that trust.

I'd decided the reason Bogey was so lonely was that he couldn't trust anybody. What makes a person's heart grow wild is the constant suspicion that he or she's going to be betrayed, or used, or made a fool of. If you have just one or two people you are able to trust implicitly, the type who makes you feel that even if they did betray or use you, you would forgive them, then you are saved from isolation.

Meeting Bogey had taught me that. That's why I'd been able to achieve happiness, and I wanted Bogey to feel the same way because that was the most necessary thing for people like us. But to win him over took a lot of energy – energy that came from deep within me. I was dealing with a wounded bear, a bear whose heart was deeply scarred.

☆

As I gradually tamed my bear, he took to giving me little tokens of affection. On his way home from a late-night mah-jong session he'd pick up some live prawns from the nearby sushi restaurant, just to please me.

'Didn't the Ginza *mama-san* ever cook for you?'

'Very occasionally, about once a year. Calamari rings and simmered radish, that sort of thing. I wouldn't eat any of it. Speaking of rings, it was she who told me about those rings you use for family planning.'

I dutifully echoed his laughter.

Bogey and I were seeing in the New Year in poverty, but also in love. Apparently the owner of the sushi restaurant owed him money (they were mah-jong buddies), so Bogey was able to bully him into supplying us with some nice festive nibbles – crab, salmon roe, tuna. Those fresh prawns might have been in lieu of a gambling debt, too. In his world, money wasn't owed because it had been borrowed but because it had been wagered and lost.

Bogey managed to roll up a little cash by playing low-stakes mah-jong in the last week of the year, and he used some of it to rent a car so we could drive down to the coast and see the sun rise over the ocean on New Year's Day. I had been back to mother's at the end of the year to help with the traditional grand house cleaning, and had been given some lessons on how to wear a kimono properly. This enabled me to please Bogey by appearing in a brand-new kimono that mother had ordered for me.

Then it was time to indulge in a few more quaint traditions –

like the first mah-jong session of the year and the first fuck of the year. Those were gentle days. Perhaps it is true that early on in a love affair you can find bliss in a state of honest poverty.

FOUR

We were heading for summer again and I turned twenty. As usual, we were broke.

My birthday. I scraped together my pocket money, bought a bottle of Akadama honey wine and a one-thousand-yen birthday cake, and sang 'Happy Birthday' to myself and the kittens that had been born in the spring. I was somewhat annoyed with Bogey, who had totally ignored my birthday.

It's not as though I'd insist on a middle-aged man swallowing his embarrassment and buying something so romantic as a bunch of flowers. I didn't expect anything elaborate. I just felt that a little something would have been nice.

'People do buy something on such occasions,' I gently pointed out to Bogey.

'Now you listen to me,' he said. 'You're talking to a man who couldn't even remember his own daughter's birthday. I never did anything for my wife on her birthday or on our wedding anniversary, not once. If you want someone who'll do that kind of thing for you, go and find yourself a younger man.'

At times like these, I couldn't help recalling mother's words: 'There's a world of difference between parting from someone while they're still alive and being parted by death. Your grandmother used to say that if someone leaves you while they're alive you remember only the nasty things about them, but if you're separated by death you remember only the good things. When somebody dies, only the happy memories remain.'

I reckoned she had it dead right. Indeed Bogey often used to say,

'I really loved my wife, you know.' He'd get all tearful as he said that.

Do guys usually go on like that? To the woman they're actually living with? That's what I thought, but since I loved Bogey I let it pass.

He often upset me with his clumsy insensitivity, but putting up with it was a lot better than having to part from him. Even so, considering what a warm and loving relationship we had, totally ignoring my birthday did seem a bit much.

Even the sight of me ostentatiously conducting my lonely little party with the cats right in front of him didn't seem to faze him at all. He just poured himself a slug of Jun *shochu* (he'd slipped a few more ranks down the booze ladder – this brand was aimed at the youth market and was even cheaper than Beni Otome) and sipped it casually, quite unaffected by the pathetic scene.

There was only one place where we could eat out and that was the sushi restaurant next to the mah-jong club. Nowhere else could Bogey have a meal without paying cash. The restaurant owner had lost a few times to Bogey at mah-jong, putting Bogey in a position to demand repayment in the form of sushi and booze. We might be reduced to drinking *shochu* at home, but here at least we could still indulge in Hennessy and Remy Martin. We'd eat just the fish on top of the sushi, spurning the rice, and swill it down with brandy and water. This was a habit we couldn't kick, however impoverished we became.

The drinks were won by gambling. Bogey was a gambler through and through, and gamblers are hunters at heart. The descendants of peasants may be content to accumulate the fruits of their labour day by day and slowly, but your hunter will stake his life on a single, fleeting chance. The difference is obvious. For hunters to survive, they need prey. They are carnivores who cannot live without victimising another living creature. And they feel no guilt. Prey is bounty sent by heaven. At the same time, even if a fish they have caught contains a dangerous poison, they will not regret losing their life so long as the fish tastes good. That, in a nutshell, was Bogey's view of life.

When Friday came, Bogey would focus his mind on mah-jong in a bid to scrape some funds together for the weekend. Recently, however, he'd found it hard going to raise enough stake money, and perhaps partly because of that he'd been losing steadily. Several times we had to endure weekends when we were so broke we couldn't go anywhere. For a kid like me and a fun-loving guy like Bogey this was unbearable.

'Oh, God, I wish we could go somewhere!'

'Just a second – didn't you say you had a credit card?'

'Yes.'

'How much cash are you allowed to draw on it?'

'I think it's 200,000 yen.'

'Fantastic! Go and borrow that right away. I'll pay you back double in no time!'

So, sacrificing my red Marui credit card, we rented a car and went sea fishing.

With a 200,000-yen campaign chest to pay for a one-night, two-day trip, Bogey was flush with confidence. And indeed his luck did seem to be turning, for we rose at three in the morning, hired a boat, and reeled in fish so thick and fast that the old boatman couldn't believe his eyes. Even I, a rank beginner, hooked a colossal sea bass. It pulled so hard I thought it would drag the boat after it, but with the dogged assistance of the bemused boat-man, I finally managed to haul it in.

'What a whopper!'

Overjoyed at the incredible catch, I clean forgot that the bass had been caught on credit.

Young people learn fast. 'Money's just money. No matter how you get hold of a ten-thousand-yen note, it is still worth ten thousand yen.' I had taken Bogey's lesson to heart: the moment the 200,000 yen popped out of the cash machine, it became the same as the easy money in his wallet. Such light money – as light as the bank notes forged out of dead leaves by raccoons in Japanese fairy tales.

That day we hurried back to Tokyo at full speed. Bogey descaled the mighty bass, sliced it up, and we ate it as sashimi.

'Bogey, the old boatman said this was a top-quality fish that would cost 2,500 yen even if you bought it right there on the dock!'

'Fantastic, eh?'

'Yes! Doesn't fish taste good when you've caught it yourself?'

'It certainly does. What a day, Saya! You really hit a home run this time.'

In the end, my unpaid credit card bill was passed to the card's guarantor – which was, of course, my mother. With her ironclad rule of avoiding debt at all costs, her reaction was predictable. I told her the truth about why I'd borrowed the money, but my honesty failed to impress her.

'You little moron. You're subhuman!'

The upshot was that she took the card away.

'Dear oh dear,' Bogey commiserated. 'You tell your ma that when I'm in the big money, I'll pay her back ten times over.'

I'd often heard Bogey say things like that, but I'd never known him pay back a penny. I felt no guilt myself. It wouldn't even bother me that much if mother severed all relations with me over it. OK, she might refuse to pay my tuition fees, but so what? College was a boring place, and I felt not the slightest attachment to it. So long as I had Bogey everything else could go to hell.

I had the cats, I had Bogey and I had a place to live in and food to eat. There was no one getting in my way and life was as cozy as could be. I particularly loved Bogey's soft cushion-like tummy. To me it was the one thing in life that was absolutely irreplaceable. So long as I had that cushion to snuggle up to, nothing else mattered.

As we became more lovey-dovey, we also spent more time in bed.

'You know, Saya, when I'm with you I somehow wind up having sex. I wasn't sex-mad like this in the old days.'

I took what he said as a compliment.

At least the Nezu apartment got plenty of sun, and our litter of kittens would frisk about in the sunlight. We had no money but plenty of cats and kittens, and the days passed by in a rosy haze of love.

☆

Then, one day a worrying news item appeared on the television. The president of Tomita Trading had been murdered, hacked to death with a sword. The assailant had made no attempt to escape, and pictures of him and the bloodied body filled the screen. By Japanese standards it was a lurid piece of news, and I instinctively covered my eyes.

All night long the shocking images were shown repeatedly, on every TV channel. Apparently Tomita Trading was a wicked company that had ripped off thousands of customers. Actually, the murderer looked quite cool – a bit like Yuya Uchida, the film star. He had an accomplice, a guy with a huge beard that made him look like a terrorist. It was just like watching a scene from a crime movie.

'Oh dear,' sighed Bogey, 'so they finally got him.'

'What?'

'Don't you remember? I told you I used to work for that company, and I knew something like this would happen sooner or later.'

'What?'

'Honestly, Saya, you really don't listen when you're not interested, do you.'

It was true. Unless something seemed like fun, it made no impression on me. I never read newspapers or any news weeklies. After the continuous misery that had been my adolescence, I had developed the habit of unconsciously screening out any information that might be depressing.

Bogey, by contrast, was a news addict. He'd sit there poring over news magazines and newspapers, while I'd be snuggled up beside him, engrossed in the dreamy world of fashion magazines and comics.

'Oh yes, you did say something about that.'

'Why don't you take a look at the newspapers now and again?'

'The ink makes my hands dirty!'

'Very funny.'

The next day there was another item in the news: the former president of Kabutocho Journal had been arrested. This time I *was* interested enough to read some of the articles. Apparently the company's illicit activities had been exposed way back in August the previous year, just after Bogey and his mates had quit, declaring it 'a dangerous company'. I hadn't even noticed that development, despite the fact that I was in a relationship with one of the people directly involved. Indeed I'd even worked there myself, although only briefly as a part-timer. So I certainly should have been interested, but I wasn't. The news just went in one ear and out the other. At the time I was too busy worrying about the Ginza *mama-san* and the abortion and so on to pay much attention to all that.

One of the photojournals carried a blurred black-and-white photo of the former president of Kabutocho Journal. Apparently he'd been hiding out overseas, but when he heard about the murder of the Tomita president he decided to turn himself in to the police before something similar happened to him.

This must be what Bogey meant when he called it 'a dangerous company'.

Then I gave a start. Among the photos of the company executives, splashed over the newspapers and magazines, was someone I knew.

So this was the president!

My mind went back to the day my boss at Kabutocho Journal had invited me to dinner at the Crescent restaurant. The man in the photo had been sitting right across the table from me. It was a funny sensation. I didn't feel scared or dirty. It was more a thrill, as if I'd had a very small part in a thriller movie. I wondered if all criminals felt the same.

I was young and healthy and knew no fear. I just couldn't take anything seriously. Everything was a load of fun. So even with incidents such as these, it never crossed my mind that something bad could happen to Bogey, far less to myself. I was just mildly surprised.

I got telephone calls from a few people who knew about Bogey and me. One of them was from Minako. I hadn't heard from her for ages.

'Are you going to carry on with Hotta despite all this?'

She was worried. She also sounded disgusted. We'd been best friends, and I know she blamed Bogey for taking me away from her. But I wasn't going to let a couple of unpleasant news stories come between Bogey and me.

'If you're going to lecture me, I'll hang up.'

Bogey and I were so close it seemed we were stuck together with glue. And it was very, very strong glue – so strong that if you tried to pull us apart, more than half my skin and flesh would be left on Bogey and I'd die right away.

Bogey and I would stick together all day and all night long. When he made a phone call from the bed, I'd be between his back and the headboard. When we went for a walk, I'd have his arm in a tight grip, or I'd be clinging to his back or shoulder, or I'd be just in front of him, leaning back against his chest and getting in the way. We'd stagger down the road all tangled up like a couple of slapstick comedians.

'Honestly, Saya, sometimes you're like one of those sucker fish.'

I had biologically morphed into a woman who couldn't live without Bogey.

As for the man himself, the recent unpleasantness had merely spurred him to renewed efforts to avoid the same fate himself. His approach to business combined elements of network and foot-work, and now he'd be out day and night, consulting with other shady businessmen about how to launch some enterprise that would be dodgy but not downright dangerous.

The summer holidays came around once more, and with Bogey out a lot I had time to kill. *I could look for a part-time job*, I thought. Mother had taken away my credit card and I was still wearing clothes I'd bought the previous year. Mind you, there weren't too many jobs suitable for a girl like me. I had no wish to do anything that involved hard work or staying power. So once more my thoughts naturally drifted in the direction of hostessing.

The first step was to find a partner. I turned to Reiko, a college friend who was relatively fashionable according to the standards of Sakura Women's University.

'Hey, wanna do some part-time work in the summer holidays? Just enough to buy some nice clothes and then quit?'

Reiko had recently ended an affair with an impoverished asso-ciate professor at another university. She'd once done a bit of waitressing in a Suntory restaurant pub, and for a serious-looking girl like her, she could actually turn on the glamour quite effec-tively, just the way customers at hostess bars liked it.

As I might have guessed, Reiko's mother had been a *mama-san* at a Ginza club before she'd married Reiko's dad, who was an elite research scientist at the Engineering Department at Tokyo University. She'd advised Reiko to hook someone like her dad and turn herself into 'a woman who looks good in jewels and furs'. Reiko had got the message. Her clothes were still on the plain side, but she laid on the make-up pretty heavily.

Now we needed to find a club. It would be awkward to ask Minako for an introduction after our recent disagreement, so I bought one of those job seekers' magazines as thick as a telephone directory, and started going through the part-time work ads in the 'night' section. It wasn't easy. Every single job that paid well sounded fishy. We didn't want to work at places where duties included sleeping with the customers. Yet every time I came across an ad offering slightly better conditions than average, I couldn't help feeling there was more to the job than met the eye.

In the end I suggested to Reiko that rather than taking a chance on some seedy club we knew nothing about, we should use one of Bogey's contacts. Bogey knew this architect, Professor Hirota, who'd just finished designing a new club – Les Arles. It was decked out in the high-tech style fashionable at the time, and the *mama-san*, in name only, was a rather well-known old chanson singer called Lulu Kitano. Perhaps because of that there was a fair sprinkling of customers from showbiz, and the girls who worked there were a mixture of would-be starlets, third-rate porn-magazine models and college girls. Quite a classy establishment, you might say.

'You can wear what you like, you get 2,500 yen an hour, which goes up to 3,000 yen if anyone asks specifically for you. So that's at least 10,000 yen a day just for sitting there for four hours. And it's in Roppongi, so it should be a smart place,' I explained.

'I see...' Reiko wasn't as decisive as I was. Her mother had browbeaten her into cramming for the university entrance exams by telling her that 'entering a good university is the first step toward finding a good husband'. Reiko had duly obliged and got into Sakura, but her ultimate objective in life was to marry the right kind of guy, as she once told me.

'Because, you see, I'm not as strong as you think. Holding down a job and bringing up children and doing housework all at the same time would be too much for a girl like me. But once I've got the children off my hands, I might take up some job, just as a hobby to keep me from getting bored.'

Although she hadn't yet found Mr Meal-Ticket, Reiko needed to make her life of ease a reality. She was always talking like that. Unlike me, she did at least have a plan for the future. What Reiko and I had in common was a certain confidence in our looks. Our aim was to sell our faces for the best price we could get while we still had something to sell.

Naturally, we both sailed through the job interviews, and that very evening found us sitting demurely at the counter of Les Arles. It was well past ten o'clock before customers started showing up, so we were free to engage in girl talk – a traditional early evening pastime in this line of work. The girls who came in around ten and stayed until two or three in the morning were a different crowd, but during the gossip sessions we learned that most of the girls on the early shift were also college students, all of them from the best schools in town.

They were decked out in the latest brand-name fashions, painfully reminding us what a dump Sakura was – a place where the likes of Reiko and me were viewed as glamorous. Once I got to know the girls better, however, it slowly dawned on me that it was a tough business maintaining that 'elite college' look. Ever since 1980, when the novel *Somehow, Crystal* got on to the bestseller lists and was turned into a hit movie, the demands on these girls had become a lot tougher. The college girls in the movie were glamorous models in their spare time, and suddenly it had become an iron rule that real college girls moonlighting in bars all had to wear designer clothes as well.

These girls weren't wearing the type of Tokyo outfits that Reiko and I hankered after. They had to be seen in the much more expensive European brands, the latest from Hermes or Ferrer, Gucci or Chanel. Take a girl with average good looks. The more self-conscious she feels, the more she has to dress up, and the more she dresses up the tougher it gets for her.

'This?' they'd say, indicating some frighteningly overpriced accessory and trying to sound as casual as possible. 'Oh, Mama bought it for me.' Or they'd embellish it with, 'Oh, Mama got it for me while we were travelling in Europe.' This would often be a barefaced lie to hide their embarrassment in the company of their friends, some of whom might be genuinely wealthy. In actual fact the dresses and accessories would be financed by long hours of part-time work in a desperate struggle to pay for these fashions that were rapidly becoming a kind of uniform. And even if their 'mamas' had bought the clothes it was more likely to be the *mama-san* of the bar they were working in than their real mother.

Still, this club was a relaxing place for us hostesses. Unlike the Cocteau, the management did not make us wear weird house-style clothing, hair, or make-up. The customers were different, too. They weren't all old lechers like the ones I'd known from the Ginza. And the club didn't have that hint of sadness that so often permeates the nightlife industry. The sales pitch here was that customers could have a drink with someone who was more like an ordinary girl than a professional. This was the fashion note of the time, and the club was designed to attract showbiz types and rising young executives.

There was usually a pretty boisterous crowd, and the showbiz folk who did turn up included several comedians. The ideal Ginza hostess was a mature, voluptuous beauty, but here they preferred younger types who could manage lively conversation. I soon became the favourite of a rather famous comedian, much to the displeasure of the professional hostesses, who'd glare at me every time he asked for me by name. Reiko did her best to cozy up to a succession of successful actors and doctors, determined to become somebody's mistress. She was through with penniless academics and was now aiming strictly for the money. And she was more than willing to go all the way – all the way to the altar, that is.

The buds of love were starting to bloom in Bogey's bosom – followed shortly by the buds of jealousy. When my shift at the club ended around midnight, he'd be waiting for me at another bar nearby. It was one of those snug counter bars run by Hirota's mistress, a former Ginza hostess, for friends only. Bogey would be there, chatting over a drink with the eminent architect himself, one of those men who still look elegant even when their hair turns grey. Hirota, whom we called the Prof, was a good drinking pal of Bogey.

Bogey hung out here for two reasons. First he knew he'd feel lonely if he went home to an empty apartment; and, second, he wanted to avoid the slightest risk that I might take off with another guy. He would often discuss this with me.

'Saya, there's one thing I won't have and that's you two-timing me with someone else. That kind of thing's all right for guys to do, because it's only a bit of fun. But when girls start fooling around they suddenly turn serious, so that's a no-no, OK? Honest, I'm not kidding. A woman will fall in love with any guy who'll give her one. Know what I mean? A woman is that kind of animal.'

'What a lot of nonsense!'

'It's not nonsense, it's the damn truth. And I know it is because of all the pain and suffering I've been through.'

I knew it was nonsense. Whoever you sleep with, if you don't love him, just doing it won't change a thing. What I would say, though, is that having sex with a guy is a good way of finding out whether or not you really love him. Bogey thought I was too naïve to understand such matters, but it was the one thing I knew only too well. It wasn't something I'd read in a book, either – it was knowledge acquired by experience. All that stuff about fooling around being OK for guys but not for girls was just self-serving male sophistry.

Anyway, it came to pass that Bogey gradually returned to Tokyo's neon-lit nightspots. His next business venture was starting to taxi down the runway. There was only one line of business open to someone like him, and that was investment consultancy. He couldn't abide work that involved hassle, hard labour, or poor returns.

Of course it was a lot more difficult to launch such a business now that the Tomita Trading and Kabutocho Journal scandals had broken. Bogey had consulted all sorts of experts in the field to figure out how to get around this little problem, and had concluded that what he needed was a bait to lure customers, to win their trust and spark their interest. He had to find a celebrity who would allow his name to be associated with the venture. Needless to say, there had to be something in it for the celebrity.

Just at that time Lulu Kitano, the retired chanteuse and *de facto mama-san* of the club where I worked, happened to be experiencing a slight cash-flow problem. The days when her mellifluous voice had made her the queen of chanson had long passed, and all that was left was a pile of debts. She'd been obliged to sell her house in Paris, her home for many years, and had returned to Japan to make a fresh start. It was Lulu that Bogey chose to approach, using the offices of the Prof, to put the proposition to her delicately and discreetly.

Lulu had just recently returned from Paris. She said she'd arrived in Tokyo with a thousand yen in her pocket and nowhere to stay. So her first condition for allowing Bogey to use her name in the new venture was setting her up in a one-room apartment in

Roppongi and taking care of her immediate living expenses. She sponged off the Prof, too, casually buying herself a 400,000-yen wardrobe on his credit card.

Lulu's great skill lay in using her fame to foster goodwill toward her. She was also a genius at sniffing out nice guys with open wallets. Above all, despite her advanced years, she was still a charming woman who could exploit people without them noticing it.

She was an old bird, well past fifty, but that didn't stop her from wearing the latest fashions and looking good in them. She was a showoff, an egomaniac, and a natural-born liar who was way over the hill but still retained an odd attraction. Your typical showbiz celeb, in short. And because she was one, people felt proud just to be seen with her – and didn't she know it!

One night there was a party at Lulu's apartment. Bogey was there, along with the Prof and a few of Lulu's friends. No one had bothered to let me know, and as dawn broke I was still waiting in Nezu for Bogey to come home. He hadn't called, which was unlike him, and I had no idea where he might be. Feeling anxious, I called the mah-jong club, all the Roppongi bars where he hung out and every decent hotel in Tokyo.

He finally called at six in the morning. He was in great spirits for that time of day.

'Why're you so upset, Saya? I've been having a drink with some friends, that's all! Just a sec, let me hand you over to the one and only Lulu Kitano!'

'Hello, this is Lulu. What? A woman?'

Her winsome tones infuriated me. I was working for nothing wages in her club, and here she was living it up at my boyfriend's expense! Just who did she think she was?

'Send Bogey back right away,' I said, bridling. Something in my voice surprised Lulu, and I heard her talking to Bogey.

'She seems terribly vehement! I haven't done anything wrong. Why's she so angry with me? I'm rather scared!'

'Uh-oh!' followed by Bogey's familiar guffaw.

As they giggled like a couple of naughty adults teasing a child, I slammed the receiver down.

Half an hour later Bogey came home. I think my telephone manner had put a damper on the party. These days Bogey never took the train – it was always a cab. I don't know where the money came from, but things were looking up a little. I had a feeling that he was diddling someone. Sometimes he and Ken-ken would dress up in supersmart business suits and set off somewhere. Bogey would say, 'Got a business appointment. On such occasions you can't let the other side know you haven't got any money.'

He had retrieved his expensive watch and gold accessories from the pawnshop, duly paying the accumulated interest, and would deck himself out in these items before leaving. When he returned home the second telephone would ring – the one I wasn't allowed to answer. No doubt it was from one of the poor saps who was being hoodwinked. Bogey would put a finger to his lips and say, 'Sshhh,' gesticulating to me to get out of the room for the duration of the call.

Anyway, wearing a sheepish grin on his face, Bogey came through the door of the apartment and started to make excuses.

'Honestly, Saya, what's the big deal? Lulu is fifty-five years old, you know! You don't really think anything could be going on between a hag in her fifties and a forty-year-old like me, do you? My aesthetic principles wouldn't allow it!'

'Then perhaps you'd care to explain why I never get a penny from you all the time I'm working my butt off in the old hag's bar while you're paying for her non-stop party lifestyle!'

'Listen, Saya, I need Lulu to do me some favours. I have to use her name, so naturally I help her out now and then.'

'Whereas I've got no name, no nothing, and I'm just a foolish kid, right? In that case why not go and shack up with Lulu instead?'

'For God's sake, Saya! Can you imagine Lulu and me having it off? What a disgusting thought!'

Lulu and Bogey were similar in build, both running to fat because of their drinking. Big face, broad back, thin arms and legs, they were built like buffaloes.

'But, but…' I ran out of words and burst into tears instead.

There was nothing I could say or do. All I knew was that I wanted to stay firmly stuck to Bogey.

From about that time I started to sense something strange in his demeanour. It wasn't just jealousy on my part. I couldn't put my finger on it, but instinctively I knew there was something about him that both worried and irritated me.

Since he'd started associating with Lulu, Bogey had gone back to extravagant partying, using his work as an all-purpose excuse. Lulu would introduce him at smart restaurants frequented by showbiz and business folk, and all of a sudden he was a regular at high-flying executive bars such as Brown's and Ooh-la-la.

Every single evening he'd hang out with the same crowd: Lulu Kitano, the Brown's *mama-san*, the Ooh-la-la's *mama-san*, and the Prof. Gradually Bogey started to include me in the circle – he'd call me from some watering hole in town and I'd head over to join them and drink the rest of the night away. We'd take a cab back to Nezu well past dawn.

I have to admit that those people were a lot of fun to hang out with. They didn't laugh at me because I was a student or hassle me for neglecting my studies. I really liked them. They treated me straight and it felt like being with old friends. Bogey also loved being with this crowd, even if they accepted him only because he picked up the tab.

✵

Autumn arrived. School started again and I quit Les Arles. I had once again been painfully reminded of how unsuited I was to hostessing as a profession. Sure it was easy money – being paid just for dressing up and having a drink with someone – but there was an emptiness about it. It didn't feel right doing that kind of work for money. Since I was supposed to be a student, I might as well act like one and get back to my studies. It would be a good way to pass the time.

Bogey wholeheartedly concurred.

'That's the spirit! Bars are places to go for a bit of fun. They're not places you want to work in or manage. Think about it for a second: in most ordinary jobs there are stages. You can go up the ladder, so even if you're still in the same line of business, at least there's some change. You get praise and are rewarded with pay rises over the years. But bar girls just do the same thing night after night, from when they're young girls to the day they retire. It's tough! I reckon that's why they get paid so much – people appreciate what a tough job it is and don't mind paying over the top.'

'So that's why the money's good, you reckon? If it didn't pay well, no one would want to do it, would they? Switching on the feminine charm every evening for some old punters you've got nothing in common with.'

At any rate it wasn't work that a lazybones like me could stick for long.

Reiko was more hardworking and she stayed. She was closing in on a promising marriage prospect she'd spotted amongst the customers. Luckily he had just broken up with his girlfriend, and Reiko was going to play tennis with him the following weekend. Not that she'd ever picked up a racquet in her life.

I'd earned enough to dress in the season's fashions, and that was good enough for me. Every day I'd head straight home after my last class, do the housework and the homework, have a bath, and then take it easy, lolling around with the cats. That would conclude the diurnal part of my day. I'd drift off to sleep until aroused around two or three in the morning by Bogey's call – the signal to commence the night shift. I'd dress up and hop in a cab to Brown's. Bogey would be unwinding after a mah-jong session, or maybe hanging out with the Prof, Lulu and the rest of the gang. Anyway there'd be a party in full swing and I would join in the fun. Eventually Bogey would call it a day and we'd catch a dawn cab. Bogey was tough. He could get along just fine on four hours' sleep.

✸

We were drunk and happy to be drunk, each and every night. Meanwhile, however, nasty little pink slips of paper were starting to accumulate in the mailbox.

Eviction order for non-payment of rent.

We'd moved in fifteen months previously and Bogey had only paid the rent for the first three months. After that he hadn't got around to paying for a whole year. We were growing alarmed at the mounting pile of eviction orders, but determined to ignore them, come what may.

'It's OK, Saya. We've got a right to live here, say I!'

Bogey made fun of any situation.

Even so, a whole year was beyond a joke. We were in arrears to the tune of one-and-a-half million yen; Bogey decided it was time to take decisive action.

'I'm going to talk to the landlord. I've seen him around the condo a few times. He's a real old gentleman: kimono, snow-white hair. I'm sure if I just explain the situation to him he'll understand and wait a little longer.'

'Really? Well, go for it!'

Bogey put on his smart suit, the same one he wore when going to 'work', had a shave for the first time in ages, and went to see the landlord. He'd been sporting a beard ever since he'd quit Kabutocho Journal, saying it was part of his 'dandyism'.

'People don't trust you if you have a beard,' he remarked. 'You can grow a beard once you've made pots of money and earned your freedom.' For Bogey, a beard was the symbol of an independent professional, of being free. A free person could grow a beard and dress casually. In other words, a beard and casual dress were symbols of wealth. Until you achieved the wealth that spelled 'freedom', you had to wear a suit – the uniform of the masses – keep your hair short, and be clean-shaven. These truths Bogey held to be self-evident. Sticking to the dress code was obligatory for all adults in contemporary Japan.

'What a guy wants to do isn't work. It's play. So doing as you please is something you have to tuck away until you've made so much money that you don't need to worry about daily expenses. That's when you can have your fun.'

Bogey often stressed this belief in the principle of deferred pleasure. But just how much money he would need to live what he considered to be a satisfying life 'without worrying about daily expenses', I couldn't begin to imagine.

Bogey came back from his talk with the landlord wreathed in smiles.

'He lives in this fantastic mansion of a place – incredible! Just as I thought, he's a big landowner. Says he built this condo as a tax write-off, so he's not too fussy about the rent. He just leaves it all to the bank and doesn't know anything about it himself. The reason he drops in now and then is because he uses one of the rooms on the ground floor to store his collection of books. That's his hobby and he comes over to look at his books sometimes.'

'He sounds like a nice old guy. But what's the deal with the rent?'

'Well, I told him I was in the process of setting up a new company and things were proving a bit awkward, and he asked me whether I had any intention of paying.'

'And?'

'And I said maybe I could pay off the rent like a loan, say 2,000 yen a month or so, and he said, "Have you any idea how many years it would take to pay it off like that?" Ha-ha-ha! The old fellow was having a good laugh about it, too. And then he says, "If that's all you can manage, don't bother. Pay it to me in a lump sum once the company's up and running." What a great guy!'

'Isn't he? One in a million!'

Thanks to our remarkably generous landlord, Bogey was able to put off paying the one-and-a-half million yen more or less forever. Seems the old man must have taken a real shine to Bogey, who had a rare ability of making the unthinkable happen.

Generosity has its limits, however, and we had to move out as part of the agreement. We parked the furniture and cats at Ken-ken's place and moved into a business hotel in Roppongi. It was a love hotel, really, dressed up to look a bit more respectable. It was within walking distance of the office Bogey had rented.

He had opened his own company in December. It was called Shinra, made up of two Chinese characters meaning 'trust' and 'prosper'. Naturally it was an investment consultancy – 'licence pending'. Bogey was full of confidence that the venture would succeed, a confidence as absolute as it was groundless. This careless fatalism was part of his gambler's personality. His favourite film was *Bonnie and Clyde*, known in Japan as *We Have No Tomorrow*, and he was not at all averse to the notion of rushing headlong to ruin.

TOKYO TANGO

'If it all goes wrong, I'll rob a bank and escape overseas. I've got it all planned out. I even know which bank I'd hit: Toa Bank. When my travel agency was in trouble all those years ago, they refused me a loan. If those bastards had only lent me a little cash, the agency wouldn't have gone bust and my wife wouldn't have died. So they've got it coming.'

He often spoke like that – half joking, but half deadly serious.

Bogey held a big party to celebrate the launch of his new company at a club in the Ginza called the Poporon. He'd got to know about the place because the Old Man, his novelist friend, had worked there as a waiter in the days when he was too poor to feed his family. It was supposed to be an ultra-deluxe club, and it was run by an old guy by the name of Koshimizu, a famous ex-TV producer. He had run a company called Atlantic TV, which made pots of money by buying the rights to American television dramas and selling the dubbed versions to Japanese networks. Unfortunately, the company went down the plughole after a bunch of scandals over blatant tax evasion, etc.

Ever since then Koshimizu had been protesting his innocence and battling with the state in long-running court actions that were also kind of famous. Meanwhile he ran this club as a hobby that would bring in some cash. He was already seventy years old, but the older he got the more he was into booze, girls and the libertine lifestyle. Reflecting its owner's personality, the interior decor of the Poporon was completely over the top.

The walls were studded with large, uncut semi-precious stones, and the floor was strewn with tiger-skin and lion-skin rugs – with the heads on, of course. Even the ceiling of the toilet was covered with the finest Nishijin brocade from Kyoto. All the Poporon girls were Koshimizu's type – classical beauties with elegant figures and long, straight, jet-black hair.

Here Koshimizu would hold court every night. He'd drape a

RIKA YOKOMORI

beautiful woman over each arm, sip a glass of thirty-year-old Ballantine whisky and occasionally slip something into his mouth – a sliver of steamed monkfish liver, a Japanese delicacy.

One reason this was Koshimizu's favourite snack was because he didn't have a single tooth in his head. He looked as if he'd just taken out his set of false teeth – though in fact he had none. He used to boast that in the old days he had lived with a beautiful blonde in a suite at the Hotel New Otani, and that at that time his front teeth were studded with diamonds. This I found hard to visualise, and certainly no evidence of his claim survived.

Yet old Koshimizu was a Ginza institution. He'd been around long enough to build up an excellent clientele. The Poporon was the kind of club where company directors entertained each other. The girls wore sophisticated cocktail gowns and they all spoke English. The house band was classy, too: it was a quartet led by a drummer who'd once been quite famous – even I had heard of him. Those boys knew the difference between a tango and a bossa nova.

If Koshimizu took a dislike to a customer, he'd warn him that it was 'six hundred thousand yen for a whisky and water', which proved pretty effective at keeping out the riff-raff. There was a thuggish undertone to the Poporon, but above all it was Koshimizu's empire.

Bogey's friend the Old Man had heard of the strange antics of Koshimizu and his club ten years previously, and had taken the bar job partly in the hope of picking up material for a book. Nowadays, however, the club's golden era was long over and the place had been in decline for years, held up only by the paint on the walls. Hence the Old Man had introduced it to Bogey as a famous Ginza nightspot that could be hired very cheaply for a party.

Shinra was launched amidst a blaze of glitter and glamour.

Lulu's name was on the list of sponsors, and many of her theatrical friends showed up at the party, along with the owners of famous restaurants, former sportsmen and old-time celebrities. Bogey was delighted. As for me, I was pounced on by old Koshimizu. The moment he caught sight of me, he grabbed me with both arms and kissed me on the cheek – or, to be strictly accurate, he licked my cheek with his slobbery, slack-jawed, toothless mouth. Ugh!

Worse was to come. Just when Bogey was well drunk and in mellow mood, Koshimizu sidled up to him and said, 'Hey, Hotta, if you're a real man, lend me this woman for my club.'

Bogey, bewitched by the Koshimizu legend and in his cups, replied, 'If she'll do, please make use of her as you like,' and agreed to what he wanted.

Koshimizu's club was on the brink of collapse, yet he still wanted to recruit fresh young women. That was what he lived for. He viewed the commercial side of the business with disdain. But in the Ginza there were more clubs making money than stars in the sky, and no bright young hostess was going to sign on at a club that was so obviously on the way down. At that party my youth made me stand out like a desert fox in an Arctic snowfield.

I had at last accomplished the long, straight-hair look. I'd dieted until I was as thin as a rake, and I had become the Koshimizu type of girl. Bogey seemed to feel a perverse pride in being asked to 'lend' his mistress to a glitzy club, albeit one in terminal decline. Without thinking about it, he simply handed me over.

'Shit, Bogey, what sort of guy lends his woman out on request?'

'There, there, Saya. Do it for Bogey. It's good to keep friendly with a guy like Koshimizu. And it's only for a couple of months after the New Year. It's a fantastic club, you know! Some very grown-up party people hang out here; you'll be able to make some interesting social observations. And I bet the money's a whole lot better than in Roppongi.'

121

That last comment was true. A four-hour stint at the Poporon, from 7:30 to 11:30 in the evening, paid 27,000 yen. And that was just the starting wage. I heard that some of the longer-serving girls were pulling in 50,000 yen a night. There was no nonsense about having to pay for your drink and then get the money off the customer, or having to pick up customers early in the evening and bring them along to the club. And since there were virtually no customers, it was really just a matter of dressing elegantly and sitting there looking like a million dollars.

After I was loaned out to the Poporon, however, I learned that there was also a less pleasant side to working there – an initiation that new girls had to go through.

The club opened for New Year on 3 January. We were supposed to wear kimono just on that day. From then on the club's employment terms specified 'formal wear only', as a rather disagreeable bartender stiffly informed me. He looked down his nose at me, evidently offended that the club had employed a whippersnapper still at college – all the other girls were at least five years older.

But I'm not the type to be defeated by such an attitude. On the contrary, it made me more determined to show them what I could do. If they didn't recognise my worth, I would damn well make them change their minds! That meant, however, that I couldn't afford to be careless about my appearance. I would go to the beauty parlour, have my hair done up in traditional Japanese style, and get them to dress me in kimono properly!

I lied to my mother, saying that I was going to a formal New Year's party with friends from a seminar group at the university, and I put on the extravagant, long-sleeved kimono that she'd given me for my coming-of-age ceremony when I'd turned twenty years old. I know it had cost well over one million yen, and never in a thousand years would she have guessed that I was dressing up to go and do the one thing she'd implored me not to – work as a bar girl. And not in a million years would she have guessed that my destination was a deluxe club in the Ginza, the very apex of the profession she so despised.

I stopped off at one of those Ginza beauty parlours that cater specifically for hostesses, where they help you to put on kimono as well as do your hair, so that even on my first day at the Poporon I had the glamorous nightclub look down to a T. I went clack-clacking down Namiki Street in my shiny lacquered sandals just when the butterflies of the night were fluttering to their places of employment. I turned a few heads in my New Year finery, and brought a sparkle to the eyes of a few jaded *mama-sans* and off-duty waiters as I tottered through the Ginza.

'Heh-heh. I'll show them.' I chuckled to myself, pretending not to notice.

No sooner had I sunk into one of the sumptuous sofas at the Poporon than Koshimizu called me.

'Hey, you, the new girl! Come over here.'

He summoned me to sit with an elegant, white-haired dandy, who seemed to be about eighty years old. He made quite an impact on me: here was a man who must have been studying the Way of Pleasure for over half a century. He had an air of gravitas, slightly weathered by the years that wafted through the space around him. He looked me over, gave a little smile, and said, 'Well, well, this is a most sophisticated young lady.'

He spoke in all earnestness and I was suitably impressed. I felt that I had just received the official imprimatur that designated me a 'first-class woman'. I had to hold back the tears. Ah, the importance of appearances!

Yes, it really is important to put on the style. The compliment went straight to my head. I got my red Marui credit card back, lying to the company that I'd lost the previous one, and set out to buy myself more finery. The time was ripe for a raid on the boutiques, for the winter sales had just begun and I was able to pick up job lots of dresses, suits and high-heels designed for Christmas parties, all at 70 per cent off! I now had the right wardrobe for the Poporon – although the clothes were crammed inside the tiny closet in the business hotel where Bogey and I were wintering. School was out for the holidays, and I felt as though I was the Number One hostess in all Japan.

I was living in a hotel and working nights in the Ginza. After work, Bogey would be waiting for me at the bar in Roppongi run by Hirota's mistress. I would take a cab over there and make my entrance in one of the Poporon gowns. It was a pretty crazy scene.

The Prof's mistress gave me the once over and made a little pout.

'Well, well, aren't we just beautiful tonight, little Saya. Fantastic. But tell me, is it true that all the girls at the club have to sleep with Koshimizu?'

You had to hand it to her – she had a brand of sarcasm that was simple to understand. Her tone and manner clearly indicated that she was a former Ginza hostess, knew the score, had indulged in every luxury imaginable, and had long since graduated from flirting with men the way her younger colleagues did. Her hair was cropped short and she was dressed in a well-cut, somewhat mannish, suit.

The Prof broke in. 'That's just a rumour, isn't it? Probably gets about because the pay's too good for a club with so little custom.'

'Bogey, did you know about this?'

'No, I didn't. But just a sec, Saya. An old fellow like him couldn't do any damage between the sheets. We're talking ancient history here.'

'Yes, I guess you're right.'

But the *mama-san* wouldn't leave the subject alone.

'Has he tried anything?' she asked with a leer.

'No, not exactly...'

'Not *exactly*...?'

'So there was something?'

'Come on, tell us what happened. Tell us.'

They all crowded around me. It was a planned assault. They'd been lying in wait for me to get back from work, hoping for a few laughs to go with the booze.

'Well,' I began cautiously, 'Miyuki and I – you know Miyuki, she was at the Christmas party, the second-youngest girl after me. We have to sit on either side of the boss...'

'And?'

'Well, tonight it got to closing time and not a single customer came in, so...'

'Not a single customer? Ha-ha-ha!'

Bogey and the Prof were really getting into it.

'Yes, but actually the work's harder when there're no customers. Because the boss has nothing to do, either. So Miyuki and me have to keep him entertained. Apparently it's an initiation rite for new girls. Once he's had a few drinks he gets quite impossible. You know the monkfish liver he always snacks on? Well, he picks up a piece with his fingers, drops it into his mouth, and then touches you without washing his hands. They're all, like, sticky. And then he kisses you with that toothless mouth of his, right after he's eaten the piece of liver, so his breath stinks of the stuff. And if you start feeling sick and try to push him away, he scolds you, saying "You can't work here with an attitude like that!"'

The Prof, Bogey and the *mama-san* looked at one another, struggling to hold back their laughter, tears of mirth glistening in their eyes.

'What then?'

'Then he deliberately starts talking about some topic Miyuki and I know nothing about, so we can't join in, and again he goes on about how we're not fit to work in his club. Then he raps us on the head with his knuckles, which doesn't hurt because he's too old and feeble.'

'That's perfectly dreadful!'

'Yes, but all of a sudden he'll say, "Oh, scratch my back, will you?"'

'What's that about?'

'Well, he hasn't looked after his health for years, his liver's bad, and he won't go to see a doctor. So when he begins drinking, he starts itching all over, especially on his back.'

'So you give him a little back-scratch, do you?'

'Yes. Apparently that's another initiation ritual I didn't know about. I just scratched his back through his shirt, so he gets all cross again: "Get your hand inside and give me a proper scratch!"'

'And then?'

'So I pull up his shirt, put my hand under it and start scratching again, but I still wasn't doing it right. Then Miyuki leans over a bit flustered and whispers in my ear: "Saya, not like that. You've got to hold your nails at right angles to the skin."'

'Eh?'

'Like this.' I flashed my long, manicured nails at my bemused audience. Most people hold their fingers at an acute angle when they scratch, but I demonstrated how to scratch at right angles.

'Then – too late! – I look at my fingernails and they're chock-full of oily skin that I'd scraped off the boss's back.'

At this, the three of them burst out laughing again. But to me it was no joke. Of course I was upset to find my beautiful fingernails full of waxy-yellow dead skin, but there was also a sad story behind Koshimizu's revolting state.

Because of his protracted legal battle with the state, he had been obliged to live apart from his wife and kids. Apparently he was being threatened by far-right groups who saw him as a traitor to his country for polluting Japanese television with filthy American dramas, and he didn't want his family involved. He'd been living on his own for many years and was too decrepit to wash his back properly, so over the years members of each generation of Poporon hostesses would take it in turns to go to his apartment and give him a good back scrub. Recently, he'd had difficulty finding the kind of girl whose devotion to duty would extend to providing this sort of personal service, and the scurf had built up to a distressing extent. The stuff about the bad liver was probably a cock-and-bull story. I reckon he simply had dirty, dry skin that got itchy naturally. Trapping new girls into scratching his back had become his habit, and keeping their nails at right angles had become their habit.

'A ninety-degree-angle scratch? It's not something you'd know about without being told, eh?'

'Well, think of it as part of your training, Saya. Might as well humour the old guy.'

It was an unfortunate turn of events, but a promise is a promise. Bogey had loaned me to the Poporon for two months. Besides, I had laid in all those smart outfits and had nothing else to do with them, so I carried on at the club.

One night we were approaching closing time after yet another quiet evening. Just one party of customers had come through the door, and now the boss was collapsed in a drunken stupor on a sofa. He obviously couldn't be left like that, so someone would have to take him home.

'Saki,' he mumbled, 'you take me home tonight. You and the new girl, Saya.'

Saki was one of the girls who had been there the longest, and a real beauty. A mumbled order was still an order, so she and I agreed to take him back to his apartment.

Koshimizu lived on the eleventh floor of a waterfront development with a magnificent view of the night lights around the bay.

But as the years passed, his possessions had accumulated all over the floor, along with a thick layer of dust, and there was hardly anywhere for us to place our feet. I was standing there, nonplussed, when Koshimizu, by now somewhat recovered, thrust a bottle of orange liquid into my hand.

'Mineral extract from Kusatsu hot spring,' he said. 'Put this in your bath and it'll make your skin silky and smooth.'

With that he started to undress before my very eyes. Saki seemed quite unconcerned. Evidently used to this performance, she busied herself tidying up odds and ends littered about the room, and then moved to the kitchen to tackle the stack of dishes in the sink.

Butt-naked, the boss calmly turned to me and said, 'Come to the bath with me, OK?'

I was thrown into confusion, but Saki had slipped into the bathroom from the kitchen without my noticing and she whispered in my ear: 'It's all right. All you have to do is be there until he gets out.'

The boss tottered over to the bath in the nude and plopped into the tub. Then he glanced over his shoulder at me. I was sitting, fully clothed and very embarrassed, in the changing area.

'Ah, there you are.'

Something about the scene made me wipe away a tear. There was a child's rubber duck floating in the bath and a plastic clockwork boat. The boss was playing with them while he soaked in the hot water, burbling some kind of song to himself.

Emerging from his ablutions, he called to Saki.

'Saki, my dear, there're some nice strawberries in the fridge. Give one pack to this lass and take one yourself.'

'OK!'

Saki put the boss to bed in a manner that showed she'd had long experience of doing this job, handed me a pack of strawberries, and washed another pack before returning it to the fridge.

I emerged from Koshimizu's place feeling I had witnessed something I shouldn't have done. Something went flip-flop in my heart. Mustn't think about it any more. Instinct kicked in and automatically stopped my train of thought stone dead. Silence reigned over my troubled heart.

I went back to the hotel, filled up the small unit bath, and added some of the Kusatsu hot spring mineral extract. Then I climbed in with Bogey and reflected hard on my present happiness.

'Phew! This bath stinks!'

'The boss gave me this stuff. Said it would make my skin silky and smooth.'

'Really? *My house may be small, but I love being here just the same...*' Bogey launched into a popular song.

'It *is* small. This bath is especially small!'

'This bath is especially smelly!'

'At least it warms you up!'

Sulfurous fumes from the Kusatsu hot springs suffused the bathroom. And not just the bathroom – the smell filtered into the bedroom and seeped under the door, along the corridor, all the way to the elevator.

☆

It was only after I had completed my promised two-month stint at the Poporon that I learned that Koshimizu did not actually have the money to pay the handsome wages that the hostesses were supposed to get. The few customers who still showed up did so only out of kindness, as they were old friends of his. The same went for the hostesses. They all had day jobs and only worked at the Poporon out of sympathy for the old man. That was the reason for all the rumours about intimate relations between him and them. They made their living by day and put on the style at night, just for the boss. To be fair, he did occasionally borrow some money and pay them a small portion of their back pay. I myself got about ten days' wages handed to me by that sour-faced bartender, who turned out to be a much nicer guy than I had judged from his appearance. It would be just enough to pay off the credit card.

At about the same time that I finished at the Poporon we stopped living in the hotel and moved back to Azabu Juban. We couldn't very well leave the cats with Ken-ken indefinitely, and living in a cramped business hotel put too much strain on a middle-aged man. Getting his new company set up was proving to be quite a battle for Bogey, and the stress was showing in his face, which was deathly pale.

'Lulu's talking about moving into a more spacious apartment in Shirogane and I, too, reckon we should make a move. Let's go back to Azabu Juban. It's near Shirogane and I like that part of town.'

We wound up in the very same white condo that we'd lived in before the move to Nezu. Our new apartment was actually slightly better than the old one. This one had one more room, but the rent was the same since it faced north and didn't get much sun. Besides, the condo wasn't as new as it had been when Bogey first moved in. We looked at several other places, but it seemed that the only vacant ones were old and filthy. The apartment we moved into had just been repainted, almost as if it had been made ready especially for us. We had to take it: it felt like fate.

FIVE

'I can't stand that Ichiro Fujiyama!'

Bogey could be harsh in his judgements about singers that he saw on television. Now that we were happily back in Azabu Juban, we could resume one of our favourite pastimes: lazing around on our big bed and eating and drinking while we watched TV.

'He always comes across like such a goody-goody. That stance, that expression, that style of singing. I just can't stand him.'

He did a brief imitation of the despised singer and took another gulp of his Hennessy and water.

'Tsk!'

Bogey was struggling to give vent to his pent-up indignation at the effrontery of Ichiro Fujiyama. Hardly surprising, really, for this particular singer happened to be Bogey's exact opposite in spirit, appearance, and especially posture. Ichiro Fujiyama had an excellent bearing, firm and upright, while Bogey's had been justly condemned by no less an authority than my mother. When I introduced Bogey to her she looked him over and was not impressed. With furrowed brow she whispered, 'His shoes, Saya, look at the heels! If you can't stop him slouching, at least get him to wear his shoes properly!'

When Bogey dressed casually, he never bothered to put his shoes on correctly. Instead he stepped on the backs of them, squashing them flat, so his shoes were more like a pair of slippers.

The first time Bogey met my mother, he wanted to make a good impression by taking her somewhere nice.

'Is there someplace we could go that your mother would like?

131

You know, somewhere she's always wanted to try but never had the chance?'

'Well, there's the Tour d'Argent at the Hotel New Otani. It's the Tokyo branch of a very famous restaurant in Paris. She was reading about it in a magazine the other day and said, "This is one place you wouldn't want to go to without a gentleman to escort you."'

'But I thought you said she has a boyfriend?'

'Yes, but he wouldn't take her to a swanky place like that. He's a major league skinflint.'

So the three of us duly dined at the Tour d'Argent. But my ma's dream restaurant was not the kind of place for Bogey, who didn't like the service and soon became irritable.

There we were – a scowling Bogey not looking his best in his crushed-down shoes, my mother looking as though she couldn't stand being in his company, while the waiters hovered around with expressions that said they didn't know how to deal with this particular party. I was terribly nervous, ate too much, and ended a triumphant evening by throwing up most of the 70,000-yen haute cuisine in one of the toilets in the hotel lobby. Bogey had scarcely eaten a thing except for the turtle soup, practically forcing me to eat two full-course dinners.

He was very scathing when we got home.

'Phew, I'm worn out! Why did all those guys – the sommelier and waiters – have to stand behind us while we were eating? And why the endless explanations about every single item? "This is a selection of foie gras and truffles air-freighted from France earlier today." I ask you, do we want to know all that? And then they hang around, checking to see if we're eating it properly. It's outrageous! We're paying for the food, so why can't they leave us alone to eat it as we please? What a nerve!'

Ill at ease to start with, he had hated everything about the place: the affected superciliousness of the other diners; the overly deferential manner of the staff; the rich, elaborately prepared dishes; and the constant reminders of what an elite establishment we were privileged to be eating in.

On top of that there was the fact that we'd spent so many months living in a hotel. Even after we came back to Azabu Juban, apart from occasional visits to the toilet or the bath, Bogey virtually lived on the bed, clad only in his briefs. On a bedside table he'd have some snacks, a bottle of Hennessy, a water jug, and an ice bucket, and he'd just wallow there like a bedridden pensioner. With a lifestyle like that, he could hardly be expected to sit through a lengthy formal dinner.

While he may have been living like a slob he was nevertheless very particular about the little nibbles he had with his drinks. Each one had to be properly prepared and served at the right time after the previous one, just like in a well-run restaurant. My cooking had improved a lot while we were living in Nezu, and now I was working as Bogey's personal chef.

On weekdays I would carefully plan a menu that appealed to his tastes, but at the weekend he would decide what he wanted to eat for dinner and we'd scour the local food stores in search of the right ingredients. He'd always buy far too much, and I would have to carry the whole lot myself. Bogey wouldn't dream of being seen in public with a supermarket bag stuffed with meat, fish and vegetables. That, he felt strongly, would violate the sacred principles of dandyism.

'Bogey, this is too heavy! Just take one bag, will you? My arm's falling off; the handles are cutting into my fingers and stopping the blood flow!'

'Saya, you look so cute with shopping bags!' he'd cackle.

He himself would be strolling along on his crushed heels in his usual nonchalant manner, with both hands in his pockets.

✡

Our personal life may have become more enjoyable for Bogey, but his mood still changed according to the ups and downs of the stock market.

Managing the investments of his new company was tough. Once again he'd be carrying a thick wad of notes in his wallet, but that didn't mean he had any cash to spare. Everything was on a totally different scale from the Nezu days: there was a lot more money going out as well as coming in. He had his employees' wages to pay and he had to support Lulu and her entourage in their accustomed lifestyle. He had cash, but he couldn't spend it on himself. In a way this situation – just looking after money before passing it on to others – was harder than having no money at all.

He was now renting an office in the Ginza as well as the one in Roppongi. He was also preparing to open a bar for Lulu, the celebrated Paris nightingale. He needed to have a special nightspot to entertain customers and gain their trust – an important aspect of the business. Lulu decided to call the bar Pile ou Face.

'That's French for "heads or tails", my dear. It's the name of a restaurant right next to the Bourse in Paris. Perfect for a bar associated with a speculative enterprise, don't you think?' said Lulu mischievously.

The bar was to be staffed by poverty-stricken good-for-nothings she had run into while out on the town. They'd only have to tell her some hard luck story and she'd exclaim, 'But my dear, you simply must come and work at my new establishment!' Among them was the *mama-san* of the Ooh-la-la – now the ex-*mama-san*, as she'd been sacked for persistent drug abuse.

Spongers and hangers-on came swarming around Bogey, and

the more dealings he had with people from the financial world, the more depressed he became.

'People in this line of business are the scum of the earth! What a rat race! Once I've made the big money, I'll be out of this dunghill so fast you won't see me for dust.'

This was how Bogey spoke about his business, and he tried to distance himself from the 'dunghill' of speculation by keeping to his presidential office in Roppongi while the bulk of the work was done at the Ginza office.

Officially, Bogey's business involved setting up networks so people could play board games such as *go* and Japanese chess via their telephone lines. This was in the days before the Internet, of course. He was perpetually embroiled in legal hassles to obtain the rights to run such a service, and he was getting nowhere fast. But that just provided a front for the real business, which, as usual, was unlicenced, barely legal, investment consulting.

Bogey's pallor was becoming truly ghastly to behold. Every morning he'd get out of bed and dash for the toilet, where he'd have a lengthy, noisy bout of diarrhoea before returning to the bedroom clutching his stomach in pain.

'God, I feel so sick! I wish I could chuck my stomach into the washing machine and give it a good cleaning.'

But he never went to see a doctor. Despite his unhealthy life-style he was surprisingly tough. Besides, he had no health insurance so he'd have had to pay any bills himself, which could amount to a hefty sum, and he didn't have the money to spend anything on himself (or on me, for that matter).

He looked so terrible that I was starting to worry about him.

'Bogey, you should see a doctor,' I said.

'Saya,' he said, looking as though he might throw up at any moment, 'I'm a person who hates government offices and hospitals. Those places are a complete drag, and the people there think they're so damn important. If I went somewhere like that, I'd end up feeling sicker than before.'

'I know, Bogey, but just look in the mirror. No way is that a healthy colour. You don't look at all well.'

He knew I was seriously concerned, but he wouldn't budge.

'It's all right, Saya. I know what's doing this to me – it's not having any money, that's all. Financial anaemia, that's the only problem with my health. Once I start making a bit, all this will clear up in no time.'

There was actually some truth in that. When the stock market went up, his health and spirits would show a marked improvement. But when the market went down again, it would be 'Would you be willing to die with me?' or 'Would you stick with me, even if we had to live in a room in a flophouse?'

He'd sound like the lyrics of some corny ballad.

On such occasions I'd just nod and say yes, yes. I'd been brought up in an overheated economy and had never known poverty. I didn't have the nous to associate business failures with double suicides. As for 'a room in a flophouse', I'd no idea what such a place might look like. I was still very young and didn't like doing much thinking. That meant I was able to feel cool about everything, even death. On the other hand, it made me a rather shallow person.

Yet the sight of Bogey's ashen face was so pitiful that it was no fun for me. *In that case it might be better for us to die together*, I would think. At the same time I'd be wondering when he was going to pay back the money he'd borrowed off me.

That money was the pittance I'd been paid for working two months at the Poporon, something like 200,000 yen, which I was planning to use to repay the debt on my credit card after buying clothes for that very same Poporon. One morning Bogey had been standing, trying to figure out how to put together the cash he needed for his activities that day, when a flash of inspiration came to him.

'Hey, Saya, didn't you say you'd just been paid by the Poporon?'

'Er, yes...'

'Really? Ha-ha-ha. Will you lend it to me?'

'But that's the money I have to pay off my credit card!'

'Well, so what? I'm only asking you to lend it to me. I'll pay it back right away. With interest, of course.'

That was a few months ago. I had already received several payment reminders, and any day now they'd be writing to the guarantor – my poor old ma – again. And I hadn't even repaid the previous 200,000 yen that Bogey and I had blown on that one-day fishing trip.

Bogey's constant pleas of poverty did not stop him from hitting the town with Lulu and all sorts of other people every single night. He might not have had the money to pay me back, but he always had the money to pick up the tab for tons of overpriced food and drink, all in the name of 'business entertainment', which was supposed to be terribly important.

At my wits' end, I finally asked him, 'When are you going to give me back the money you owe me?'

He flew into a towering rage. 'What the fuck's all this about paying back loans?! You're supposed to be my woman, not my fucking bank manager! You're nothing to do with me any more! Get the hell out of here!'

I was too frightened to raise the matter again. I just kept quiet and waited for the storm to pass. Whatever happened, I couldn't face parting from Bogey. Our life together was the one and only solid thing I had to hold on to. If he was taken away I'd have nothing.

In the end my mother had to pay off my debt again. This time she didn't even get angry with me - she realised it would be a waste of time, that nothing she or anyone else did or said was going to make me leave Bogey until I saw the need to do this myself. Instead she gave me more of her practical advice.

'Men who go into business have good times and bad times. Your grandmother knew that. When your grandfather's business was going well, she always took care to squirrel away a little cash for a rainy day - without telling him, you know.'

She spoke in a weary voice, then lapsed into silence and quietly placed a bank envelope containing the latest 200,000 yen on the table between us.

'When you're living like a lord, this sort of thing is bound to happen sometimes. So in the future, when Mister Bogey's business is doing well, be sure to set some money aside for yourself. Just a little here and there, OK? So that he doesn't notice. And then one day, just supposing something goes wrong, that money could be your salvation.'

Whatever happened, I was still obsessed with Bogey. Right now he was showing his rough side, just like he did when he was at Kabutocho Journal, but underneath it all I was convinced that he was still the same old sweetie-pie. Once the money started flowing in, he'd revert to the nice guy he was at heart. I alone knew the true nature of this man. I really believed that.

✡

Meanwhile, Lulu's bar, the Pile ou Face, was finally ready to open. Bogey loaned me out to help get it up and running. At least that meant I once more had a use for the gowns I'd bought for the Poporon. Now that I was 'family,' however, I wasn't going to be paid, as Bogey briefly explained to me.

'You're one of us, so no pay, right? If you need money, just ask me.'

And that was that. No doubt Bogey felt it would be demeaning to pay his own woman a salary.

The new establishment was decorated like an old-fashioned adult bar, a style favoured by Bogey and Lulu. The furniture and light fittings were art nouveau replicas. The customers were all Lulu's friends and associates. Having been around for so long, she'd acquired a wide circle of acquaintances. Her lax attitude toward money had alienated quite a few, but new ones always came along. Showbiz people's acquaintances seem to multiply and divide like cancer cells, and cultivating admirers is an essential talent for people in that line. Whenever Lulu was out eating or drinking – invariably at another person's expense – someone would be bound to say, 'Look! It's Lulu Kitano!' Their eyes would meet and before you knew it she'd be chatting up a perfect stranger, who would then be brought in tow to the Pile ou Face.

I had to be impressed by this knack of hers, but at the same time I hated Lulu because she was squeezing as much money as she could out of Bogey, and the net result of this was that he was squeezing me. Moreover, she rode roughshod over my predominating desire to monopolise Bogey's attention. Bogey was obsessed with Lulu because he had got it into his head that being friends with an attractive and famous person brought hopes for a bright future. I was strictly secondary in importance.

With her glittering career in chanson, Lulu certainly had a distinctive singing style, but when it came to running a business she was a complete and utter amateur. She so longed to be adored that at the drop of a hat she would give customers discounts, or even let them off paying altogether. Then, when the bar closed for the night, she'd just help herself to cash from the night's takings and invite everyone out to some other watering hole. The silly cow!

As well as helping out at the bar, I was instructed by Bogey to keep an eye on the cash register.

The Pile ou Face was just as weird as the Poporon. It had a transvestite floor show with gloomy old queens, too ugly to get a job at the many transvestite bars around Tokyo, wearing kimono. There was also a gypsy-type hostess who would tell your fortune and a gay pianist called Glen Kitazawa, poached from Les Arles, who would give piano recitals dressed in a suit, complete with heavy make-up and a moustache.

Behind the counter, an unemployed actor called Také performed the role of bartender. The cashier was an avant-garde girl with plucked eyebrows just back from Paris, invariably decked out in a skin-tight mini dress. And when big-shot customers needed to be entertained, Lulu would be assisted by Michi, the former *mama-san* of the Ooh-la-la in Shinjuku.

I liked Michi better than Lulu. At first glance, with her smartly cropped hair and tanned skin, she could easily be mistaken for a man. She had a certain charisma that appealed to people in the same profession. She'd been involved in all the fashionable new businesses that started up in the 1970s, and had once starred in a film made by a well-known director. In the world of showbiz she was often described as 'a true genius'.

None of Michi's activities had ever developed into a proper occupation, however. This was because her excessive individualism, coupled with a weak character, had turned her into a junkie. Just when she was about to make it big in some venture or other, she'd be busted for drugs. Whenever she went to the toilet, you could smell the marijuana fumes drifting out beneath the door, and every night at around three, just before closing time, her druggy friends would start to gather at the bar – men working in nightclubs who used to be popular fashion models, photographers, designers, etc. When the bar closed, they'd take her along to carry on in a more private place somewhere else. It was clearly only a matter of time before she got arrested again.

Sure enough, just three months after the Pile ou Face opened, the drug squad searched Michi's apartment. One of her friends had ratted on her.

The Prof, who was well versed in such matters, shook his head sadly.

'It's not as though I didn't warn her. If you've got to do something dangerous like that, never do it with more than one other person. Once there are three or more people involved, someone's bound to spill the beans.'

I didn't really understand what it was all about, but at Lulu's suggestion we all went to the trial and sat in the public gallery. There was a good turnout in support of Michi – even her mother was there, an elegant old lady in kimono. The courtroom was a grim and plainly furnished place, almost totally silent, like a church. We party animals weren't used to such an ambiance and got childishly excited. We'd look at each other and giggle. We just couldn't help it.

Michi was cheekily dressed for the convict look in a smart black-and-white striped T-shirt, with a rope tied around her waist as if to prevent her escaping. It was way over the top. She looked up and gave us a little grin. Of course she didn't think she'd done anything wrong.

'Wow, look at Michi – still playing to the gallery!'

'The accused was found to be in possession of a small brown receptacle containing 0.003 grams of cocaine.'

'What, all this fuss just over 0.003 grams? Ridiculous!'

'How did they find such a tiny amount?'

'Silence in court.'

Even Michi's mother couldn't help joining in the chatter: 'In the old days, you know, you could find hemp plants growing outside anybody's front door.'

I was suitably impressed. 'Really? I had no idea!'

'Oh yes, dear. Hemp leaves were a popular pattern on kimono, too. Along the hem, you know.'

'Hemp hems, eh?'

'*Silence in court!*'

But was marijuana made from hemp leaves? I thought they were different somehow. I was still pondering the matter when the trial ended. Michi was found guilty.

✶

While I was keeping an eye on the Pile ou Face every night, Bogey was keeping his eye on another woman.

I first got wind of it on my birthday. He came home blind drunk and stinking of perfume – nothing unusual about that – and in his hand he was carrying a box with a birthday cake in it. He had evidently bought it some hours before, since the dry ice had melted and the cake was somewhat squashed and messy.

'Here you are, Saya! Look, I've got you a birthday cake! The first one I've ever bought in my life! I never did anything like this for my wife or kids, you know! I really love you! Come on, aren't you going to open it?'

The cake had been bought from a French restaurant near Bogey's office. It was a pleasant-looking bistro actually, and I'd been thinking it'd be nice to go there sometime. Was Bogey the sort to venture into a swish restaurant like that all by himself? I thought not. He'd only go to a place like that if he were with … a woman. I had it figured out in an instant.

That morning I'd told him it was my birthday, with no great expectations.

'Oh, your birthday? I've got a lot of work today, and I'm not sure when I'll be able to get back.'

142

He'd said that in an excessively careful way, which immediately aroused my suspicions.

Bogey never bought me anything for my birthday, and now he was being so affectionate. He even said he loved me. Had I ever heard those words from him before?

It is often said, with much truth, that men treat their wives especially well when they've got something going on the side. By chance Bogey had made a dinner date with some fox from a club on my birthday, and he'd felt the prickings of conscience. Probably he'd mentioned it to her and she'd chosen the cake for him as a measure of good manners.

Huh! She needn't have bothered.

Bogey's new playmate was the *mama-san* of a club called the Salon de Marie, located near his office. Everything was turning out the way it was when he was at Kabutocho Journal. As the risks got bigger, Bogey felt the need for more than one woman. He seemed to think that since he was enduring so much stress he deserved extra female attention to soothe his fevered brow when he came off duty.

Our days of living happily together in honest poverty were over. I remembered the misery of those long nights, waiting for him to come home: those nights when I'd call all the bars, all the mah-jong parlours, all the places where I thought he might possibly be. And if I still couldn't find him, I'd start working through the hotels in the phone book.

My jealousy of this woman, whose face I'd never seen, caused me to imagine the two of them doing things together – all sorts of things. I'd drift off to sleep, still prey to those dark imaginings, and the movie would carry on in my dreams – a woman I'd never met, with long, black hair. I could see the two of them doing it right there in front of my eyes. It was incredibly realistic, and I'd wake up alone, weeping tears of hopeless rage. I'd drift back to sleep and straight into the same dream again. An all-night triple bill at the Cinema of Jealousy. I thought I'd seen the last of those tortured nights, but now they came back to haunt me once more.

The next day, there was Bogey, smirking at the sight of my eyes all red and swollen from weeping and the pillow I'd just hurled across the room at him.

'There's nothing to worry about, Saya. She's an old lady over thirty, past her prime.'

'It's that woman from the Marie, right?'

'How did you know?'

(Well, the matchboxes in Bogey's pockets with 'Salon de Marie' written on them were a dead giveaway, as was the *mama-san*'s calling card with feminine, rounded corners.)

He giggled nervously. 'What a to-do. She's got a tired old cunt as well, I can tell you.'

A moment's silence.

'I can't believe this,' I said.

Perhaps because his work was a form of fraud, Bogey hated having secrets in his private life. Once his adultery had been exposed, he would try to make a big joke of it and tell me all about it. I was quite used to this. He would then assuage my anger by taking me on a trip somewhere or giving me some money, a kind of fine. That was the deal.

Bogey's excuses for his infidelities always went like this: 'You do know, Saya, that you're the only woman I really love.'

Whenever Bogey was cheating on me, he was sure to start making frequent references to his love for me.

'I wouldn't get serious with a nightclub girl like her, you know that. You're respectable, that's why you deserve to be my "home woman". You see, men, especially in my line of work, don't look the part unless they've got at least one professional hussy on the side.'

That was it – the distinction between 'respectable women' and 'professional women'. That, and the notion that adultery was the right and proper thing for men. On top of which, I know it made him feel proud that his 'outside women' were top-class Ginza and Roppongi *mama-sans*, while his 'home woman' was a student at a famous women's university. His deceased wife had been even more of a refined young lady. Bogey liked to think of himself as a social outcast, but he was really an orthodox Japanese male.

'Once I've hit the big bucks, I'll let you have my baby. When we've got some security, like property, even if it's just a lease on a shop or something, we'll chuck away the IUD and make kiddies.'

That was Bogey's way of expressing affection. I fell for it every time.

'That'd be great. By the way, if I have a baby, I'd like to have it at Aiiku Hospital. The cherry blossoms there are lovely, and the old-fashioned European-style building is just gorgeous, don't you think?'

I used to think about marriage occasionally. I'd left it far too late in my college career for any serious job-hunting, and even if I didn't get married to Bogey I'd still be with him for the duration, so it might be fun to have a wedding ceremony after I'd graduated. I wanted to wear one of those dazzling white brocade kimonos, or maybe a Western-style wedding dress with a long train – or maybe both. We could have a big party, and it would be a real laugh! That was the extent of my thoughts on the subject.

I did try to think about what I was going to do after graduation, but as it was my habit to avoid serious reflection, I could never come to a conclusion by myself. And if I asked other people's advice, they wouldn't take it seriously because they could see that I wasn't that serious about it myself.

I asked my mother what she thought I should do.

'A woman's happiness depends on her man,' she stated. 'Even

if a woman gets a job in some company, she'll only be allowed to make tea. So I think you should go along with what Bogey says and see if he'll let you do some kind of light part-time work that'll keep you from getting bored.'

I also asked Bogey for career advice, but that proved futile.

'Saya, I've got it! You're small and light, so why don't you see about riding one of those motorboats in the races? There's already one woman doing it, and she's in all the magazines! They call her "the Hiroko Yakushimaru of motorboat racing". It'd be a great job for you. Great money, too, and you'll be famous in no time!'

He showed me a series of sexy photos of this female motorboat racer in one of the weeklies. She bore a very slight resemblance to the movie star Hiroko Yakushimaru.

'Kind of cute, eh? You'll be idolised by all the dirty old gamblers!'

'But I can't swim a stroke. If the boat capsized, I'd drown for sure.'

'I was forgetting that. Hmm.'

My worries were featherlight, and they soon floated away. I never thought too deeply about myself. All I wanted was to keep enjoying the wild ride of my life with Bogey. Somewhere at the back of my mind lay the thought that it wasn't a good idea for a woman to work. If I did, I'd end up like my ma and pa, which I didn't want, so maybe it was better for me just to stay at home. So long as I depended on Bogey for everything, I could still be a cute young thing that he would look after and never abandon. Deep down Bogey was tough, so I would be OK, provided I stuck with him. He had the composure to laugh about things, even when his fortunes hit rock-bottom. He'd always do his best to enjoy life.

When we were living in Nezu, even when we were poor as church mice, he'd bully the sushi bar owner into giving him shrimp and sea urchin and the marbled pink tuna we both loved, and bring them home to me. I felt as though I was living in the middle of the jungle, and this lynx was bringing back its kill to share with me.

He had that animal toughness about him. If a gang of ruffians ever attacked me, he'd risk his life in my defence. If I were about to be run over by a car, he'd hurl his body in front of mine. I felt that kind of trust in him, which I'd never felt with another man.

Bogey was enchantingly masculine. Never mean-spirited, he was a gorgeous man. But what I hadn't yet realised was that there was no place for a man like him in Japanese society. Beset by fantasies of death, Bogey enjoyed putting his life on the line. That's why he drank like crazy, spent money like crazy, fucked like crazy. In his work he was always fighting with his back to the wall. It struck me as magnificent. Never mind the details about his work – he was a real man. Bewitched by the glamour, I felt deeply in love.

✫

Sometime later, after much rowing and fussing, Bogey broke up with the Marie *mama-san*. But to my utter disgust his next 'outside woman' turned out to be none other than Miyuki, who'd been the second-youngest girl after me at the Poporon!

I only found out about what was going on when it had already just about finished. I had befriended Bogey's secretary, who was my age, and after the affair with the Marie *mama-san* we had got in the habit of pooling information about him. When Bogey was breaking up with Miyuki, he bought her a piano as a farewell present – she had hopes of becoming a jazz singer. The bill for the piano came to Bogey's company and the secretary tipped me off. I hurled another pillow at him.

'What? That? Well, you see, after the Poporon went bust, Miyuki moved to a new club and she sort of got in touch with me.'

'And you just go and sleep with anybody who "gets in touch with you", do you? Even someone I know?'

'I did think it was a bit off, but what could I do? She came on to me!'

There it was. It was the woman's fault for making advances. To refuse the woman would have meant displaying a lack of masculine gallantry, so what could he do?

This time I wasn't going to let him off so easily. This time I *did* know the face of the other woman. She and I had sat on either side of old Koshimizu night after night for two whole months. And since there were hardly any customers at the Poporon, we'd had four hours a night to chat and, well, I guess you could say we had become good friends.

Not only had he slept with her, he'd bought her a very expensive present, something he'd never done for me. Could anything have been calculated to infuriate me more?

'A piano eh? A matter of about half a million yen? You blow tens of millions of yen on that Lulu, you casually splash half a million on a present for Miyuki, but what about me? A soggy birthday cake, picked up on your way back from fucking another woman, that's all you've ever given me!'

I was sobbing hard as I screamed at him, yet he kept his cool.

'Saya, after a man's had a quick bang, it's only right to show his appreciation to mark the end of the affair. Half a million's no big deal – cheap enough, considering that it's payment for clearing off. If I die, you know that my company and everything I own will be yours, all yours! That's not too shabby, eh?'

Even I wasn't that dumb. Bogey might have easy money passing through his wallet, but no way could he possibly leave any assets behind if he should die. Really rich people get rich by being mean and stingy, not by throwing it around like confetti. That much I had grasped.

I had a good grumble about the situation with the Prof.

'Well,' he said with a little laugh, 'even if Hotta left more debts than assets, you could avoid responsibility for his debts by renouncing any claim to his assets.'

You never could tell how serious he was.

I told myself to forgive everything, as it was Bogey. But as I struggled to accept his outrageous behaviour, my lifestyle gradually moved in an unhealthy direction.

For a start, my dieting escalated to pathological levels. Since the women Bogey went for were pencil-thin, I ate virtually nothing but diet foods except when I was with him. I checked out every gym, fitness club and aerobics studio for miles around, before finally settling on the Sweden Centre. It was the closest to home and I could go there every day.

Patrons of the Sweden Centre included famous actresses and TV folk, and wealthy housewives who lived in the neighborhood. The only other youngster apart from myself was a soft-porn star who was well known among aficionados of late-night TV. So, of course, when the ladies of leisure saw me walk into the sauna, they assumed I must be in the same line of business and eyed me coldly. As for the porn actress herself, she shot me a glance that said, *Who the hell are you? I don't want to know, anyway.*

I also started going to an 'aesthetic beauty salon' on Sundays. Now that Bogey was beginning to make money, he had resumed attendance at the bicycle races on that day, leaving me to my own devices.

Like the gym, *mama-sans*, upper-class ladies and business-women frequented this beauty salon. I had young, smooth skin that didn't need anything done to it, nevertheless I was given treatments designed for the middle-aged that left my face stinging. Still, I gritted my teeth and continued going there. I couldn't think of anything else to do.

Reiko was busy preparing for her wedding and I had no friends to hang out with. Every Sunday I would sit in that beauty salon as the tip of my nose was slowly turned red by unnecessary exfoliation, listening to the ladies of leisure discussing their toy-boys while having dead skin removed from every inch of their bodies. Even that was better than staying at home on Sundays. After I finished at the salon, I wouldn't go home until about five o'clock, which was when Bogey generally got back from the races. I'd just wander around on my own and shop a little, for want of anything better to do. To compensate for my loneliness I had started buying more clothes than I needed.

Since the salesgirls were working in the stores to earn a living, they would at least talk to me, and I could talk to them without feeling inferior. Hey, I was the one paying, so I could do as I pleased. I was starting to think and act like Bogey.

I began to spend money the way he did, treating it like so much waste paper, using it for meaningless things in a desperate bid to soothe the strange discomfort in my heart. I used to be disgusted by the things he did with money, but now I was doing the same myself. Bogey knew this and he didn't object – how could he when he was burning money faster than ever? – and he didn't want to give me ammunition to use against him in the future.

Before setting out for the bicycle races or the horses, he got into the habit of slipping me several hundred thousand yen as pocket money.

'Here, get yourself some clothes or something with this.'

He considered it money well spent since it would guarantee him a smiling welcome, even if he came home in a bad mood when he lost.

Every Sunday he would leave me to myself. On the other hand, he also left me enough money to buy the sort of clothes that most young women only dreamed of. So I accepted the situation.

Bogey's habit of doing exactly as he pleased gradually spread from Sunday to the rest of the week, and I became increasingly irritable and despondent. I took to having a few drinks on my own during the long nights I spent waiting up for him. I was quietly drifting into alcoholism.

During the nights when he didn't come home at all, because he was playing mah-jong or having it off with a woman, I'd empty a bottle of Chivas Regal or Hennessy and wake up in the cold light of morning lying on the floor with the empty bottle beside me. I'd pick myself up and tidy the mess. He never saw any of this since he wouldn't come home until much later, sometimes not till the following day.

✼

At the end of January I handed in a graduation thesis that was just passable and promptly settled into the last spring vacation of my student career. The fortunes of Bogey's company were continuing to pitch and toss with the vagaries of the stock market, and, as ever, when the market was down, Bogey would get dead drunk and his face would turn ashen.

As my graduation approached, Bogey expressed a new concern in his drunken ramblings.

'You won't want me after you've graduated. You'll find a bright young fellow and marry him. I know. I can see it all.'

When he drifted off to sleep, his fears would emerge from his subconscious, and I'd hear him moaning 'Oh, oh … Saya, Saya, where have you gone?'

His worry that I was about to leave him escalated rapidly.

'I bet you reckon love's one thing and marriage is another, or that marriage is something you do with a young man, right?'

'I keep telling you, I don't think that way!'

Indeed, although I was developing something of a victim complex living with Bogey, I had no intention of leaving him. I loved him, and however badly he behaved I found myself shrugging it off, thinking, *It can't be helped*. Or, to put it more honestly, I didn't have a thing in my head except him. My love for Bogey counted for more than the whole world.

Moreover, I had no desire to get married. Probably my parents' failed marriage had something to do with it, but I couldn't summon up the smallest speck of interest in settling down to a steady life, whether that meant marriage or anything else. Listening to sermons from my friends about the importance of marrying a guy with the 'three highs' – height, high education and high income – I really couldn't understand what all the fuss was about. I was just as bemused when they talked about getting a job at a good company, and so on.

Seeing the miserable state Bogey had got himself into, however, it seemed to me that perhaps marriage was the only cure for his type of the blues. If marriage would make him happy then what the hell? Might as well go for it!

Ever since I'd first met Bogey, I'd made it my mission in life to keep him from feeling sad. That was my *raison d'être*. Anytime, anyplace – never for a moment was his shadow out of my mind. For several years, now, pathetically enough, I'd thought of nothing but him.

I still hesitated about actually marrying the guy. Marriage would mean taking on the social responsibility of being a legal couple, and it sounded like heavy baggage to me. Still, it would be better than plunging Bogey into despair. Besides, it was no fun being together when he was constantly fretting about my commitment to him. So I made up my mind and raised the matter.

'Bogey, wouldn't it be fun to get married? The wedding could be cool, and you could leave all the arrangements to me.'

'Wh-What?'

Bogey was astounded, to say the least. Guys of his generation didn't expect women to take the initiative in proposing marriage, unless perhaps it was some older woman from the hostessing world.

I had talked myself into it by telling myself that since I was about to lose my role of 'student', I might as well replace it with one as 'housewife'. Here in Japan, I reasoned, you couldn't get by without some kind of job title or label, even it was only 'house-wife'. Maybe the status of a married couple would pep up my relationship with Bogey, which had been a bit stale of late.

Bogey hesitated. He was a little embarrassed about getting married at his age; but he was also genuinely concerned about my future. I was very young, and although his business was now up and running, the fact remained that he was still straining the limits of legality in the world of finance. He felt he ought to think of marriage only after he had become established in a more legitimate line, when he had made the move from the back street to the high street. Otherwise it would be unkind to drag me into his affairs. We had come together when I was still a naïve nineteen-year-old, and I had been plunged into the deep end of the back-street lifestyle. If I got it into my head that it was a sensible lifestyle, I'd be no good for anything else if something should happen to him. In his mind's eye, my image merged with that of his late wife, and he didn't want to be the ruin of the second woman he'd loved.

I, for my part, was relaxed about all this; indeed, such heavy concerns never entered my head. I just thought we might as well get hitched, but Bogey poured cold water on the idea.

'Saya, before you get married and become a housewife, don't you think you should take a stab at working at a job, earning a salary, renting an apartment, and all that? That's all part of acquiring life skills.'

'What do you mean?' I wasn't having any of that. 'I wouldn't be able to get any decent job at this late date – the deadline for applications is long past. All my girlfriends have been job-hunting like crazy, and they can't get proper jobs, even after four years at university. If you're a woman they won't let you do anything except make tea and do boring office chores. I'm not gonna do stuff like that! Besides, you don't want your woman making tea for some old boss, do you?'

'Saya, no one does that stuff because they want to. They're all gritting their teeth and bearing it, living in some filthy apartment with start-up wages of 130,000 yen a month.'

'That little? If you have to pay the rent out of that money, how can you live on what's left over?'

'Believe it or not, Saya darling, people do live on that kind of money. That's how ordinary people live!'

'I could never do that. I'd sooner die!'

'If an ordinary office girl could hear you, she'd be pretty angry, you know.'

'But it's not fair, Bogey! Look at your own lifestyle! You can't live like this and expect me to put up with that!'

'Talk about self-indulgence! Listen to the little lady!'

Since I was the one looking after Bogey, I considered it natural that I should enjoy the perks that came with the job.

Besides, even if I did as Bogey suggested, he wouldn't like the new me, grimly battling in the poverty of the 'respectable' world. Whatever he might say, the fact was that he wanted his woman to be self-indulgent. A respectable woman would be too prim and proper for him; it would be like having a school-teacher at his side the whole time, and he'd feel constrained and ill at ease.

Beset by all kinds of thoughts, I lapsed into a sulky silence.

'You're hopeless, Saya. You couldn't do a thing without your

Bogey there to hold your hand, could you? Oh, all right, then, do as you please!'

'Really?'

I promptly went right ahead and did just that. It was February, close to Valentine's Day in fact. The following Sunday I dragged Bogey, ready to die of embarrassment, to the Tiffany jewellery counter at the Mitsukoshi department store in the Ginza.

In my mind's eye was the glittering diamond on the engagement ring that Reiko had graciously allowed me a quick look at after she'd landed her man.

'This ring usually costs one-and-a-half million yen,' she'd proudly told me. 'But his dad's got a friend who runs a jewellery store, so he got it for half price. Even so, that's 750,000 yen! Scary, isn't it? I daren't wear it!'

Silly Reiko, is that the only way she can measure a man's love? That's what I thought, but at the same time I have to admit I was jealous. Bogey had never given me anything valuable.

He had said I could do as I pleased. OK! It would please me a lot to have the kind of engagement ring that would make Reiko's look like a schoolgirl's trinket. Such were my thoughts as I dragged Bogey into Tiffany's.

Bogey looked at the price tags of the rings in the showcases and blanched.

'One – One million six hundred thousand yen? Just a minute! There's a shop you can place off-course bets just across from here.'

To Bogey, any sum in excess of one million yen was seed money with the potential to 'grow'. But I wasn't going to lose my engagement ring money to some stupid horse or cyclist.

'Oh no, no, no! You'll blow all your money there, and then you won't be able to afford a brass curtain ring!'

'But I haven't got that kind of money on me! Can't we buy it another time?'

If Tiffany's wasn't on, I'd have to settle for second-best. I took him to a less fancy counter on the second floor. I knew I had to get him to buy it that day, otherwise the cheapskate would definitely try to marry me without giving me an engagement ring. And I had no intention of letting him get away with that.

'Bogey, look at this one. It's lovely, isn't it? And the price is so reasonable, too.'

I got the salesgirl to open the showcase and take out a nice little ring with a cluster of tiny diamonds set in the shape of a heart.

OK, so it's not as expensive as Reiko's. But at least it's a Nina Ricci, so I can say it's fashionable.

'We need it as an engagement ring,' I proudly told the salesgirl as I slipped it on the ring finger of my left hand. Fate was at work again – it was a perfect fit.

'I must say it suits madam remarkably well,' she said very helpfully.

Bogey looked sick. The price was 290,000 yen, almost exactly what he had in his wallet at that moment.

✻

The next morning I paid a sudden visit to the nearest place I could think of where they did wedding receptions, which happened to be the Nogi Banqueting Hall.

'Er, I want to get married right away. When's the next available date? It's got to be a Saturday or Sunday, though – it would spoil everything if the stock market crashed on the morning of the wedding.'

'Pardon?'

I felt myself getting irritated. I wanted to get everything nailed down before I changed my own mind. Also, because of the nonsense about June weddings being more romantic, Reiko was getting married in June, and I was damn well going to beat her to the altar. Such were the foolish thoughts racing through my mind.

'Do I have the honour of addressing the bride-to-be?'

'Yes, you do!'

No wonder the saleswoman was a little perplexed. Usually people contemplating marriage would phone in advance to make an appointment, and the prospective groom and probably several other members of the two families would accompany the bride-to-be as well. Also, they'd probably want to check out the facilities before committing themselves to the expense of a wedding reception.

'And you want to know the earliest possible date?'

'Yes.'

'Er, just a moment, please.'

She leafed through a weighty, leather-bound appointment book.

'If you want a *tai-an* day, I'm afraid we're booked solid. People who want that date book at least six months in advance, if not a year.'

Tai-an was the luckiest day on the calendar for weddings.

'Aren't there any days available?'

'Well, people who really can't manage it any other way will even get married on a *butsumetsu* day, although that's considered terribly unlucky. But just a moment! We seem to have a free slot on Saturday, March 28. It's a *shakku* day, not quite as bad as a *butsumetsu*, though the only time available is in the late afternoon.'

'OK, we'll have it on the day you've just said!'

'Don't you need to consult the other party first?'

'No. He's leaving all the arrangements to me. Besides, it's his second, so I think it'll be a pretty informal affair.'

'I see.'

'What would be the minimum number of people we'd need to make it a decent show?'

The saleswoman's jaw fell open and stayed that way for a while.

✡

I became very busy. Or rather I made myself very busy for fear of having time on my hands to wonder about life after graduation, which would only depress me. Questions about Life – deep questions, long questions, much-too-difficult questions. So for now I just avoided thinking as much as possible.

There was a two-month gap between submitting my graduation thesis and the actual graduation, and most of my college friends took the opportunity to travel somewhere to celebrate this milestone. I was invited to go along with some of them, but I turned down the invitation without a moment's hesitation. I was too worried about Bogey to go off and leave him on his own.

I'm all right. I've got plenty to do.

Indeed, I was down at the Nogi Banqueting Hall almost every day, setting up the wedding in a great rush while the bemused saleswoman patiently taught me all the things I needed to know, and there were many: from ordering a rather dull wedding ring to renting the traditional clothes and wig, to drawing up the guest list and composing the text to be printed on the invitation cards. All this I accomplished by myself. I even chose the customary gifts for guests to take home afterwards.

Bogey had the bright idea of asking the Prof and his wife to act as the ceremonial go-betweens. He even steeled himself and visited my mother to ask her for my hand formally, and he introduced me to his parents.

As he was already middle-aged, his parents were rather old. Bogey resembled his mother slightly more than his father, I thought. She was a very charming and sprightly lady. His father, whom Bogey had always bad-mouthed for being weak and useless, struck me as a most civilised, elegant gentleman.

The two of them were shocked at my youth, and then the astonishment on their faces gave way to pity.

'What a perfectly marvellous young lady! Really, Takashi, how could you?!'

His mother talked apologetically, as if her son was setting out to ruin an innocent girl. Meanwhile her husband just sat there, gazing out of the restaurant window at the early-blooming cherry trees in the garden.

Both of them were opposed to the marriage. Partly they felt sorry for me, but their main concern was for their grandchildren, Bogey's kids by his previous marriage who were now living with his wife's family.

When the meal was over I left early while Bogey talked things over with his parents. When he arrived home later he said to me, 'My mother thinks we should wait until the kids have grown up. She says that for their sake I should show some restraint and put up with a little hardship because they've had to put up with so much. That kind of thing. Well, she does have a point. It's only a few years since their mother died and here I am getting married to a woman who's closer in age to them than to me. You'd expect that to hurt, I guess.'

He spoke quietly and in a straightforward manner. For the first time I sensed genuine contrition.

Come to think of it, Bogey's mother's qualms were justified. His oldest daughter was only seven years younger than I was. Seeing myself in her shoes, I could imagine how painful it would be. Especially considering how unnatural her death had been.

But we had already booked the reception hall and everything else, and had put down the deposit. And it wasn't as if Bogey was of an age where he needed parental consent.

'Oh well, never mind,' he said, 'we'll just have to go ahead without inviting my relatives. I'll get Lulu and the gang to sit on my side of the hall, along with some guys from my company. By the way, what are you going to do about your dad?'

'What? Oh, whatever. We don't have anything to do with his family. Perhaps I'll ask the barber next door if he can fill in for dad.'

'Whatever you say. Ha-ha-ha!'

Bogey could be very gracious. Once he'd decided that something didn't really matter, it was just a question of getting on with the show. And in the case of our wedding, the show did indeed go on. But our 'Qué será será' approach resulted in a shambles.

For a start, the guest list was not at all balanced. My side was missing my father and his relatives, while Bogey's side had no relatives at all – just a few of his employees and some nightclubbing buddies. Between us we could only muster enough guests to fill about one-third of the smallest hall in the building, and they were served an equally unbalanced assortment of Japanese and Western-style dishes. Even so, we had the works: I was constantly attended by a professional bridesmaid, and several assistants helped me to get in and out of the various gorgeous costumes I had to wear. Bogey and I sat in front of an ornate golden folding screen at the head table, and all the guests gave us a proper send-off once it was over. This made it feel even stranger. Everything was being done to please little me. The adults, including Bogey, were indulging a kid, staging an overpriced school play just so that I could have my moment of glory on stage.

My mother had made the wedding an excuse to go back to the kimono store and splash out three million yen on a magnificent formal kimono. All the other guests duly showed up in their Sunday best, clutching gifts of cash in decorative envelopes that they deposited at the door on their way in, just like they did at a real wedding. The whole thing was weird.

The Prof looked totally out of place in his role as the formal go-between, which involved giving one of the main speeches. He had managed to find himself a respectable morning suit from somewhere, but he could not stop giggling and his white wavy hair was in total disarray. On top of that, his loathing of dentists meant that his long-lost front tooth had never been replaced. As for Lulu, she didn't have any formal eveningwear, so she was dressed in her usual eccentric, vaguely Parisienne, style. 'Oh, this is absolutely amazing,' she trilled. 'It's the first time I've ever been to a genuine Japanese-style wedding!' – And she cackled merrily like an old witch. My professional bridesmaid stared blankly, jaw agape.

Oh well, it was all part of the show. I was happy just to see everyone getting into the festive spirit.

When Bogey saw me in my thick, all-white bridal make-up, with my traditional wig and hood and long white kimono, he got embarrassed and became overly deferential to the guests, acting in an unnaturally jovial manner. For a cynic like him, who was used to getting people into a good mood and then taking advantage of them, there was nothing more confusing than being the star of the show himself.

I myself was as cool as a cucumber and thoroughly enjoying the new experience of partying in an all-white, antique-style wedding kimono. Yes, fashion is a truly splendid thing. Appearances *do* matter, because when you are dressed like the real thing you *feel* like the real thing.

The professional bridesmaid led me toward the Shinto altar to say my vows. It was the last Saturday in March. The previous Saturday I'd been dressed in a different kind of formal wear – the sober skirt and top required for university graduation. I reckoned it was a pretty smart idea to get these ceremonies of life tidied away. Once they'd been sorted out, I could sit down and think quietly about my future.

My mother had made another trip to the kimono store to order me a plain smart kimono for everyday use, with the family crest on it, along with two mourning kimono, one for summer and one for winter. In principle she didn't want to give anything to her capricious daughter, but with my graduation and wedding both occurring in the space of a week, pride dictated that the customary bride's wardrobe be provided.

Trussed up in the heavy wedding kimono, with ornate head-gear stacked on my head, the corridor leading to the altar seemed extremely long. As I painfully progressed along it, I was thinking to myself, *This means that the foundation of your life is solid.* Once we were properly settled down, I could start to build my life on that foundation.

In my youthful innocence I had no idea how overly optimistic those thoughts were. I simply believed in the old Japanese myth that a woman and the man she marries are somehow linked by a long, red thread of fate, even before they are born. The bridal finery in which I was clad and the atmosphere of the surroundings inspired such romantic thoughts.

The wedding itself was held at dusk, at a Shinto shrine in a small wood in the grounds of the wedding hall. The little altar was already wrapped in purplish light as we approached it, and the twilight was thickening. By the time the shrine maidens had fin-ished their sacred dance on the cypress-wood stage before the altar, and the last notes of the ancient instruments had died away, and we had sipped our ceremonial cups of saké, we were envel-oped in darkness. Nogi Shrine at dusk: a suggestive, foreboding scene. Bogey was tense in a way that was out of character, and as we exchanged rings I noticed his fingers were trembling slightly.

SIX

Although we had the wedding reception, in the end we didn't get married in any legal sense. Bogey felt that he should respect his mother's concerns about the feelings of his children, and also see how his company progressed before registering our marriage with the civil authorities.

'I still don't know how things are going to turn out with the company,' he said. 'If I get into some kind of trouble, I don't want you dragged into it. As for the children, well, the older one's big enough to look after herself, but the younger one's just going through adolescence and seems to be turning into a difficult teenager. I'm thinking of meeting up and talking things over...'

Bogey spoke in an apologetic tone, but he needn't have worried about hurting my feelings. To me, registering our marriage was just a boring bureaucratic procedure, and I couldn't care less whether we did this or not. So when Bogey asked if I minded postponing the formalities for the time being, I replied, 'Sure, no problem.'

'Really?' Bogey sounded slightly suspicious.

'Sure. Like I said, we should think of the wedding as a kind of "event".'

I wasn't saying this just to make Bogey feel at ease. It was what I really believed and I was telling him straight.

'*Reelly*?' He put on that mock childish voice he used when he was feeling playful or embarrassed.

'Yes. *Reelly*!'

Bogey seemed suitably relieved, but at the same time disconcerted to have got through a tricky situation without taking any flak.

Yet it was true. To me, a marriage certificate was nothing more than a scrap of paper. I was glad we'd held the wedding, because it had calmed Bogey down and it had been a lot of fun for all, including me.

As was customary, after the reception we had several more parties that evening, of gradually decreasing formality. The second party was held at a Chinese club in Roppongi. It had a glittering golden interior and an outrageous disco floor, complete with a Filipino band. Bogey was in a white suit by Monsieur Nicole that I'd persuaded him to hire from a boutique, and I was in an off-the-peg wedding dress from Parco in Shibuya.

It was only a simple seventy-thousand-yen white calf-length dress, but it meant a great deal to me to have my own wedding dress. I was happy to rent everything else for the wedding, but the dress – and the tiara – I wanted to buy and keep as mementos. Though I didn't care a hoot about the legal and social significance of marriage, the ceremony did have a dreamy, girlish romance to it.

The palatial stage of the disco was framed by neon tubing, along which multicoloured lights flashed rhythmically to the music. Bogey and I got things rolling by pouring cheap pink champagne into a wobbly pyramid of champagne glasses and sending it cascading down from glass to glass in the customary manner, a performance greeted by boisterous cheers and applause. This was followed by one speech after another, one present after another, and then the two of us walked off the stage and into the crowd, filling people's glasses with Hennessy. It was a really gaudy party.

All the guests were getting into the swing of it – all the glitterbugs and gangsters, the whole *nouveau riche* tribe. The grand finale was Bogey and Ken-ken singing 'Brotherly Honour', the theme song from an old *yakuza* movie, and myself making some closing remarks not entirely fitting for a blushing bride: 'Everybody, please don't think about anything. Just enjoy yourselves as much as you can tonight. After all, that's what life's for – having fun!'

After these rather meaningless words, I led the assembly in the three rounds of rhythmic clapping that signified the end of the formal proceedings.

I dare say Bogey's friends had been to such events before, but for my young friends it was their first experience of a gangster-style blowout, and they were understandably surprised. When, however, they saw that the groom was actually a charming middle-aged fellow and not some scary underworld type they soon warmed to him. Bogey, for his part, was doing his best to put everyone in a relaxed and cheerful mood, leading them in a spot of go-go dancing on the disco floor.

When the party ended, Bogey and I adjourned, laden with flowers and gifts, to the honeymoon suite at the ultra-upmarket Miyako Hotel. Bogey's mates had reserved it as another wedding present for us. The bridal bed was colossal – I believe it was wider than it was long.

Alas, however, Bogey was too tired from the strain of being on his best behaviour – as well as from the second, third and fourth follow-up parties – to appreciate the sumptuous surroundings. He just rolled over on the bed and was off, snoring like a hippopotamus. The romantic suite reverberated with the loudest snores I'd ever heard: ceremonial wedding snores. The Madonna-style lacy white underwear that I had chosen to match the wedding dress went to waste.

✧

The day after our wedding Bogey handed me 300,000 yen and said, 'Now that you're a full-time housewife, take this and see if you can make it last a month.' The graduation and wedding ceremonies might have been merely enjoyable events for me, but here was hard evidence that I had made the real transition from student to housewife.

'I see. "Full-time housewife", eh?'

I had never been fully aware of what I was doing, and since I didn't know where to begin, I started from appearances. I wasn't used to rings, but the one I now wore was my wedding ring, so I must never take it off. Because I drank too much my fingers had swollen, and I couldn't get the thing off anyway. I tended to put on airs, but since I was duly married I took to dressing in a manner becoming a young bride: demure but winsome.

I also lavished far more care on the apartment, telling myself that this was now 'my job'. I draped a stylish cover over the grubby sofa and selected flowers that matched the colours of it, placing them in strategic locations to set off the sofa. I hung modern art silkscreens on the walls. I used the gifts of cash we'd received from the guests to buy a wardrobe and chest of drawers. The 30,000 yen left over was just enough to pick up a cheap and cheerful dressing table. With all the tangible elements of newly-wed life in place, I reckoned I was set to enjoy the life itself.

Bogey, too, was in high spirits. Every time he went drinking, his pals would tease him about his 'young bride', and when he came home drunk he'd give me a big hug and say, 'So you're my wife now, Saya. Dear wife, how I love you. Ooops, just listen to me!'

He'd crave my indulgence in all sorts of ways, some of them slightly off-putting. One morning, for instance, on his way to the toilet, he said, 'Come along with Bogey and see what he can do.'

'What?'

'Come on, Saya, now that we're married it's only natural. I read somewhere that Tomisaburo Wakayama's wife always looks at his crap in the morning to check on the state of his health. Now that's a sign of true love, right?'

'Tomisaburo Wakayama?'

Newly-wed bliss is all very well, but there are limits. I didn't want to be compared with the scrawny wife of some fading samurai movie star, and I certainly had no wish to inspect Bogey's lavatorial productions. I didn't want to hurt his feelings, however, so I accompanied him as far as the toilet door and hung around outside, pretending to feign interest by craning my neck as if to get a better view.

'Ah, Saya, you don't love me after all,' he sighed. Married life in Japan is tough indeed if love is measured by a willingness to inspect your husband's crap.

Bogey was, however, now more considerate towards me than he had been in our unmarried days. Also, I still had plenty of bridal duties to occupy me, such as writing thank-you letters to the guests, ordering extra copies of photographs to go with the letters and generally tidying up loose ends. Additionally, there were other weddings to attend and help out at; Bogey's secretary was getting hitched, and so, of course, was Reiko.

I performed all these duties briskly and efficiently, as befitted a bright young wife. I went with Bogey to the other weddings as if we were a real married couple. Although we had no honeymoon as such, we took a pleasant trip to our favourite hot-spring hotel and another to Kyoto for the horse-racing. It felt like proper, grown-up married life, fresh and invigorating.

Around spring that year, Japan's overheated economy reached boiling point, making Bogey a very busy man and putting a lot of easy cash in his pocket. Everyone was making so much money that it was coming out of their ears. And the more they made the more they wanted. Making money became a kind of crazy game that was all the rage.

Bogey's company was raking in profits like gangbusters, and he was so preoccupied with this that he hardly had time to visit the office in Roppongi that was supposed to house his legitimate business. Instead, he was permanently encamped at the investment consultancy office in the Ginza. His lifestyle was just the same as it had been in the Kabutocho Journal days. He virtually abandoned all planning for the 'proper' business that was supposed to bring him in an honest income, and as the big money started to roll in he turned with renewed excitement to his favourite pastime – manipulating stocks to make big money bigger still.

To Bogey, stock trading was just another form of gambling – only it required bigger stakes than a wad of notes in the pocket of an individual punter. That meant he had to get his stake together by persuading other people to put him in charge of their money. And like all true gamblers, he never believed for a moment that he might lose. He didn't think he was swindling people on false pretences either, for he genuinely believed he was on to a good thing every time. I didn't know anything about what he was up to, but I knew that what he was doing was much the same as what he had been doing at Kabutocho Journal. I also knew that there was no malevolence in the man.

Bogey was a born gambler. He gambled for work; he gambled for pleasure. He didn't feel alive if he was not gambling. It wasn't a rational thing. There'd be about as much point in telling Bogey to stop gambling as in telling a carnivorous animal to stop killing other animals for food.

Of course the work wasn't all fun. Every night he'd be somewhere in the Ginza, swapping stock tips or wining and dining potential investors. In the days when he used to hang out at the Roppongi office he'd be out every night drinking for pleasure with the Prof, but these days he no longer had time to go drinking with people just because he liked them. Now his drinking partners were middle-aged men involved in the finance business. Apparently he'd also sometimes knock around with *yakuza*. Every night he'd wear his dark suit and come home around three in the morning, utterly exhausted from all the entertaining and the wheeler-dealing.

'Oh dear, I don't know how much more I can take, Saya. Tonight they all insisted on going to the karaoke bar and singing. They love those *enka* ballads, you know.'

Enka aren't as popular as they used to be, but there are still a lot of people who have a soft spot for these old-fashioned, melancholy, slightly sentimental songs. I remember making sarcastic comments about a boring *enka* programme on TV one night and drawing a mild rebuke from Bogey.

'You say those things because you're young. But mark my words, one of these days when you're older, some of those *enka* lyrics will bring a tear to your eye and a lump to your throat.' He said that, but in a way he was poking fun at the genre himself.

'What about you, Bogey? When you're with a group like that, you can't get away without singing a number or two. So what do you go for when it's your turn? Moody songs? Pops?'

'Why, you little...'

'Thought so! *Enka*, right?'

'I don't sing them because I like them. And don't get it into your head that I'm one of those idiots who loves the sound of his own voice. I have to do it, just to be sociable, OK? Give me a break!'

The more stressful his work and his socialising became, the more he gambled. His face would go that horrible pale colour again, and he would start burning money with a fury. I wonder why money seems to have this effect on people, so that the more you make the more dissolute you become, and you end up wasting it as if it were bath water or toilet paper.

Once Bogey even got arrested , when the police busted an illegal high-stakes mah-jong game where he was playing with some retired pro baseball players. I got a phone call from the Osaki police asking me to bring spare clothes to the station where he was being held for questioning. It was a bit of a blow; no matter how much effort I put into beautifying myself and the apartment, and however carefully I prepared dinner, he seemed to leave me alone almost all the time. And now, instead of Bogey walking through the front door, it was a call from the police station.

I was getting to be as dissolute as Bogey. We'd only been married a month, and already I'd become the kind of bitch who keeps the score in her relationship with her man. I was providing such-and-such services, therefore I had a right to expect such-and-such in return.

I'd browse through travel magazines, find a nice place to go for the weekend, and wheedle Bogey into taking me there. My birthday, for instance, was a very different affair from the previous year's soggy cake. This time I had him take me to the Hotel Seiyo, one of the most luxurious in Tokyo, the jewel of the Ginza. Bogey agreed at once when I asked in my usual coaxing manner. I think he had a guilty conscience because he'd left me on my own so much.

We invited Ken-ken and a few of the boys from the office after work, and broke out the Dom Perignon. Then we adjourned to Kitcho, the legendary Japanese restaurant in the hotel's basement, before hitting the Ginza for a night on the town. Again we failed to make full use of the accommodation. I was left sitting in our lovely suite – in a hotel that only had suites, I might add – with a marble bathroom the size of an average family's living room – looking at Bogey lying in another of his drunken stupors, while his mighty snores rang out once more.

✫

Since Bogey was always drunk as a lord when he came home at night, our sex life took place in the morning, just before he set off to work.

'Saya, you just have your morning "injection" and then go straight back to sleep! That's why you're so fit and lively.'

It was one of Bogey's favourite little jokes – but it was true. By the time I woke up after our morning's lovemaking, he'd be long gone. And by the time I got out of bed, it'd be past noon. I'd have a shower, clean up the apartment in a desultory way, and head off to the beauty parlour or English conversation school. If I didn't feel like it, I could always cancel. There was nothing that I absolutely had to do, which was relaxing, but also sad. My one mission was to keep Bogey from feeling lonely by always being on call, looking my best and ready to fly to him at the drop of a hat if and when he phoned. This was before the days of mobile phones, so it meant spending a lot of time at home.

In short, once the rites of spring were over, my life became extremely empty and uneventful, like a broad expanse of beach after the tide has gone out. I was back to square one. I had graduated from university and I had got married, but these events didn't seem to have made any difference to my life. At first it had been a pleasant change of pace, but once I'd got used to my new status, I felt the old depression seeping back. Until I'd solved my fundamental problem – whatever that might be – I would not truly be able to enjoy anything that I did.

A lot of the creeping depression seemed to stem from the change in status. From frivolous college girl to – what? Frumpy housewife? I suddenly found the new title weighing on me like a ton of lead.

I was getting into the habit of nagging Bogey when he got home.

'I keep telling you, Saya, you're free to do whatever you like.'

But I wasn't free. I was shackled by my status as surely as if it were a ball and chain. As a housewife I somehow couldn't be bothered to do anything. All the college friends from my year had got jobs and were terribly busy. Of course, I had younger friends who were still students, but I didn't feel like hanging out with them. And so I was all by myself, morning, noon and night.

'I'm so bored I think I'll take driving lessons. How about buying a car, Bogey?'

This was one request that was not going to be met.

'No, we're not getting a car. Anything else, but not that.'

Bogey had a phobia about women drivers stemming from the traffic accident that killed his wife.

'Women are emotional creatures. That's why they're no good at making decisions in emergencies. You often read in newspapers about women drivers getting into accidents, like driving out of the garage and accidentally slipping the car into reverse and crushing their own children to death. Or seeing some guy right in front of them and getting all flustered and stepping on the accelerator instead of the brake.'

'Do things like that really happen?'

'Of course. You never watch the news on TV or read the newspapers, otherwise you'd know. But the fact is that stupid accidents happen all the time, and more often or not they're caused by women.'

'That's a damn lie. The most dangerous drivers are young men who have just got their licence. I know because that's what they told us at driving school. I did have a go at getting a licence in my first year at college, you know.'

(I didn't get it. I was too busy partying and ran out of time.)

'Anyway, the answer's no, and that's final! The way to ride in a car is to sit in the back with a chauffeur at the wheel. I'll sort that out one of these days, but until then you'll just have to make do with cabs!'

Since we'd got married, Bogey had become more prone to worry about my well being and more willing to spoil me. But I didn't want to be chauffeured. I wanted to do something myself for once.

'Ah, what a bore!'

'Oh, for goodness sake! It's tough, I know, but life isn't one endless party! Most people lead a boring life – that's usual. With all the goodies you get, you're one of the lucky ones!'

'Well, if ordinary people have boring lives, I don't wanna be ordinary. I'd rather be weird.'

'Anyway – no car!'

The more Bogey spoiled me, the worse I became. I was now your typical rich bitch.

'Well, if you're not going to let me get a driving licence, at least get me a kimono, OK?'

'Wh-What?'

I was no longer satisfied going around in fashionable Western-style clothes and felt it was time I had a few proper kimonos. After all, Bogey liked beautiful Japanese women who looked good in kimono. More than that, I felt that a man of his means should buy his wife a nice kimono now and then. I was getting accustomed to buying whatever I wanted right away. Shopping was about the only aspect of my life where I didn't encounter any frustration.

As it happened, Bogey's company was doing fantastically well at this point, which meant that Bogey had pots of money but no time to spend with me.

'How much is this kimono?'

'A million yen on the nail. I can get a discount because a friend of mine runs the shop.'

'Phew! That's on the high side, isn't it?'

What's he got to grumble about? A million yen's nothing to him, I thought and coldly added, 'I'll choose a cheap sash to go with it.'

Since I was leading this tedious life for Bogey's sake, I reasoned that the least he could do was buy me some decent clothes occasionally. That's how arrogant I'd become.

Moreover, by decking myself out in kimono at every opportunity, I'd become the kind of woman who looks right in a kimono. I also had all the leisure I needed to get my hair done at beauty parlours that specialised in traditional Japanese hairstyles. To be the elegant woman Bogey could be proud of was my job.

Eventually the new kimono was finished. I gave a bored little sigh: 'I know, maybe I'll show it to Ma.'

That was the first thing I did with it. Since Bogey didn't have much time for me, I'd taken to visiting my mother more often. I'd paid back every penny of the money I owed her, out of the increasingly generous pocket money that Bogey had been giving me.

'You do have exotic tastes,' was her comment. 'Only professional geishas wear that kind of kimono.'

She didn't mean that it was loud and gaudy, quite the opposite. Actually, the design was plain but elegant. I think she was rather pleased to think of me and Bogey maintaining the kind of old-fashioned relationship she associated with the look.

'You see this tacking thread? You should leave just a little of it in place and ask your husband who bought the kimono to pull it out himself. That's the traditional way of doing it. It's his dependability as a breadwinner that allows his wife to look attractive. You don't know how lucky you are. I used to buy stuff for your dad, but he never bought a thing for me. Not once!'

Instead of the girlish kimono mother had chosen for me, with bright colours and floral designs, the one I was now wearing was very adult in style – dark, austere and elegant. Mother was enchanted. I saw the glow of pleasure on her face and knew I'd made the right decision – and not just with the kimono. What a lucky girl I must be!

As it happened, Bogey and my mother shared the same values. My escalating material demands scandalised him, but in a weird way they also pleased him, for my extravagance was a visible reflection of his wealth. Make the wife look good and let her live a life of luxury. That was the old-fashioned masculine ideal – a *yakuza* aesthetic if you will.

He liked me to live this lifestyle – detached from reality with nothing much to do except sleep, wake up, complain and occasionally pout, all the time being spoiled rotten.

'You know what,' Bogey said, 'men aren't attracted to women who work for a living. They like to let their women live in luxury, just to indulge in one or two enjoyable pastimes, hobbies or something.'

He wanted his wife to live in luxury. Or put another way, he wanted her to live in such idleness that she was at his beck and call and he could assume that she would be thinking only of him at all times. Also, so that he could take her to any place he felt like going, anytime, safe in the knowledge that she would look smart enough for him to feel good.

You could say there was a slight element of male chauvinism in his thinking! Even so, I did my best to consider myself happy. He was a man of the world, and had fallen in love with me at first sight. That, I told myself, proved my worth as a woman.

'I'll get out of this rut by finding myself a hobby.'

It sounded easy, but I soon realised that finding a fun pastime was very hard. At first I told myself that everything was fine, that I was a lucky girl. Bogey was happy, my mother was happy, and as a housewife I could go to the local English conversation school, gym, and beauty parlour as much as I liked.

But however much English I learned, and however fit and beautiful I became, I had nowhere to make use of these skills and attributes. There's nothing sadder than slaving away at something that's totally unnecessary.

Apart from the rare occasions when Bogey took me out, I spent nearly all my time lying around at home with the four cats. It started to feel as if life was passing me by.

I tried to soothe my anxieties by calling up the outside world to see how it was getting on. Whenever I phoned a friend from college, she'd say something like 'God, I'm so busy! I'm so envious of all that time and money you have to do as you please'. My friends'd complain bitterly, but I thought I also detected a note of happiness in their voices, too. They were having a tough time, but they were doing their best to get used to the world of work, and their voices had a lively bounce.

As for me, I had leisure and money to excess and I was supposed to be happy, but my heart was always covered in thick, dark clouds. My friends grumbled about being too busy, but they were lucky to have something that needed doing. Without that, all the partying and spending was no fun at all.

When I was still at college, Bogey and I thought we were so clever. We looked down at people who were struggling to scrape together a living. Most of them were idiots, and the whole world seemed designed for idiots. It was just too boring and silly for us to be bothered with it. Now, however, it began to dawn on me that, possibly, the real idiots might be us.

✻

'Why not have a go at scriptwriting?' said Reiko, between spoon-fuls of the seafood risotto she was stuffing into her mouth.

I had browbeaten Reiko into having lunch with me at the café in the health club where she was doing her maternity swimming. I hated to ask her advice about anything, since it would seem as though I was admitting that she was doing better than me, but I didn't have anyone else to talk to.

It was a very snooty health club. Reiko's father-in-law had a lifetime family membership, so Reiko had become a member when she got married. It was the kind of club where they carried out background checks into your professional and family circumstances before they'd let you join. Money alone wouldn't be enough to get them to issue a membership card to someone like Bogey.

I felt a twinge of inferiority. I'd never had that feeling before, not with Reiko, anyway.

'Scriptwriting?'

'Yeah. It's a hard, time-consuming job that doesn't pay too well, so there aren't many people doing it. And coming from our university literature department will help you get work.'

The literature department... Hmm. I was no literary bluestocking. I'd drifted into that department because it'd seemed harmless.

'But how do you go about becoming a scriptwriter?'

'Well, first you go to a scriptwriting school. It's not like you have to go every day – they have this night school option where you just show up one evening a week. Basically they give you homework for the following week, along with comments and corrections on the previous week's homework. You can pick up a graduation certificate in six months or a year, and after that it's a matter of trying to sell your stuff. The teachers at the school will help you with introductions, and if you get a lucky break you can make your debut right away. Excuse me, could I have another one of these?'

This last was directed at the waitress. Reiko was now eating for two, and she needed double risotto.

'I eat and eat and I still feel hungry. It's terrible. The doctor told me it would be bad if I put on any more weight.'

'But Reiko, how come you know all this stuff about script-writing?'

'I'd been thinking of doing it myself. It seemed a shame not to make any use of that college education, so I was looking around for some profession I could combine with being a housewife. I figured this was quite a high-status, intellectual thing I could do from home, and if I made a go of it I might get famous and all that, so I sent off for the prospectus. But then this happened, which kind of put the lid on it.'

Reiko stroked her stomach. It was certainly exhibiting rapid growth. Thinking of the happy event it portended, and about Reiko's life in general, I had to be impressed by how meticulously she'd planned everything out.

Through the café window I could see the muscular bodies of elite businessmen cruising up and down the swimming pool. I hated to admit it, but could it be that these were the guys destined to be winners in the great game of Life? For the first time it occurred to me that Reiko – this girl I'd taken to be the same kind of listless, lazy type as myself – had in fact been a member of that winning set, right from the word go. I, on the other hand, had unthinkingly gone straight from 'college girl' to 'gangster's bimbo'.

I thought of what Bogey had once said to me in the days when his company was struggling to get started and he'd ask me if I was willing to die with him: 'My mother and father never taught me about how society works, so I made mistakes. In Japanese society, if you go to a good university and then to a good company, the work may be dull, but if you stick with it you eventually get to a position where you can move big money around. You get to handle huge amounts that are on a totally different scale from my kind of money. OK, maybe what you get to keep is only a modest salary, but there is no comparison as far as satisfaction and social status are concerned. You may be living an average life, but you have pride, you have distinction. I didn't understand all that, so I drifted off-course midway and into this kind of world. So when I compare myself with my old acquaintances who stuck to the orthodox road, there's only one way I can avoid feeling that I've messed up, and that's by grabbing more money than they could hope to make in a lifetime.'

I'd always looked down on Reiko and her bourgeois life strategy, for thinking like a middle-aged woman when she was still in her early twenties. Now, however, her approach suddenly seemed very mature and admirable.

'Reiko, you're great, you know.'

'Not really. It's not like I actually did any scriptwriting. I just checked it out. But you're not planning on having kids right away, are you? If you've got time on your hands, why not give it a try? The school's in Aoyama, I seem to recall. Actually, I've still got the brochure at my parents' house. I'll give my mother a call and ask her to send it to you.'

'Thanks very much!'

I snatched up the bill and made a dash for the cash desk. It was a habit I'd learned from Bogey – when you feel inferior to 'proper' people, the one thing you can do to maintain your pride is pay the bill, because money is the only department where we've got the edge.

'Oh, are you treating me? Thank you so much! I wish I were rich like you. My husband may be a doctor, but he only works for a salary at his dad's clinic. His parents paid the deposit on our apartment, but we still have to make monthly repayments on the mortgage and it's a struggle to make ends meet. And soon we're going to have to buy a lot more stuff, too.'

She stroked her belly again. Then she dropped her voice to a conspiratorial whisper and said, 'We can't afford to do anything fancy until the old man toddles off.'

179

Still the same calculating Reiko, I thought to myself. I said nothing, however, and when the application form for the scriptwriting school arrived, I hurriedly filled it in.

I'll sign up for the evening course. Bogey is never home on weekday evenings, anyway. Maybe I'll make some friends. Maybe we could go for a drink after class.

These faint hopes were crushed five seconds after I walked through the door of the night school. God, it was a horrible place! It was the shabbiest room you'd ever seen, with about twenty of the grimmest students you'd ever met. They were all ages – the oldest being a woman who looked about fifty. They all had day-jobs, which left them worn-out and sullen by the time they got to the school. They seemed to exude an aura of resentment.

For many of them, this school was the last-chance saloon, a desperate attempt to lay their hands on a ticket to something better than their dead-end jobs. An air of desperation pervaded the classroom. There wasn't a single person who looked like a possible friend. On the contrary, most of them took an intense dislike to me the moment we introduced ourselves.

There I was, glittering with jewellery in my beautifully coordinated and ostentatious clothes, with my long, glossy hair immaculately groomed as if to demonstrate I had limitless time to devote to it, my skin smooth and glowing, and my long nails beautifully manicured. The others had all arrived in frayed and tatty clothing, hotfoot from a hard day's work, and were paying for their lessons with money earned by their own blood, sweat and tears. I had paid for my lessons with money given to me by Bogey, to whom it was only spare change, so being there was no more than a way of killing time. I wasn't grateful for the opportunity the course presented. No wonder they hated me.

Even if it wasn't going to be fun, however, I could always go home and moan about my fellow students to Bogey. He enjoyed that kind of thing, because my grumbles about the outside world bore eloquent testimony to the superiority of his world, in which he dearly wanted me to believe.

'It's just too dull to bear! The students are so unbelievably shabby that they make me sick! I'm sure they've all got poverty dwarves tailing them.'

'Poverty dwarves? What are they?'

'I read about them in a picture book when I was little. Some people have poverty dwarves following them around. The dwarves are really good at hiding, so they never get caught. But the people they follow never become rich, however hard they work.'

Bogey had a good laugh about that.

'The teachers are pathetic, too. They're supposed to be big-name scriptwriters, but those boring old types couldn't produce an interesting script if their lives depended on it.'

'You're dead right, Saya. Guys with no experience of life can't possibly write anything interesting by just sitting at their desk and thinking about it. Tell you what, one of these days I'll write you a novel that will make people sit up and take notice. I've got loads of ideas for the plot.'

Bogey had not yet given up his dream of becoming a novelist. He still bought every book by Kenzo Kitakata the moment it came out, and he also read most of the novels that won literary prizes, or even just made the shortlist, or got discussed in the media. I'd sit next to him while he read such radical new fiction, engrossed as usual in my fashion magazines and comic books.

In the end I stuck it out at the scriptwriting school, wearing the plainest clothes I could find in my wardrobe, sitting in class and not saying anything, handing in my homework and going straight home. That still left me with tons of time on my hands, since assignments involved writing only one short script per week, plenty for someone with a full-time job but not nearly enough for someone like me with a whole week to kill.

'Oh God, I'm *soooo* bored!'

Desperate for ideas, I went to see Michi, the former *mama-san* of the Ooh-la-la. After she'd finished doing time for the cocaine bust, she'd been put in charge of a small gallery by a wealthy patron in the fine arts business. Surely Michi would be able to set me up with a pleasantly arty part-time job?

At that time, trendy English job descriptions such as 'space designer' and 'interior planner' were seeping into the Japanese language. I secretly longed to be part of that world – creative, classy, cutting-edge! And since I was a literature graduate, I should be able to do something in publishing, too. Or so I thought.

Michi didn't fail me. She introduced me to a super-smart production and publishing company called Arts Cool. The president was a *yakuza*-type guy, known as a mover and shaker in the art business. He saw me as a kindred spirit the moment we met, and I was promptly employed.

Among its various activities, Arts Cool organised showy events and parties that were all the rage in the high-flying bubble economy of the late 1980s. My job was to help run these gatherings, theoretically at least. In fact the company already had a perfectly efficient secretary and accountant to deal with all that, so my job didn't really exist. Instead, I served as a kind of glorified 'companion', a decorative accessory at parties, who was taken along on drinking sessions by the president and his cronies, like a pet.

Even so, I was in seventh heaven when I landed the job. Fashionable young people would read the stuff in Arts Cool magazines and consider themselves to be tapping right into the avant-garde. I used to do the same myself. And now I was on the team making those magazines! It was enough to send me into raptures. At last I had somewhere to go in my designer clothes, and people would make a fuss of me again. I felt happier than I had been for a long time.

OK, so maybe I was only the receptionist at these events, but I still got to see in the flesh all the famous people in the art and fashion world I'd read about in the magazines. This was happening at the height of the bubble economy, when lots of people had unlimited expense accounts. And I was right there, every evening, listening to the gossip about the latest trends and the rumours about the people who made the trends. Somehow I became deluded that I, too, was a creative, intelligent person.

The people I mingled with had travelled all over the world. They'd explored high-tech cities and hidden wildernesses in search of the most interesting and most delicious items. They were fascinating to listen to, and they tickled my intellectual curiosity.

When a person who doesn't think about anything starts to think, the thoughts quickly turn into emotions. Suddenly my days were full of glitter, and the next thing I knew I was tormented by envy – envy of these people who'd lived abroad, who were gifted and who had interesting careers.

I was surrounded by writers, designers and artists. They had built up successful careers with their own talents. They were full of energy, leading free and enjoyable lives – and I was a nobody. I couldn't bear it. They'd look at me with eyes that said, *Don't know that face... Who the hell is that?* At which point the president would say: 'To avoid any misunderstanding I'd better say that this isn't my girlfriend. She's a wealthy housewife, and she comes and hangs out when she feels like it.'

He tried to make a diverting anecdote out of it, but no one paid the slightest attention and the conversation would move on.

To the president, there was a touch of class in having an unusually young, unusually wealthy housewife, with unusual amounts of spare time, at his social events. But I was no more than an accessory and nobody bothered to talk to me, since I did nothing and had no talents of my own. The only people who would give me the time of day were older guys who were happy just to be in the company of a young woman.

Meanwhile the economy had reached a point where there was so much money sloshing around that people didn't know what to do with it. More culture and art seemed like a good idea, and the newspapers were full of stories about the importance of cultivating 'spiritual wealth'. Artists and writers gained new respect as authorities on the tricky business of turning material wealth into spiritual wealth. They were only too willing to lend their assistance.

As well as my chagrin at being ignored by this glamorous crowd, I also started having new and unfamiliar thoughts, such as, *Who am I? I have no idea.*

Now that Bogey was spoiling me so much, I no longer felt the same love for him as I had in the days when I was desperately trying to monopolise his attention. Now that I was sure of his affections, the balance of power had shifted my way. After years of self-sacrifice and devotion to him, I began to think about myself instead of him.

Since my work involved mingling with artistic and literary types, I started paying more attention to cultural stuff. I suddenly wanted to talk about art and about trends, and I started to get fussier about my own lifestyle. I also began to take a more critical look at the man with whom I shared my life. Some of Bogey's personal habits, which I had cheerfully accepted as charming eccentricities, I now found hard to put up with.

✻

Around this time a regrettable incident occurred in a Chinese restaurant. It was a stylish establishment in Daikanyama, the trendy district near Shibuya. I dragged Bogey there, in the face of stiff protests, because I thought that it was about time he developed more fashionable eating habits. I shouldn't have bothered.

Every Sunday Bogey would go to the off-course betting centre in Shibuya, after giving me some money to fritter away in the bijou boutiques of Daikanyama. That particular Sunday he was in a bad mood because he'd been losing on the horses, so it wasn't the best of days to take him to an arty restaurant.

At this kind of place they'd only fuss over you if you were a reasonably well-known media celebrity. Status was not just a matter of money, and the staff made no attempt to pretend they wanted customers like Bogey.

'Give us the menu.'

'Being lunchtime, there are only three options: the A lunch, B lunch, or C lunch.'

'ABC?'

'Yes, Bogey, look at this.' I drew his attention to the laminated plastic menu that doubled as a placemat.

'OK, OK, but you've got a real menu as well, right? The à la carte menu? Be a good chap and bring me that one, will you?'

'At lunchtime, we only have this menu.'

'Bogey, it doesn't matter. Come on, why don't we have a B and a C to share? And a couple of Tsingtao beers.'

'Certainly, madam.'

As the obnoxious waiter turned away, Bogey muttered under his breath. 'Huh! Not very flexible, are they?! And they haven't even given us an ashtray. *Hey, garçon!*'

Everyone turned to look as Bogey bellowed for service. I scurried over to a nearby table and fetched him an ashtray.

When the food came, it was very artistically arranged but did not meet Bogey's exacting standards in terms of taste or volume.

He got even more irritable and asked the waiter for another bowl of soup.

The waiter didn't like Bogey. Here he was, the great waiter who served famous people of culture, and here was this vulgar *nouveau riche* cad who thought that just because he'd made some money he was entitled to an extra bowl of soup.

'Extra helpings are not permitted on the set menu,' he said, with all the icy spite he could muster.

Bogey lost his temper. He was ready for a fight now.

'Look, I'll pay for it, OK? Just bring the damn soup!'

The waiter was not to be swayed, however.

'The house rules do not permit it, *sir*.'

And with that he turned on his heel and beat a swift retreat. Bogey flew into a towering rage.

'That does it! The bastard! I'll take no more! Come on, we're out of here!'

He stomped over to the cash desk, tossed some money on the counter, and stormed out without waiting for the change. I was mortified. Why did he have to behave like that?

Bogey never ordered the set menu as a matter of principle. His way was to order a whole load of dishes from the à la carte menu, sometimes more than he could eat. He had no time for the economical alternative of ordering a lunchtime special or a set-course dinner. He used to call that 'getting rations'.

Even if we were at some very ordinary fish-bar at the seaside, one that served only set meals, he'd still come up with something like, 'I'll pay double, so could you give me a double-size helping of mackerel?' And he really hated people who wouldn't do as he said. As for this waiter, who'd refused him an extra bowl of soup just like that – well, he'd made an enemy for life.

Bogey loved soup, to an unnatural degree. At our regular Chinese restaurant in Azabu Juban, he always ordered *tanmen*, noodles in broth, but he'd just have the soup and leave most of the noodles untouched. He wouldn't eat anything derived from potatoes or beans because they made him thirsty, and nearly all his meals were washed down with Hennessy and water.

'It's true what they say, Saya, that when a guy starts to age, his teeth, eyes and cock are the first to suffer.'

Actually, the last two items on Bogey's list appeared to be in pretty good working order, and the reason his teeth were a mess had nothing to do with old age. He just hated brushing his teeth or going to dentists.

'For heaven's sake, Bogey, brush your teeth! You'll ruin them and your gums as well if you don't.'

I'd told him that a thousand times, but to no effect. He'd squeeze toothpaste on the toothbrush, put it in his mouth, then rinse out his mouth without brushing. These days the only thing he could still chew was his beloved abalone. So eating some not-very-tasty set lunch with no soup – no way! Plus he'd lost at the races that morning.

I gave an inward sigh. Bogey was still adorable, but he was also becoming embarrassing. Much as I loved him, I preferred to keep the old fellow hidden from my friends.

✻

Bogey always did exactly as he pleased, and it never bothered him what other people thought. That was his strength, yet I now found myself alienated by his unique personality. Though I had only dabbled in the world of work, it was enough to make me more particular about the impression I was creating. People's views were starting to matter more. Was I not a bit of an embarrassment? Was I not somehow disgusting? Or contemptible? These fears of mine wouldn't leave me alone.

I got Bogey an Issey Miyake shirt with a stand collar. If we happened to bump into some of the Arts Cool crowd in the street, I didn't want them thinking I was knocking about with a shabby old guy dressed like a *yakuza*.

Maybe I was no more than a party escort, but I was still glad to belong to the gang at Arts Cool. I bought even more expensive clothes, but still I wasn't satisfied. Even if I had nothing to do there, Arts Cool had become the main focus of my life. When I was at the office, I used to ask the president and other people for careers advice.

'What would be the best thing for someone like me to do?'

What an idiot I was! No one was going to bother to think up a proper answer to a silly question like that. It made me sound as though I was still at school. It was a tough world out there and they were all very busy. Why should they offer advice to someone who wasn't even in trouble?

I was a girl without a thought in her head, always relying on others, wandering through life not knowing what she really wanted. There's only one thing someone like that gets, and it isn't careers advice. It's a man.

The man in question was a coordinator based in New York, who often came to Arts Cool when he was in Tokyo. A coordinator – at least in the Arts Cool sense of the word – is someone who lives abroad and helps visiting people in the creative field gather materials for the arts. This particular coordinator also used to write articles in fashion magazines about the latest trends in the United States, a civilised activity that made him look cooler still.

The man had lived in New York for ten years and was doing a cultural job. He used a lot of English words in his conversation, yet somehow managed to avoid seeming pretentious. His manner had something appealingly foreign about it – I just loved his cosmopolitan air. He was refined and charming, and when he placed an international phone call, he yammered away in English like a native. What a guy! It was only a matter of time before my admiration for him started to shade into love.

SEVEN

His name was Kaoru Nakatani. He was embodied with lust and glided smoothly around in a casual suit by Comme des Garçons Homme.

It was a hot, sticky summer night, and the big city air was heavy with pheromones. I was light-headed from the heat, booze and youth. We were just emerging from a bar in Roppongi when the Arts Cool president turned to Kaoru and said, 'I'm going in the opposite direction, so do me a favour and take Saya home, will you?' And he let the two of us take the cab he'd called from the bar.

Because the economy was bubbling so hard, you'd emerge from a bar after a late night drinking session and there wouldn't be a cab in sight. Even if your company had a standing arrangement with one of the cab firms, it could be a struggle to get through on the phone, and even then you might have to wait another hour for the cab to show up. As for an ordinary, non-corporate individual trying to call one – well, you'd end up kicking your heels in an all-night bar until morning.

'Hooray! Lucky old me!'

It wasn't just the fact of having captured one of these scarce rides that made me mutter these words to myself. I was far from displeased at the prospect of sharing the back seat with Kaoru. Not that he'd shown any sign of coming on to me; it was just nice to get a little closer to a guy whom I happened to rather like. I had no idea that he was a wolf in designer clothing.

For a Japanese guy, he sure was a fast mover. Hardly had the cab set off when he jumped me. His barrage of kisses took me totally by surprise and I offered no resistance. We were heading for the Akasaka hotel district, and I was high as a kite and afraid of nothing.

I returned to Azabu Juban around dawn, covered with love bites like little rose blossoms. A devil-may-care feeling outweighed my fear of being found out by Bogey. Let the chips fall where they may – that's how exhilarated I felt. For the first time in ages I had a sense of release. Oh, it had been such fun! I had just been pleasured to my heart's content, and I didn't give a damn about what anybody thought. Since I'd first got to know Bogey, I'd never before been able to go out and enjoy myself without thinking about him. Amazing!

I couldn't go home sober, so I'd had a couple more drinks in the hotel room before setting off. For what it was worth, I did have an excuse planned: I'd claim I'd been out drinking all night. What with the refreshing air of the early summer morning, the light beer buzz over the top of last night's hangover, the lack of sleep and the unexpected ecstasy of new love, I was glowing all over and walking on clouds.

I hadn't felt so fantastic in all my life. People are only perfectly free when they're enjoying themselves with no thoughts of the past or future. I felt so marvellous I couldn't care less what happened next. I pushed open the door to the apartment.

Bogey wasn't there.

Well, wouldn't you know it? All-night mah-jong again, I suppose.

I was relieved, but also somewhat disappointed.

It was scary to think of losing everything that mattered to me, but I was even ready to believe that making a fresh start might be better than carrying on being bored. I wanted a change, but I didn't have the courage or energy to make that happen myself. I had dieted to the point of anorexia: it was all very well being attractive, but my waif's body was so dehydrated that I was permanently lightheaded. For me, dieting was like foot-binding – an unnatural constraint, endured to please men. I was totally dependent on Bogey for everything, and I literally could not take a single step under my own steam.

Bogey finally came home after dark the following day. He was in a huff, and the first thing he said was, 'So where were you last night?'

Uh-oh, he knows.

Bogey was in the habit of calling me up from the mah-jong club now and again, just for fun. Sometimes he wouldn't phone all day, but if he did call and I wasn't there to pick up the phone he'd immediately become irritated and start calling every thirty minutes to check whether or not I was at home. This habit of his scared me, which was why I'd got a ten-metre extension cord so that the phone was within reach, even when I was in the bath.

If he called and I wasn't there to answer him, his temper would immediately flare up. He was that self-indulgent. He thought nothing of leaving me on my own for days on end, but if he felt that *he* was being neglected, even for a few minutes, he just couldn't handle it.

From the moment we'd met, I'd felt restricted by his possessiveness. Although you could say that this quality was what made me fall in love with him. At that time I'd been so lonely that I'd wanted to matter enough for someone to impose that kind of demand upon me. I'd entered willingly into captivity and had been happy in my cage.

Now his possessiveness felt like a curse, and it weighed more heavily on me every day.

I also thought he should stop behaving like a spoiled brat. After all, I had no idea when he was going to phone. Sometimes days would pass without a call from him. When he was busy with some other woman, for instance, he wasn't exactly going to call me from her boudoir.

Even when he did phone, he never had anything much to say. He'd just check that I was at the apartment so that he could stop worrying and devote his full attention to the game at hand.

'Ah, Saya, there you are. I don't know what time I'll be home, but have some dinner ready and wait for me, OK?'

He'd say this in a silly voice to entertain his mah-jong buddies, and I'd hear them roar with laughter in the background as he hung up.

'I went for a few drinks with Minako,' I said casually. 'I haven't seen her for ages.'

✡

Once I'd sobered up, I realised that I had no intention of leaving Bogey because of a fling with Kaoru. Bogey was my old blanket and, like Linus with his, I couldn't dispose of this comforting item so easily. I didn't have the courage to let go.

Deep down I was hoping someone else would come along and sort out the situation for me. I felt as if I were sitting in a lukewarm bath, not hot enough to be enjoyable, but not cold enough to make me get out – unless somebody did something. Kaoru Nakatani was that somebody. He'd flown into my life like a shiny pebble thrown into still waters, and the ripples kept spreading with the passing of time.

✡

Autumn came and I was given a new position, manning the reception desk at a gallery run by Arts Cool. Normally I'd rather die than take a job like that, but this was different – Kaoru had been appointed curator of the same gallery. I gladly accepted the job, simply because it would give me the chance to see more of him.

At first Kaoru tried to escape from me. He had just turned thirty and wanted to carry on screwing whoever he fancied for a few more years. He found my intense attachment too much to take.

I was a married woman with a husband, and a pretty tough husband at that, so he reckoned he could make a quick 'snack' of me, say thanks very much, and move on to the next tasty dish. But I wasn't going to let him go that easily. I could be surprisingly stubborn about odd things. Kaoru wasn't really worth making too much fuss about, but once I saw that he was trying to make his excuses and leave, I dug in my heels. I wasn't going to let a guy of his calibre treat me like a cheap plaything.

The more I struggled to satisfy Kaoru's mighty libido, however, the more I came to share his hunger for sex.

'When you have sex with a guy, you gradually get to be like him.' That was Minako's theory. 'I reckon something in the guy's jism gets into you. Have you noticed that girls who only sleep with black guys start to look kind of negroid themselves?'

Maybe there was something in that theory. Anyhow, Kaoru's pheromones seemed to have seeped into me, and the more we fucked the more I wanted it. Kaoru was your stereotypical oversexed male – hair all over his body but prematurely bald up top. And now I, too, was crazy for sex.

I was so horny it scared me. Once you started to take sex seriously, it was amazing what you could do. We didn't do anything you'd call perverted, exactly, but that still left plenty of activities, and we did them all – repeatedly and with feeling. It made my previous sexual experiences seem like child's play.

This was the first time I'd experienced love that leads directly to lust. Until now I hadn't had sex because I wanted to – I'd let the guy do it to me as a favour.

It was very different now. Every time I met Kaoru I'd be begging for it. I couldn't control myself. Even when we were walking along the street, I'd pull him into some dark alleyway between buildings and throw myself at him. I'd be French kissing him at the slightest opportunity – on back stairs, in elevators, in cabs – any fleeting moment of privacy was OK. I'd do anything with him – any way, any where, any time. I had well and truly caught the lust bug.

I was addicted to Kaoru. I recalled Bogey's cynical comment: 'A woman will fall in love with any guy who'll give her one.' Maybe with the wisdom of his years Bogey knew what he was talking about, after all.

Any guy!

Kaoru certainly was no gentleman. His public face was so appealing and his private behaviour so disgusting that you'd almost wonder if he had a dual personality. He was in love with himself, he put on all sorts of airs, and he didn't possess the slightest particle of love for any other human being. And he was a real skinflint, too – a guy with no money to spare and no love to give. He'd take his pleasure whenever he could, and he'd hurt a woman's feelings without a second thought.

Once he kept me waiting in a hotel lobby for three-and-a-half hours. But the more coldly he treated me, the more I wanted him. I would lie in wait for him at the gallery and, if he showed up, invite him for dinner. I started dressing to please him, switching over to the Comme des Garçons look he favoured. I took him to trendy Italian restaurants, bars, art galleries and cinemas that I could never hope to drag Bogey to, and immersed myself in an elegant, cultured, starry-eyed mood.

When Kaoru wasn't available, I'd make do with romantic movies, romantic novels, and generally graze on romance. I used to think such things were nonsense, manufactured for silly women, but right then I was just that type of woman.

And I didn't only fall for Kaoru. I became increasingly obsessed with New York, the city that was his base. I wanted to know what it was like to live there. I wanted to be cool and cosmopolitan. I didn't want to just pop over a foreign country for a few days' vacation. No, I wanted to live there long enough to get so good at English that I could jabber away in the language like a native.

Probably the main reason I fell for Kaoru was because he held out the possibility of taking me somewhere that was fun. He used to go on about his travels in search of art and culture – to the Caribbean, Latin America, or remote parts of Africa, India and China. I knew he was just showing off, but how my eyes would sparkle when he was spinning those yarns!

How fulfilling it must be to live like that, and what a lot of fun, too! If two people share the same values, they don't have to hide their true feelings out of consideration for the other. They can enjoy everything together.

So it was with Kaoru and me. We liked the same movies and the same restaurants. Whether it was a French movie at an art cinema, or an exhibition at a modern art gallery, our responses always matched perfectly. How different from Bogey! I would never be able to get Bogey to set foot inside an art gallery, and the only films he liked were gangster movies. Even then it had to be very simple fare, for a gangster movie with artistic pretensions such as *Once Upon A Time in America* would send him to sleep, and the cinema would reverberate with his mighty snores.

Every weekend he'd go the races – either horses or bicycles – and when he lost and came home early he'd just sprawl on the bed for hours on end, feeding his face, knocking back the booze, and watching TV or some *yakuza* movie. Now that I was going out with Kaoru, Bogey's slovenly lifestyle struck me as sterile and meaningless. It repelled me. Was I really going to spend a lifetime with him like this? If so, a lifetime was way too long.

✳

Being obsessed with Kaoru was fun, but it could also be a trial. When I met Bogey he was already mature, and I could say what I liked without worrying about annoying him, but Kaoru had a real temper. I had to watch my words carefully when talking to him, or face an angry outburst. We'd get into a fight in no time at all, and it was very unpleasant for both of us. Maybe that's why our sex life was so passionate. 'The more you fight, the better you get on' is another of those old Japanese sayings that suddenly didn't seem so dumb after all. Maybe conflict really is good for a love affair.

It was just the opposite with Bogey. 'It's true, Saya, you and me are the best of buddies!'

Indeed, we got on too well. We had never fought over anything. Maybe Bogey and I were really cut out to be father and daughter rather than lovers. I was nineteen years old when I'd met him, and still a kid. Four years had gone by without my thinking much about it, but now I was becoming an adult. It no longer satisfied me simply to snuggle up to my big daddy bear.

However, leaving Bogey, earning my own living, and having a relationship only with Kaoru wouldn't be an easy matter. It would be like climbing out of a warm bath and leaping naked into freezing snow. 'Tolerance' wasn't a word you would find in Kaoru's dictionary.

My affair with Kaoru was like a roller-coaster ride. I used not to like roller-coasters because they were scary, but fear had now turned into ecstasy. I was still frightened, but I wanted another ride just the same. I was frightened, too, at the change in myself.

I began to imagine what life with Kaoru might be like. As things stood, this was no more than a dream, but nevertheless I started to think how wonderful it would be to become emotionally and economically independent and live a meaningful, cultured life. Although I had yet to break my material and emotional dependence on Bogey, I fondly dreamed of a scenario where I could be on an equal footing with a man and live a more creative, more fun-filled existence.

That was never going to happen as long as I stayed with Bogey. I would never escape from the hell of dependency. My body would get old, while my inner self would remain forever frozen at the age of nineteen. That was one prospect I simply could not bear to contemplate.

✫

However, there was more to becoming an independent woman than wearing off-the-peg clothing from Comme des Garçons. I wanted to achieve independence by working at something cultural, but nothing in that line presented itself and I fell prey to a deepening anxiety.

I'd finished the six-month course at the scriptwriting school without feeling any great urge to pursue the subject further. That was hardly surprising; after all, I'd only joined the course in the first place because a friend had recommended it.

Whenever I thought about taking on a new project, all kinds of self-indulgent objections would come floating out of my subconscious and I'd lose all enthusiasm. When your life's one of total idleness, you start to think you could do anything if you put your mind to it, but at the same time you feel there's not one job in the whole wide world that you could master. But however depressed I became, Bogey was always around to comfort me.

'Even if you've got nothing else, you've always got your Bogey,' he'd say. 'That's good enough, isn't it? Just do what you like,

199

darling. You don't have to look for something to do if that's not what you want.'

Even so I was getting panicky. I couldn't conceal my affair with Kaoru forever, and I was constantly dreaming of an ideal life whilst living an unsatisfactory existence with Bogey. It was just too miserable. To cap it all, the economy was still booming away fit to bust, and Bogey's style became more and more like that of a gangster as the money poured in.

His office in the Ginza now featured a gigantic table made of a single slab of marble that must have cost millions of yen, and the walls were draped with expensive, tasteless tapestries. Back home, our apartment was dominated by a massive 40-inch television set that he'd bought from an acquaintance who sold off the furniture and fittings of companies that had gone bankrupt. A lot of the time Bogey just sat there staring at this giant screen: sports pro- grammes, horse-racing, *yakuza* movies. I became more painfully aware of the gap in our tastes – a gap that seemed to be widening into an unbridgeable canyon.

I continued to sit at the art gallery reception desk, but I also started taking on small writing assignments for the art magazine that the company published. There was no way I'd ever make a living from writing, but I'd try anything. I wanted to hasten the day when I would become cultured and independent, a woman fit to hang out with Kaoru. He was my motivation as I struggled to make a life of my own.

The new me was like a rudely awoken baby. This bald and hairy guy had interrupted my peaceful slumber, triggering all sorts of awkward thoughts about myself, and now I was ready to burst out crying. I still wanted to suck my thumb and curl up in the warmth of Bogey's love, but Kaoru made me feel uneasy about such child- ish desires. My feelings were drifting further and further away from Bogey, and it felt scary.

Sometimes I would come home from yet another sizzling session with Kaoru to find Bogey already at home, having come back early. I'd hug his great warm tummy and indulge in some comfort. I'd give him a playful pinch. Here he was, the only person on earth who'd let me carry on being a baby. But apart from the emotional complications, other more practical reasons also made it hard to spend time with Bogey.

As well as doing small writing jobs in my spare time, I still had to be at the gallery at ten o'clock every morning. At night I had my business socialising, and when Kaoru was in town back from New York I had to find time to play with my new toy. With one thing and another, I was short of time, just like an overworked businessman.

By the time I got home I'd be exhausted. Even so, at around three or four in the morning all the lights would be switched on and I'd hear, 'Honey, I'm home! Where's dinner?'

On such occasions I wanted to say, *Get your own stupid dinner! I've got work tomorrow and I need to sleep!* But I was still far from making a living wage, so I was in no position to protest as strongly as that. Nor could I very well tell Bogey that I needed my sleep to get in shape for the next steamy session with Kaoru.

Of course, my work meant nothing to Bogey. It was just a handy way for a leisured housewife to kill time, and as for my business socialising, that was strictly a matter of play, not work. I didn't like the fact that Bogey thought only about his own convenience – the idea that I might also have a schedule never entered his head. And because I wasn't making enough money to support myself I had to put up with it all.

I'd be ashamed of my own weakness, but rubbing my sleepy eyes I'd grudgingly get up, prepare some snacks, and take them to where he lay sprawled across the bed. I felt very indignant that my rights were being violated. One night my resentment rose momentarily to the surface, and instead of quietly placing his chopsticks on the tray of food I tossed them down. Bogey was not surprisingly irate.

'Hey! You threw those chopsticks down!'

'I didn't. I dropped them by accident.'

The excuse popped out, just like that. After all, I wasn't going to get very far if I tried to lecture Bogey on human rights. As far as he was concerned, although girls might have some kind of existence, they certainly didn't have any rights.

'I see. That had better be the truth!'

So saying, he went straight off to sleep, not bothering to eat what I'd prepared.

I stood there fuming. I should have seen it coming. Bogey had to be the star in any situation. People with him weren't supposed to have a life – they had to sign it over to him. They were to have nothing but him in their thoughts.

Not that Bogey was totally unreasonable. He would look after your economic needs to leave you free to concentrate on him, and that's exactly what he was doing with me. He wouldn't want me to lead my own life and take care of him only in my spare time. His pride would never allow that. In the old days I used to think that a woman's ultimate happiness lay in being with a man like him. Now, however, I was beginning to resent my subordinate position.

It never rains but it pours. That was in 1987, and on 19 October stock exchanges around the world came crashing down. Black Monday dealt a heavy blow to Bogey, and once again he was asking if I'd be willing to die with him, and so on. I was utterly fed up with the whole scene. So long as he continued dealing in stocks, these drastic mood swings would never end. And every time they happened I'd not only be tortured by anxiety but be expected to prepare for death!

It was intolerable, for being Bogey's wife meant placing my life in his hands, in the most literal sense. I had no desire to go to my death now or at any time soon.

There had been a time when I thought I'd willingly die with him, but now the spell was broken. When everything goes wrong, do you give up in despair and commit suicide? No thank you! That was for losers. If I could earn enough to support myself, I could get out of this fix and avoid dying like a dog in the gutter.

As it happened, the stock market soon went up again.

✫

'Oh me, oh my, I'm so tired,' he said one weekend. 'Let's go to a hot spring.'

With his usual impulsiveness, he decided to visit to a hot spring hotel we occasionally went to in the mountains of Izu. As always, he didn't bother asking me if it suited my schedule. I had a deadline for an article on Monday, and I'd been counting on Bogey to make his regular trip to the races over the weekend so I could work.

I couldn't refuse to go, but I expressed a sullen opposition by bringing my word processor along. After taking a bath in the mineral waters of the spa, I wrapped a towel around my head and unpacked the machine.

'What do you think you're playing at?'

I took a deep breath, put the word processor back in its case, combed my hair, and sat down for a cup of saké with Bogey.

I can't stand it any more.

I had a drink with Bogey, even though I wasn't in the mood. In the old days, when I had so much free time, I'd always been in the mood for a drink with Bogey, or able to get in the mood. Nowadays, however, I hated doing anything to please someone else that was the slightest bother.

I started talking about splitting up.

But it was easier said than done. We'd been living together for three-and-a-half years and we'd just had a wedding, so the two of us had become a sort of family. Also, apart from the emotional aspect, there were practical problems. Bogey needed an understanding woman to look after him, and I needed Bogey's money.

That's nowhere near enough to live on, I thought with a doleful sigh as I inspected my bank statement. I wasn't making enough in a month to finance one shopping expedition, let alone a life. I felt all my resolve ebbing away as I gazed at the figures. So instead of plucking up courage to leave Bogey, I did the usual thing: play psychological tricks on myself to stop thinking too deeply about the present. Idleness brought dark thoughts, so I deliberately made myself busy. I stepped up my English lessons, abandoning the local American housewife who'd been teaching me in favour of a more businesslike school I could go to every evening. I wrote a few film scripts, entered them in competitions, and got nowhere.

Time weighed heavily on me. Since my standard of living was not related to my activities, I never put my heart into them. That, in turn, meant that no one bothered to make any demands on me, and I still felt the burden of all that free time weighing me down. Some words of my mother's always lingered at the back of my mind.

'A woman like you will never be any good at a job. Why, Saya, you haven't even got the gumption to go out and buy your own lipstick. You might as well forget it.'

I was approaching rock bottom. I felt so down I could hardly get out of bed. When my eyes opened, they were full of tears.

No doubt about it, I had to leave Bogey, however hard that might be. If I didn't, I would never do anything. If I stayed I'd go to my grave tormented by that vague dissatisfaction, that longing for something undefinable, but unable to do anything about it and as depressed as ever.

I had to leave him. With tears in my eyes I went to him and asked him a second time to let me go.

'I can't make it without you. I told you, didn't I? Just stick with me and you can do whatever you like. It's all this sitting around at home that's making you depressed. Here, take this and go on a spree. A bit of shopping will make you feel better.' So saying, he placed the usual pile of crumpled bank notes on the bedside table – 200,000 yen or so – and left.

He just doesn't get it.

The sadder I got, the kinder Bogey became. Every weekend he'd take me to a swish hotel, calling it 'family service' – the way salaried workers talk about taking their kids to Disneyland. It was just like the old days when we were on the run from the Ginza *mama-san*, only this time no one was in pursuit.

And that wasn't all. He even made the effort to dress for the occasion. 'It's good for a couple to dress up and go out on the town occasionally,' he'd say, and would present himself at the hotel bar in a stiff, formal suit. This was quite a change from his usual style – which entailed flopping down on the bed in his briefs within minutes of checking into the hotel.

Bogey even took to lavishing attention on me on weekday nights. It was as if he were trying to make a fresh start to our married life. He'd make me wear my smartest clothes and take me to ridiculously expensive restaurants, as though I were some kind of princess.

The Hotel Seiyo, formerly a special treat to be enjoyed only on my birthday, was now a regular haunt of ours. Or we'd stay in a suite in the still more luxurious Hotel Okura and knock back non-birthday Dom Perignon. And I wouldn't feel a bit grateful.

I even had my body washed by an attendant in the Okura Hotel's massage room, not that I was sick or anything. But when a common lass like me gets treated like a royal maiden who's never had to wash herself, it feels strange and uncomfortable.

The more meaningless the luxury, the more miserable I became. I was getting all the goodies and doing nothing to deserve them. I was just making myself look pretty to please Bogey and receive his beneficence. I could no longer see any value whatsoever in the exercise.

The sadder I got, the more horny Bogey became. There was a time when I used to give him the come-on, but now it was the other way round. He used to say he wasn't all that interested in sex, but these days he'd loudly proclaim, 'It's Sex Day today!' and shove me down on the bed. If he tried a more subtle approach I would pretend not to notice. He'd let it pass, but make me pay for it first thing the next morning.

'You knew I wanted it last night. Why did you refuse? Don't you love me any more?'

He'd go on about it endlessly. Worse still, he'd give me a long, lascivious look, letting his eyes rove over my body as if he were licking me with them, and then he'd start talking in a deliberately lecherous tone:

'Mmm, you're a sexy tart these days. Got yourself a new boyfriend, have you?'

'Wh-What?'

Bogey was beginning to sense that I had something going on the side. It was hardly surprising. In my struggle to ward off depression, I was deliberately focusing my thoughts on Kaoru, the guy I loved. I figured he was my way out. I was seeing a lot of him on his frequent trips to Tokyo, and the affair was becoming more intense, both emotionally and physically.

My life was like that of a tired old whore. Fucking all day, fucking all night. It got to the point where I'd notice jism trickling down my leg and wouldn't know which of my two men it came from. I was a sex object for men, and the fact that they were getting it on was the only evidence, if you could call it that, of my continuing existence.

Even if I didn't feel in the mood for sex, there was no particular reason to refuse if they came on strong enough. In my depression I had quit everything – job, English lessons, the lot. I had nothing whatever to do – not tomorrow, not the day after. My only job was to stay in bed and be fucked.

It wasn't as if I hated Bogey, but I didn't want to break up with Kaoru. Given the choice, I'd sooner go to bed with Kaoru, but I didn't particularly mind doing it with Bogey. I knew my life was at rock bottom, but my only solution was to put more passion into sex. The only time I could forget my worries was when I was doing it.

What was on my mind when I went out with Kaoru? I knew I couldn't carry on with my present life, but I also knew that I lacked the guts, the energy and the spirit to break out of it by myself. And having had a taste of utter luxury in Tokyo, I doubted whether I'd be able to adjust to a normal life in Japan. I needed a bigger, cleaner break. So I was hoping that Kaoru would take me to New York.

Take me with you, darling. Let's run away together. Huh! It was just like another corny old ballad.

Kaoru wouldn't take me to New York. 'You mustn't trust me,' he said. 'I'm three thousand times more irresponsible than you think. What I'm doing with you is totally despicable, but I can't control myself. What else can I do?'

He always spoke in that slightly bitter tone.

I wanted to leave Bogey, but Kaoru wouldn't have me. I was like a pet dog or cat. I couldn't exist on my own, or rather it didn't even occur to me to do anything on my own.

'You can do it if you try hard enough' is almost the Japanese national motto, but I never felt that way. What if I got sick? What if I had an accident? What if I ran out of cash? The moment I started thinking like that, I'd get so scared I wouldn't dare step outside.

Even if I became bedridden, Bogey was the one person who

would not abandon me. That thought stopped me in my tracks whenever I tried to leave him. Kaoru, by contrast, would be out the door in a flash if I so much as ran short of money.

I had considerable confidence in my intuition about other people. It was just me that I couldn't understand, a consequence of long years of doing my best not to think about myself.

✼

I had another reason to feel depressed. Bogey was in touch with his children again and frequently spoke to them on the phone. His oldest daughter was coming to Tokyo to cram for college entrance exams at a summer school, and he was offering to find a place for her in Tokyo, evidently pleased at being able to help. When he was on the phone to his kids I was not allowed to make a sound. As far as his daughter knew, Bogey was living by himself.

'If she means that much to you, why don't you have her to stay with you?' I maliciously suggested. 'I'll go and find somewhere on my own.'

Bogey took it as a joke. 'Honestly, Saya, look at my lifestyle! Would this be good for a child's upbringing?'

To me it wasn't funny. I felt overwhelmed by sadness. It suddenly seemed as if I'd lost half my role in Bogey's life. He used to tell me I was like a daughter, but now he had a real daughter to fuss over and I was just another woman. The blood bond between parent and child was exclusive, and outsiders weren't allowed in. *I had to make my own family sooner or later. Otherwise I'd spend my life in misery.*

So I invested all my dreams in Kaoru and pushed the relationship as far, and as fast, as I could. Our early-afternoon rendezvous had given way to more extended sessions of two or three nights. Shamelessly lying that I was going with Minako, I'd pop off somewhere with Kaoru for a dirty weekend or a midweek getaway. Left on his own, Bogey would stay at the Hotel Okura, which had become a second home to him.

After the second of these illicit trips I went along to the Okura to join Bogey. Outside the door was a room-service tray from the previous night, with an empty bottle of Dom Perignon, some half-eaten hors d'oeuvres and a champagne glass with red lipstick on it.

I wasn't particularly shocked. In fact I thought it was natural. I knew very well that Bogey couldn't bear to be alone for a single day. Something like this was bound to happen, but it didn't stop me carrying on with Kaoru. It meant that our accounts somewhat balanced. Somehow along the way I had acquired this instinctive understanding.

I entered the room. There was Bogey, reading the newspaper in bed as if nothing had happened. It obviously hadn't occurred to him that the maid might not have got around to removing the tray before I arrived. The indifference was typical.

'Hi, I'm back!'

'Ah, Saya, you've come home. I was a lonely Bogey, you know.'

And with that we had a quick fuck, just to say hello.

Bogey went back to sleep after that, while I popped down to the beauty parlour in the hotel basement. I was planning to have my hair styled really short. Kaoru had criticised my looks during our trips.

'Your hair's too long. And I don't like the way your fringe is cut so that it sticks up like that. It seems all out of tune.'

He was right. I'd grown my hair long to please Bogey. Ever since I was a kid I'd always worn it short. It suited me that way.

This was my technique for getting through life, you see. Make myself the way men liked me to be, fool the guys into thinking it was the natural me, and console myself with the success of the deception. I couldn't do anything straight – I'd have to take the long way round, every time. A hopeless case – but at least I could make myself feel better with a new hairstyle.

I didn't have the guts to go for the pageboy look I had in mind, and so I compromised (as usual) with a shoulder-length cut and perm. I went back to the hotel room, where Bogey was reading the newspaper. The moment he saw my hair he thwacked the newspaper down on the table and started shouting.

'And who said you could cut your hair? What's the meaning of this? Had a change of heart, eh?'

I stood there stock-still and silent. *A woman who can't feed herself doesn't have the right to get her hair cut,* I thought, but I said nothing.

'Right! I've had enough!' roared Bogey. 'You and me are through!'

And with that he strode out of the room.

I wasn't surprised. I even heaved a sigh of relief. Free at last! This caged bird was looking at an open door.

✳

I went back to the apartment in Azabu Juban, fed the cats, and started gathering my belongings. Just then the phone rang. It was Kaoru. I told him what had happened.

'I see. Meet me right now.'

It had taken a while, but Kaoru was beginning to show some honesty in his dealings with me. I was happy about that. I wanted to believe that we had both fallen in love, rather than just me alone. In high spirits I dressed smartly and headed for the café he had suggested. I had managed to leave Bogey and now Kaoru was surely going to take me to New York.

In fact, Kaoru turned out to be thinking things through in a surprisingly cool, practical way.

210

'Saya, I'd like you to stay in Tokyo a little longer,' he said. 'I'm going back to New York next month, but I'll be busy at first, getting the office sorted out and so on. So I won't be ready for you for a while.'

'But if it means I've got to rent my own apartment, I'd rather rent it in New York than in Tokyo. Tokyo apartments are cramped and pricey.'

'Go back to your mother's. Just for the autumn. It won't do you any harm.'

'Back to Ma's? How could I, after all this?'

The two of us chattered in a lighthearted vein for a while. We were talking about something of enormous significance for both of us, but somehow we were remarkably composed. I was delighted that we could finally devote ourselves to loving each other without feeling any scruples about somebody else.

It's a terrible thing, lust. We'd only just got back from the dirtiest of dirty weekends, but sorrow about parting from Bogey was the last thing on my mind. Off we went to a love hotel and were at it again. At daybreak I returned to the Azabu Juban apartment, expecting to find it empty.

When I entered, however, I noticed the remains of a home-delivery Chinese meal by the bed and a fat letter lying nearby. It was from Bogey. I liked his stylish handwriting. I recalled our first night together at the Akasaka Prince Hotel, watching him sign the check-in form. *Yes, this is a lovely, grown-up guy,* I'd thought.

Now, however, I cast a colder eye over his handwriting. It was a long, rambling letter, full of regrets, apologies and grief. I finished it without feeling the need to think up a response. Instead I stretched out on the bed. Being alone in a cold bed had never felt this good before. Maybe I really didn't need Bogey any more.

✦

I'd only been asleep for an hour or so when the phone rang summoning me to the Okura Hotel.

'I think I know you better than anyone,' Bogey said, 'and I haven't the slightest intention of parting from you. You need some time alone to think about yourself, right? I won't get in the way. Saya, you're the only one I love. You're my salvation. I'm staying here at the Okura, so you can have the apartment, OK? I need someone to give me support. I'm not going to marry anyone else. I'll give you all the money you need, and you can do whatever you like. Only please don't leave me.'

Bogey persuaded me to give it a try.

But exactly what was I supposed to do alone in the apartment? Reflecting coolly and carefully, I found I was once more losing my way. What was I, what did I want to do, which man did I really need?

Kaoru said he didn't want me to come to New York, and even though Bogey and I had split up I still had nothing to do. At the end of the day, maybe that meaningless dissolute lifestyle was made for empty little me.

Back at the apartment I phoned Kaoru: 'What should I do?'

'How the hell should I know?'

'But – '

'It's just too bad. It's how things are.'

Despairing of my indecisiveness, Kaoru hung up on me. Plunged again into a mood of willful self-neglect, I passed a number of dim and hazy days in the apartment, alone save for the cats.

As the days drifted by, my feelings began to change. My love for Kaoru, which had seemed so strong and pure, began to fade, and I began to feel nostalgic for Bogey. I didn't seem to be able to live unless somebody wanted me. A person who wants you is like a mirror you can see yourself in. Without that person, I didn't exist.

Perhaps the truth of the matter was that as long as if one of them wanted me, it didn't really matter which one it was. Had falling for Kaoru made me want to leave Bogey? Or had I just got sick of living with Bogey and turned to Kaoru as a way out? Right now, neither explanation felt right. Probably I was just bored, plain and simple.

One evening Bogey came to the apartment and announced he was staying the night. It was his apartment so I could hardly object. We had a couple of drinks and then slept together like two strangers.

I awoke around dawn to find Bogey sitting astride me with his hands around my throat.

'Who's your fancy boy, eh? Tell me his name or I'll kill you right now.'

I could sense from his grip that he meant it. But I said nothing. So what if he killed me? Whatever I tried to think about, I always ended up chasing my own tail, around and around. Life was a pain, so what was the point of living? I felt Bogey's hands tightening.

'I'm not fucking joking! Gimme his name or I'll fucking kill you!'

I was ready to die. But just as I was about to have my last breath wrung out of me, something inside betrayed me and I heard myself spluttering out a confession in whispered fragments.

'A guy ... called ... Nakatani ... Kaoru Nakatani.'

And I even managed an awkward, useless excuse.

'He's not anyone you know!'

Bogey relaxed his hands. When he spoke, he sounded like no man I knew. His voice was low and threatening.

'All right. I'll settle it with him. I don't hang out with *yakuza* just for fun, you know! You're a fucking disgrace. There's no way I'm letting you go now! Get that through your thick head!'

He stormed out of the room. There was always something of the *yakuza* in Bogey's style, of course, but I never thought he might really be one. Even so, this scene could have come straight out of the *yakuza* videos he was always watching. He acted just like those media gangsters.

I was still lying there, stunned at the turn of events, when Bogey telephoned. Presumably he'd just got back to the hotel and couldn't wait to give me another piece of his mind. His voice sounded quite insane as he screamed at me down the line.

'Who the fucking hell do you think pays your way, you fucking whore?! Have you thought about that? We've been married less than a year! Have you any idea what a fucking idiot I look? You're gonna stay with me and pay for this – day by fucking day! Know what I mean? You set one foot outside that apartment and I'll have you murdered right there. I could kill you like a fly – it's that easy. Got it?'

I didn't know what to say. More than the fear of being murdered, more than the shame of being called a whore, the bit about 'who do you think pays your way' really shook me.

I couldn't believe he was the kind of man to say something like that. I thought the money he spent on me was an expression of love. He often used to say, 'The cats, the apartment, the money – they're all yours, Saya!' And I believed him. Believing him was what had made me content with that life of drifting idleness.

Because say what you like, I'd been happy until I met Kaoru. The reason I'd been able to have all that fun was my confidence that Bogey loved me more than anyone else in the world – more than himself.

Whatever might happen to him, however much he might change, I had believed he would always defend me. But in the end, all the money he lavished on me was just money, like the bank notes that flew in and out of his wallet. In which case, I really was a whore. No wonder he spoke to me like that. I slept with Bogey for money. I was a common whore, sadly deluded into thinking she was queen of some fantasy land.

My knees were trembling, but my mind was unbelievably clear. Up until now this man had manipulated me into thinking I was something special. He had pampered me, indulged my every whim, put me in high spirits, and the two of us had created a fictional twosome – Bogey and his cute little sidekick, Saya. Now, however, I could see my true self: a common whore, controlled by money, fooled into thinking it was love and subjected to this stream of abuse as if I were a contemptible beggar in the street.

Soon there was another call from Bogey.

'Tell me the phone number of that guy who owns the company where you used to work!'

'But it's nothing to do with him!'

'Shut up! That Nakatani's got something to do with the company, right? I'm going to report him to his boss! I'm gonna make them pay for this!'

His voice sounded dangerous. There was nothing for it but to play along. The moment I'd given him the phone number of the Arts Cool boss, I rang the latter to warn him of what was coming and apologise. Then I called Kaoru.

'He's found out. You could get killed.'

'No kidding.'

Until Kaoru came along, no one had dared lay a finger on me because everyone knew I belonged to a *yakuza*-type guy, but Kaoru had never thought it would come to this.

Replacing the receiver, I sank to my knees before the telephone, my mind a blank. *What am I going to do?*

Night fell and the telephone rang again. This time it was a husky, sophisticated female voice.

'This is the first time we've spoken, but I have to inform you that Mr Hotta and I have been having a relationship for about a year and a-half.'

So Bogey and I had been playing the same game all this time! But a year-and-a-half? He was in a totally different league from me! I knew he'd had the occasional fling, but I would never have guessed he was going steady.

'I heard about what's been happening from Hotta. Please think over your hasty decision and go back to him. He really loves you. If you leave him now, all my suffering will have been in vain. You see, however hard I tried to make him love me, his heart was always with you. Now he's lost you, he's a complete mess. I can't bear to see him like this. Please, please, reconsider. If you take him back, I will accept defeat gracefully and end my relationship with him.'

I just didn't get it. At a time like this, why did I have to listen to some woman I'd never met calling me up out of the blue and discussing conditions for surrendering Bogey as if he were some kind of spoils of war?

'I think this is a matter that concerns Mr Hotta and myself and no one else,' I said coldly. That changed her tone.

'You have a nerve! A little bitch like you wouldn't be able to live the way you live even if you turned ten tricks a day! Everything you've got is thanks to Mr Hotta! And how do you show your gratitude? By swanning off and screwing the first fancy boy that comes your way!'

There seemed no point in answering.

'Are you listening to me? I'm telling you that if you stop trying to leave Mr Hotta, and if you look after him properly and do the housework, I'm going to give him back to you!'

I quietly hung up. I didn't want to hear any more. We weren't on the same wavelength so communication was impossible.

She was probably a nice person. Judging from her refined voice, I'd have said she was a high-ranking Ginza woman no longer in the first flush of youth. For Bogey's sake, she had swallowed her pride and called the wife of the man she was sleeping with to deliver that sermon. But I'd had enough sermons from glamorous older women.

What these people had was more money than most folk would know what to do with. They had extravagant lifestyles and possessed the assets of beauty and cunning that were needed to acquire all that material wealth. They belonged to the world of money. Bogey lived in that world, but I had thought that he was different. I still believed that once he had been different. But at the end of the day people are like chameleons and they change to fit their environment. You become what you do.

It seemed that I had understood nothing. Believing that Bogey was immune to his surroundings had been my big mistake, and I'd been lost in a fog of ignorance. Now, however, I had finally managed to understand one fundamental truth: My values were different from theirs.

I had thought that as long as Bogey and me hit it off, there was no need to worry about the people around us. That was another big mistake. People aren't that strong. Anyway, I had to get out, even if it meant risking death. Once I was sure that Bogey's lust for revenge was not going to threaten the lives of Kaoru or my former boss, I'd be on my way.

I rang up my mother and told her what had been going on. She wasn't too surprised. I guess she thought that something like this was bound to happen, sooner or later.

While I was waiting to see how events would unfold, Bogey kept calling me up all day long to heap further abuse on me.

'Just think about it, will you? When a guy's thirty-eight or thirty-nine he's in his prime! I spent the best years of my life on you! We're talking about a man's life here! Have you any idea what that means?'

I had never heard this shrill, hysterical voice before. I thought back to the old Bogey – relaxed, mature, suave and kind – and I wept with fear and grief at his terrible transformation.

'I'm a guy who's already ended his life once,' he used to say, modestly implying that his present life was of no consequence. That was in the days when he liked to smother me with tenderness. Now that he was on the attack, he was saying just the opposite – his life was very important and I had messed it up.

I eventually heard that Bogey had spoken to Kaoru and the Arts Cool boss in a calm, controlled manner. He spoke to each separately, calling the boss to the hotel bar and then talking to Kaoru in his hotel room. He told them that he didn't want Kaoru to see me any more, and that he would be obliged to use force if the relationship continued. The threat was quietly but clearly implied.

As the days passed, Bogey gradually regained his composure and switched his approach, trying to persuade me to change my mind. But I had no intention of doing that.

When a woman moves out on a man in movies or plays, she usually takes only the jewellery she's wearing, or she may toss a couple of valuables into her handbag on the way out. Then she walks off down the street, freed of her shackles and looking terribly cool. My departure was a lot less elegant.

During my college years, I'd brought ever more stuff from home to put in Bogey's apartment – prized possessions from childhood, books that had impressed me, photo albums, records, holiday souvenirs, clothes and shoes I'd bought over the years, as well as knick-knacks from the wedding. I couldn't shake my attachment to all this junk, which meant that I wasn't in a position to walk straight out of the apartment.

Strength in adversity is a speciality of women. Despite my misery and weariness, I set about moving out in a surprisingly efficient manner, called a removals company, and was ready for the movers when they arrived.

That morning Bogey came over from the Okura Hotel to observe this last scene of our life together.

'So you're really leaving, eh?'

Despite all the abuse he'd hurled at me, I still couldn't look at him without feeling the pain of separation. A sudden pang sent me into floods. I looked at his face, blurred through my tears.

'There's no other way ... no other way.' That was all I could manage to blurt out in farewell.

'It's a shame it had to end this way.'

Holding back his own tears, Bogey left the room. I continued to weep. A boy from the removals company asked if I was OK. I wiped away my tears with tissue paper and put on sunglasses to conceal my puffy eyes. I was ready to go.

The lazy cats had already settled down for their midday nap. All the females were asleep, but our solitary male, a white Persian called Fana, sensed something amiss, opened his eyes, and followed my progress unblinking as I walked to the door and left.

EIGHT

I went back to my mother's house, but it didn't make me any less sad. I felt terribly lonely sleeping by myself, and every night just lay on my bed and cried. The worst of it was that I still hadn't found anything to do. Whenever I made an effort to think purposefully all I found in my mind was thick fog.

Bogey was just as idle as I was, and he used to call every evening.

'How're you doing, Saya? Know what? Now that you've had a good taste of luxury, you'll never be able to lead an ordinary life. I've left the apartment just as it was, so you can come back any time.'

When I heard him talk in those warm, intimate tones, I was almost ready to forget all the troubles and rush back to him.

Almost, but not quite. Once relations between a man and a woman have broken down, the wounds only become deeper each time they meet. The only way I could see out of my misery was to escape to New York with Kaoru. If I could just get to New York the fog in my head would surely lift. But, alas, I lacked the courage to go there by myself – all I could do was wait for Kaoru to take me.

Bogey moved from the Hotel Okura to the Hilltop Hotel. He chose it because of its reputation as the haunt of the literati. He reckoned that the reason I'd gone off with Kaoru was because he, Bogey, was not engaged in work of a sufficiently cultural nature. So he shut himself away in the hotel and set about the novel he'd always dreamed of writing.

Sequestering an author in a hotel is a practice often used by publishers for their literary superstars. When a hot-selling writer can't finish a manuscript that's dreadfully overdue, the publisher will foot the bill to closet him in a good hotel and keep him from all distractions until the great work is completed. Any young writer would love that kind of treatment, especially in the smart but bohemian Hilltop. Paying for the room yourself isn't quite the same, though.

Bogey didn't physically write the novel but dictated it into a tape recorder. Then he called my mother and asked her to come and listen to it. By this time she'd met him several times and had a good idea of what he was like, so she knew he wouldn't try anything weird. She went to his room as he'd asked.

Bogey was a gentleman and he was kind. The terrifying transformation I'd witnessed was no more than a momentary madness brought on by great anger. I was the cause.

Mother dutifully listened to the tape for two solid hours. Dictating a novel was something Bogey had thought of doing many times. 'I'll sit in a hotel room and speak a masterpiece. Will you type it for me on your word processor, Saya? We'd be like some famous Western novelist and his secretary. Wouldn't that be grand?'

He was a person who thought in images.

'Well,' I'd say, 'in that case, how about the Oriental Hotel in Bangkok? It's famous for its writers. You could wear a white linen suit and I could do the typing on the veranda.'

I had enjoyed sharing his dream. I had been able to enjoy such things once upon a time.

What my mother heard was a novel about me – about how much Bogey loved me. After he'd finished playing the tape he switched off the recorder and said quietly, 'That's how things are. I wish you'd tell Saya to come back to me.'

She told me all this when she got home.

'You shouldn't see him. He's no longer normal. It's a shame – a clever fellow like him going crazy like that. Next time he calls, I'm going to say you're out. And I don't want you answering the telephone any more. It was a very good thing you didn't get legally married – fate played a role, if you ask me.'

But I did not stop seeing Bogey. A woman who has no self-esteem can only get a sense of her own existence when she's wanted. The only way I could maintain any pride was to drape myself in expensive clothing and place it in a luxurious setting next to a wealthy gent who would do me the favour of loving me.

Then there was the fact that we'd been together all those years. Lovers can't become total strangers in a flash. Keeping it secret from my mother, we would still meet for the occasional date. Bogey reckoned that he would succeed in melting my frosty heart this way.

But he was wrong. My feelings only got colder. At one time our relationship had been something of a rarity. I was a young lady with beauty and brains; he was an older gentleman with plenty of easy cash; and I was a slave to love. But now we were just another bubble-era couple of the kind you could find anywhere in Tokyo – a girl-crazy old geezer loaded with money, arm in arm with a flashy young woman who thought she was something special.

Whether the economic bubble was pumping harder than before, or whether I had been detrimental to Bogey's business, I don't know, but the fact is that after we split up his company profits went through the roof. Bogey was now the bubble-gentleman personified: he got bubblier every day.

He made a tremendous effort to look the part, dressing in smart designer threads. He still hoped to win me back, and had even prepared a new love nest for us.

'The apartment in Azabu Juban's got too many unpleasant memories,' he said. 'Let's rent a new place and start afresh. I had a word with the Prof, and he helped me to select a pad in a brand-new, high-tech condominium that I know you're going to love.'

He showed me around the new place. It was a very classy condo in Moto-Azabu, designed for jet-setting foreign businessmen and diplomats.

'You were just a kid, so I never took you out on proper dates.' That was another of his lines. Now he tried to make up for this by taking me for walks in Sannomaru Park and sitting on one of the benches in the sun.

We went to designer boutiques together and he'd actually pick out clothes for me: 'This would look good on you, Saya.'

And when my birthday came around he bought me a big bouquet of roses in an expensive vase.

Bogey was merely running through the time-tested routines used by men to impress women, but there was something about the new-style Bogey that didn't feel right. He carried my bags for me; he went to art cinemas with me; he sat through underground movies from New York. He even accompanied me to galleries of modern art, though I knew he didn't have the slightest interest in doing this. Doubtless he meant well, but it just wasn't him.

The Bogey I knew couldn't understand the merits of a cultured lifestyle or of avant-garde fashions. The real Bogey was a total anachronism – an old-school male chauvinist, an ingrained dandy with enough confidence to rule out making any compromise to 'modern' women. That was what I liked about him. It disgusted me to see him throw away his old character through loneliness and try to remake it to suit my tastes. Somehow this was worse than not being able to see him at all.

He even bought a car. This man, whose charm lay precisely in his lack of the common sense associated with real adults, went out and bought a car – about the most conventional thing you can do. Worse still, it was a top-of-the-line Toyota Crown – an imposing, almost offensively comfortable, symbol of wealth, unaccompanied by an ounce of imagination.

'It's good to have a car,' he said. 'I didn't think I needed stuff like a car or a house, but now I realise that the things most people hanker after really are worth having. Now to save up enough money to build that house by the sea!'

He spoke with such earnestness. Bogey was rapidly becoming just another middle-aged guy in search of security and stability.

In his hotel room, his expensive gold-nib Parker pen lay gathering dust next to a thick pile of unsullied writing paper. These days business was going so well that he had all the free time he needed – yet the first line of the great novel remained unwritten. One day, in a serious tone that heralded more homespun philosophy, he told me the reason.

'You know, Saya, all these years I've been forgetting what the most important thing in life is. Do you know what it is? It's having something to live for. So long as you've got that, money and everything else will follow. That's the truth. And if you haven't got that something, all the money in the world can't prevent you from feeling empty. Right now, Bogey's a happy man. And why? Because I've got that something special. And you know what it is? It's you.'

Bogey's love was getting to be a big drag. It was just too heavy. My heart had already drifted away and I didn't want to be like a child or a pet any more. Pets are cute because they're powerless. And because they're powerless they're pathetic. I'd had enough of being pathetic.

Anyway, a guy who couldn't find anything worth living for on his own was too sad to be with. I told him very clearly that our relationship was over. His eyes filled with tears.

'Poor old me. I wonder why I love you so much, Saya.'

I had left him in spirit, but removing myself physically was not easy. I felt like a butterfly that was suffocating in its cocoon.

But I had no sympathy to spare for Bogey. It was as much as I could do to save myself. I just wanted to be me.

At long last Kaoru came to my rescue and I escaped.

✿

When I got to New York, however, I still lacked any clear objective, so I fell into deeper isolation.

In order to keep me, Kaoru took on more work and was rushed off his feet. He had little time for me and I felt neglected, so because I was lonely I began to nag him. He nagged back, since he was doing his best to earn enough for the two of us. We fought constantly, and I took to screaming at him through my tears like a hysterical banshee.

I was even more depressed than when I'd been in Japan, and resorted to drink and drugs. I'd buy cheap cocaine on the street, snort it at the apartment, and exit reality. The comedown would leave me in a filthy temper, from which the only release was alcohol-induced sleep. Repeating this cycle over and over merely fueled my hysteria, and I was starting to frighten Kaoru. It seemed I could do nothing about the abject state I was in.

I was a junkie for six months. Every night in my dreams I saw Bogey and the cats, every night my pillow was wet from the bitter tears I shed because I had abandoned them. Life with Kaoru was sex and squabbling, and nothing else. Worn out in body and soul, I sent an SOS letter to Bogey.

I didn't feel at home in Kaoru's apartment, with him trying to work and me seething with irritation all the time, so I moved in with a Japanese woman who'd been introduced to me by Minako. In an irresponsible moment I wrote down the telephone number of this friend-of-a-friend in my letter to Bogey.

One day, just before dusk, I got a call from him.

'Saya? I got your letter. I'm in New York. Can you come over?'

Brimming with bliss, I headed for the Plaza Hotel, where he was staying. I was convinced he'd come to New York to see me. In fact he'd brought his new girlfriend with him.

He made me wait in a dark bar at the back of the lobby so his girlfriend wouldn't see me if she happened to pass by.

Silly bitch. I cursed my own stupidity. Bogey wasn't the type to go all the way to New York by himself. Yet I had somehow believed that being invited to his hotel automatically meant that I could join him in his room. *Silly bitch.*

Even so, I couldn't keep the tears from welling up at the sight of him.

'You all right? You're not, are you! I was already on my way to the airport when my secretary called to say that there was a letter from you. So I rushed back to the office to pick it up.'

'What brings you to New York?'

'Just a holiday. Felt like taking a quick look at the town you're living in.'

'Er, are you with that woman who gave me a call once?'

'No, not her. Actually you know this girl. Remember the club I took you to a few times, La Vie en Rose? There was a funny girl working there who called herself Uruka. The one who looked like a man.'

'Ah, the one who was a good singer?'

'Yes.'

Despite everything, I was glad. She was a weird girl who'd keep Bogey from getting bored. I would have been worried if he'd taken up with a more womanly woman, like the one on the telephone. No doubt she'd give Bogey plenty of love and sex and all that, but he'd be bound to tire of her sooner or later. Uruka was a cheerful, open-hearted girl, the kind I could imagine being friends with myself.

'Bogey, have you lost weight?'

'Yes. Been having some trouble with the old appendix. I'm supposed to go to the hospital, actually, but I just couldn't bear being in Japan, so I took some medicine to hold it off and hopped on the plane. A lot of stuff's happened, you know. To be honest, I'm in a bit of a fix right now.'

'A bit of a fix?'

'It's the company. I say, Saya, why don't we go out for sushi? Japanese restaurants in New York are pretty good, I hear. Let's go and talk over some nice sushi.'

I took Bogey to an uptown Japanese restaurant. He sat down, looked me keenly in the eye, and tutted. 'God, you're thin. I bet you haven't eaten any decent food in months. Go on, have some sushi.'

But my tears wouldn't stop and I couldn't get the sushi down. I couldn't tell him that my anorexic condition was caused by co-caine. It wouldn't be fair to make such a dreadful admission after he had suffered so much to free me from my gilded cage and allow my flight to independence.

Right now I was just a junkie and nothing more.

'There's so much I want to say that I don't know where to start.'

'You can start by eating something, young lady.'

Still weeping, I struggled to get some sushi down. Bogey looked on with kindly eyes. Come to think of it, that's how it had always been between us. He had the sort of love that made him delight in giving me tasty things to eat. And my love for him was the sort that eagerly and innocently accepted the banquet.

'Yep,' he said, 'old Bogey's in hot water these days. After you left, the inspectors came to check out the company. As you know, Bogey's business is always a little on the dodgy side, right? Not that I'm the only guy involved in this type of thing. There're plenty of others. But you know how the cops and journalists are – every now and then they like to make an example of someone, *pour encourager les autres*, sort of thing. Well, this time yours truly's the fall guy.'

To tell the truth, the gravity of his remarks hadn't the slightest effect on me. All I knew was that Bogey was with me again. That fact alone occupied me entirely. That old familiar face, the face that had kept me warm all that time.

'Bogey, may I touch your face?'

'All right.'

The touch of Bogey's skin proved too much. The floodgates opened and the tears came in torrents. I clung to him and wept my heart out.

✻

It was the saving of me, that evening in New York when he poured the saké and I poured out my grief. I emerged from it with a single resolution in my ever-irresolute heart.

Having abandoned my beloved Bogey to come to New York in search of a dream, I could not go back to Japan without finding anything – it would mean being knocked all the way down to zero. And once in Japan I'd be too weak to resist all the negative vibes around me. Until I found something meaningful, I was going to stay in New York and live my own life. That's what I decided.

I had been shuttling back and forth between two men, unable to bear the prospect of my own company. But I had known long ago that I was never going to get started that way.

To begin with, I had to have my own apartment. I asked Bogey if he could let me have one of the cats – Fana – for company. Fana, the white Persian male, was terribly snooty and choosy – he loved to be spoiled, but only by Bogey or me. I'd felt a special bond with that cat the moment I'd set eyes on him.

229

'All right. As a matter of fact, Fana can't seem to manage without you. After you left he wouldn't eat properly, so I've had to board him at the pet store all this time. I'm just here for the New Year, and I'll be going back on the third of January. So come and collect him on the fourth or thereabouts.'

'Thank you, Bogey.'

'That's the first time you've ever thanked me, Saya.'

'I guess you're right. But thank you anyway – really!'

'Oh, stop saying that, Saya. It's not you. More to the point, what are you going to do in New York?'

'I don't know yet. I just want to live as an ordinary person to start with. Then I can look for something I really want to do.'

Bogey looked at me with eyes that said, *What is she going on about, the dear silly thing*?

'Until I'm clear about who I am, I don't think I can go back to Japan. I can't wear the "student" or the "housewife" label any more. I'd rot away if I went back. Until I've found something, I'm not planning on going back.'

I wanted to make a fresh start and live normally. In that alone I was deadly serious. Never mind all that stuff about 'purifying the soul' – I simply wanted to start again.

'Got enough to live on?'

'Yeah, I have some savings.'

Bogey gave a slightly cynical laugh. He wouldn't believe it, but while I was with him, I'd been saving a little money. Sometimes he'd give me quite a hefty sum as a 'fine' for another infidelity, or as compensation for leaving me alone while he went off gambling. I was supposed to blow all that money on expensive clothes, but there was a limit. Whenever I had some cash left over, I'd put it by, little by little, just as my mother had advised me to do.

'How much will it cost to rent an apartment?'

'About 500,000 yen.'

'There you go.'

From his wallet Bogey extracted a thick, chocolate-bar-sized wad of ten-thousand-yen notes and quickly counted out fifty. I tried to refuse. 'It's all right Bogey. I've got my own stash.'

'Go on, take it. A little farewell present from Bogey. You want to quit hanging around with that guy right now and get a place of your own.'

'Is it really OK, Bogey?'

'Yes, yes, take it. It's only cash, after all. I'm going to Vegas and I'll make ten times that.'

'Vegas?'

'Yes. After New York, it's LA and then on to Las Vegas. I'm going to have a little flutter.'

Still the same old Bogey. I felt relieved. I gratefully accepted the donation and promptly used it to rent an apartment.

✩

There was a tempestuous parting from Kaoru, and I briefly dashed over to Japan while rushing around arranging the move. Bogey had again switched hotels and was now staying at the ANA Hotel in Tameike.

Back in Japan after all this time. As I headed for the hotel, the cab radio was announcing the death of Emperor Hirohito. That afternoon, the government proclaimed the end of Hirohito's Showa era and the start of the new imperial reign, the Heisei era.

Shocked at my skeletal frame, Bogey insisted on taking me to fancy restaurants and made me eat globefish and other delicacies. 'Must feed the girl,' he said, as if talking about one of his cats.

I went back to my mother's house and cooked some dishes that used to be Bogey's favourites in the old days. I put them in Tupperware containers and took them to his hotel.

'It's not fresh from the stove so it won't taste all that good, but eat it anyway, OK?'

We also went to Brown's, our old haunt where we used to drink away many a night.

We were the best of friends, Bogey and I, but, as we both knew, that didn't mean we could ever live together again.

I later learned that Bogey was already in debt at this time. I have no doubt that he was dying to get his hands on my nest egg, but he refrained from asking for it through sympathy for my pathetic situation. He never said a word about being short of cash.

Six months of cocaine abuse had left my body in a mess, and on top of that I'd developed pelvic peritonitis. The IUD that had saved me from pregnancy for so many years was to blame. Bogey took me to a posh back-street gynaecological clinic, a stylish place frequented by upper-class ladies, and I had the coil removed.

I couldn't tell the doctor about my cocaine habit, but the anaesthetic hardly had any effect. I proved a very awkward patient as I had to be held down by four nurses, which left me with bruises on all my limbs.

'You seem to have developed considerable narcotic resistance,' said the doctor. 'If you'd told us, I'd have given you a stronger anaesthetic.'

I took the pain as punishment for my sins, gritted my teeth, and saw the operation through.

Now that I'd got rid of the coil, I had no intention of having sex with anybody. I wasn't going to be a slave to lust any more.

I picked up Fana from the pet store and Bogey took me to the airport. There he handed me an envelope containing another fifty of those ten-thousand-yen notes.

'Get yourself some furniture and things with this, OK? You'll feel lonely and you won't be able to get anything done if you don't have the basic necessities. If you get into trouble, just give Bogey a call. Wherever I am I'll make sure you can always reach me. All I ask is that you do the same, OK? Wherever you go, make sure you tell old Bogey your address and phone number.'

'Sure. As soon as I get a telephone, I'll give you the number. Thanks for everything, Bogey.'

'Stop saying all that thank-you stuff. What are we, strangers?'

Bogey didn't want my gratitude. He wanted me to accept his kindness as a matter of course. That was how I had behaved when we were together – it was an unspoken understanding between us.

When we parted at Narita Airport, Bogey murmured one last thought in my ear.

'If only you and I had been about the same age, we could have had lots of fun, don't you think?'

'Yeah.'

Absolutely. It was so true. I wanted to say that, but the words wouldn't come.

✳

Back in New York, I was at first consumed by loneliness in my unaccustomed solitary lifestyle. Every night I would drink myself half to death and make pathetic calls to Bogey.

'I want to go back to Japan and be looked after by my Bogey,' I sobbed into the phone.

'I'm afraid it wouldn't do, Saya, not the way things are right now. I don't want to get you mixed up in my affairs. There's no need for you to see the dirty side of things. People shouldn't suffer unnecessarily. For the time being you're better off in New York.'

Apparently Bogey was being investigated by the police, and the media instinctively rallied behind the celebrity in the case. Lulu Kitano was portrayed as a victim of Bogey's deceptions, an innocent who had let her good name be abused by this smooth operator. To think that when she arrived back in Japan she'd only had one thousand yen in her pocket and had depended on Bogey for everything, down to the last hairpin.

'I still feel almost one hundred per cent certain I'm going to be OK,' said Bogey, with his characteristic gambler's optimism, 'but the only trouble is that, as the boss, I might be held responsible for what my staff did. They could put me away for a few years. For now you'd better get on with your life, as if Bogey didn't exist.'

'Are you OK, Bogey?'

'Sure I'm OK. I'm tough, you know that. And besides, you get it easy in prison if it's white-collar crime. They just put you in charge of the library. I'll be far from the madding crowd. I'll be able to write that novel at last.'

Now, even Bogey was deserting me, and I was all alone in the world. Worse still, he was on the verge of being put behind bars, and all I could do was hide away in New York and fear for him. Prison = Scary. That was the limit of my thinking about the subject.

Paralysis of the mind. I was totally exhausted. In fact the events of the past year had been too heavy for someone like me. On reflection, everything had been my fault. I wanted to kill myself and make an end of it. But when I thought of that dark and silent future, I realised that even dying was beyond me.

So long as I was alive, my days of tearful loneliness, insecurity and guilt over abandoning Bogey were interrupted by the occasional growling of an empty stomach and the need to go to the toilet. I despised myself for these physical signs of good health.

I might be able to manage some noodles.

Still weeping, I'd boil some up and eat them.

Mmm, tasty.

Even in my deepest depression I noticed how good the noodles tasted. And that made me burst into tears again.

As my eyes were all puffy from weeping, I'd put on sunglasses to go shopping for the cat and myself. Outdoors was the freezing New York winter, and indoors there was no one to keep me warm, no one to snuggle up to.

I'd buy cat litter and cat food, fruit and mineral water, and a six-pack of beer to help me sleep. All this weighed a ton, and I'd struggle home with the handles of the supermarket shopping bags cutting into my frozen fingers.

I'd trudge through the snow, shopping bags dangling from both hands, bundled up in thick clothes, hair all over the place, nose dribbling. But however suffused with tragic sadness I might feel, I looked just like any other New York bag lady shuffling along.

When spring gradually approached and the weather improved, my outlook also brightened. Increasingly often I found I could leave the house without sunglasses. As my spirits rose, I started to realise that although I was living alone in this city I was gaining acquaintances at the rate of about one per day. The janitor at the apartment building; the old lady in the apartment next to mine; the Korean family that ran the deli on the corner; the kids about my age I met in the park or at the coin laundry. Whenever I caught someone's eye they'd smile at me.

And they'd talk to me. About how nice the weather was, or that tasty whatever-it-was they had for lunch, or this or that thing that happened to them and what they thought about it. What they felt, what they thought, what their opinion was. They'd tell you straight and at length, even if you didn't especially want to know. In Tokyo I'd only ever been able to talk that freely with Bogey.

New Yorkers were so open! Whether they were genuinely interested in people, or whether they happened to remember my face because I lived in the neighborhood, whatever the reason, they noticed me.

'Hi, got over that cold you had?'

'Yes, thank you. I'm a little better.'

I'd respond to their greetings in my broken English and give an embarrassed laugh.

'That's the spirit! Keep smiling!'

They were only simple fragments of conversation, but they warmed me to the bottom of my heart.

'That's a nice jacket you've got on today!'

'Hey, you're looking better than yesterday!'

I was a nobody, but they still paid due attention to me as a fellow human being. All I did was eat, sleep and stay alive, yet I didn't feel, as I used to in Japan, that the world was leaving me behind.

✣

Right then, what am I going to do for a living?

It was May, and by the time I was ready to start thinking about this, the whole of New York had revived with the warm weather. I was twenty-four years old.

Once I was settled enough to sit down and ask myself about my hopes for the future, it dawned on me that all I wanted to do was make clothes. It had been my childhood dream, and I'd abandoned it for the sake of my mother. Come to think of it, that was where everything had started to go wrong for me. I'd gone to a good university to please my mother, and I'd entered the literature department because it was the respectable thing to do. I'd done all that simply because I wanted my mother's approval and love.

But living for somebody else had been my big mistake. Later on, all I'd been able to do was change what I was seeking – from the love and approval of my mother to the love and approval of a man who became a father figure. All that had changed was the identity of the person feeding me. Once I'd focused on my new object of dependency, I'd proceeded to remake myself in an image designed to please him. This clumsy survival technique was all I'd had.

I now set my sights on entering FIT – the Fashion Institute of Technology – a design college on Seventh Avenue. I knew I needed much more English to get in, so I started by enrolling at a language school and making a few simple garments at home. Pushing this project forward felt like the best way of getting my act together.

As I slowly progressed, I started to tire of the gloomy calls that would occasionally come from Bogey.

'Ken-ken betrayed me. He was getting into some heavy stuff behind my back – real fraud, you know – and he told the cops he'd been doing it on orders from the boss – me.'

As his voice kept whining away, it felt as if cold water were being poured over my modest attempts to sort out my life. But there was nothing I could do to help him. Theoretically I could go back to Tokyo and make as much money as I could out of hostessing or prostitution to support Bogey. But I wasn't that strong.

You couldn't meet Bogey's financial requirements with any respectable profession. The sums of money involved were on a totally different scale. Besides, if I were to keep Bogey the way he used to keep me, his male chauvinist pride would be injured. Anyway, I refused to do what I didn't feel like doing out of a sense of duty. I could see how it would end – I'd mess up my life and eventually mess up his, too. This much I had learned from my experiences of the last few years.

Finally, afraid of receiving more calls, I disconnected the telephone. I felt guilty enough about running away from Bogey without having him rub it in. Having him guilt-tripping on me would do him no good. I wasn't going to throw away my life and prospects just for love.

With all my expenses of rent, English lessons and buying dressmaking stuff, I had just about exhausted my secret savings. If I got into FIT, I was going to have to come up with more money. I resolved to try and get my mother to make a contribution by proposing it as a career investment.

I wrote a forceful begging letter, then flew to Japan during the Obon holidays in August to see her and collect the cash. I had no intention of meeting Bogey while I was there. If I did, I knew he'd play on my sympathy and I'd end up being distracted from my real purpose.

Since Bogey couldn't get through to me in New York any more, he'd taken to calling my mother. Once I picked up the receiver and it was him. He sounded remarkably cross considering he was asking for a date.

'I'm at the Café La Mille in Roppongi. Come over right away. And don't stand me up. Got it?'

There was another reason why I didn't want to see Bogey. My personal renewal project in New York had involved putting on some weight – twenty-two pounds, in fact. I'd taken to scoffing giant hamburgers and striding down the street with my mouth full. I'd kicked cocaine and given up my previous diet, and I'd got fat, just like that.

My hair was a mess as well, because these days I was cutting it myself, and since I was too chubby to get into my smart clothes I'd resorted to wearing jeans and a T-shirt. I was bulging out all over and bore no resemblance to my former elegant self – but it didn't bother me one bit. The girl in me had disappeared when I left Bogey. I was now in much better shape: I looked healthier and my body was stronger. Bogey was the one person in the world to whom I did not want to show the present me. I'd much rather he remembered me as I'd been at our last meeting – a pretty, pitiful waif.

Still, I made one last effort to present myself in a way Bogey approved of, just to try and stop him getting angry with me. I put on my striped linen summer dress, the only dress I could still get into. It used to be loose, but now it was a snug fit. I also parted my hair on one side to look a little more like the refined miss of bygone days. It didn't work.

It had been six months since I'd dressed to please another person. Sure enough, Bogey was angry.

'God, you're fat! Just look at you! How did you get like this? Food? Booze?' His attitude was one of total contempt.

I knew this was how it would turn out. Bogey often said he knew me better than anyone else, but the person he knew was just a fantasy of his own creation. He knew a teenage girl who was slim, delicate, fragile, and so weak that she was unable to survive without his protection; a girl who would satisfy his desire to possess another human being completely. Despite all the time we'd been apart he still hadn't lost that sense of ownership.

I went straight into a sulk. I hadn't wanted to see him, anyway. What gave him the right to order me over and then get mad at me? It was my body, so why couldn't I get as fat as I pleased?

Keeping these thoughts to myself, I sat there in stony silence.

'When did you get back?'

'Day before yesterday.'

'Why didn't you call me?'

I didn't feel like explaining. Whatever I said would just be a waste of breath.

The next thing Bogey came out with was: 'So it was the money, just as I thought.'

'Eh?'

'Just as I thought – you decided to hang out with me for the money.'

'What do you mean?'

My jaw fell. Once he started talking like that, he was going to spoil everything we'd ever had.

To be fair, there were two possible responses to this accusation.

I could deny it, or I could admit it. After all, a Bogey without money was not a true Bogey. A Bogey in cheap, shabby clothes wasn't a real Bogey. Even he knew that.

A big, expansive guy, far too big-hearted to get by in ordinary society; a guy who loved to play and to love, that was Bogey.

Between us we'd spent money like water and had a really good time. Only a young thing like me could indulge his whims without a second thought and make him feel good. Bogey wanted to make piles of money and then enjoy blowing it in the company of a woman with whom he could feel relaxed and intimate, a woman who could be a friend as well as a lover.

Between Bogey and me, money was the essential bond, just as children are the essential bond between many couples. The two key phrases of our life together were 'Got any cash?' and 'Have you eaten?'

I took that to be love. If it was really just a matter of cozying up to a guy for his money then our special relationship might as well never have existed.

I maintained my sullen silence until Bogey said, 'Shall we go then?'

As we emerged on the tree-lined avenue, he abruptly pulled me behind one of the trees, grabbed me by my collar, hauled me up on tiptoe, and demanded money.

'If you'd rushed over to see me I'd have let you go without any trouble. But you've got the wrong attitude, young lady! If you want to leave me, give me back my million yen! That's my price for letting you go!'

Bogey pressed a slip of paper into my hand with his bank account number scribbled on it. Then, aware of passers-by looking at us, he turned on his heel and strode away.

I went home and asked my mother what I should do. I had nowhere near a million yen. Hardly had I started explaining the situation, though, when the telephone rang. It was Bogey – same story, this time with more explanations and more shouting.

'You may think that the money I spent on you was nothing compared with the tens of millions I was blowing on gambling and Lulu and all that, but you can't ignore the two bundles of five hundred thousand I gave you at the end! That money came straight from the heart, you know! It meant something to me!'

I wondered what had happened to Bogey's famous principle that 'money's only money'. Apparently it had gone out of the window.

'But Bogey, I've already spent it. I haven't got a million yen!'

'Too bad! It's your own stupid fault! Get the fucking money any way you can – sell your body if you have to! You've got one week to send a million yen to my bank! Give me back my million yen and I won't contact you again!'

After he hung up I stood with the receiver in my hand, speechless. My mother broke the silence. Bogey had been shouting so loudly that she'd heard the entire conversation.

'OK. Let me have Bogey's account number.'

'Mother…'

'When children get into trouble, mothers clear up the mess. It's only natural. And one more thing – no answering the telephone any more, OK?'

My mother and I went to the bank and sent the money to Bogey.

'Still, he must be in quite a fix to act like that. Who'd believe it, a nice man like him coming to this?'

That night my mother got drunk for the first time in years and told me many things.

'It's better if you stay away from Japan for a while. If you're really serious about it, you should go to that dressmaking school in New York. I'll take care of the fees. I've been thinking about things, and I reckon maybe I should have given you more freedom to do what you wanted when you were a kid. Well, now you're an adult you should do what you like for a change.'

'Do you really mean that, Ma?'

'I hate to admit it, but yes. After all that trouble you went through, I realised that I was partly to blame. Anyone who's got a nice kid wants to keep her close by, and having you around makes me feel good. Whatever I do, you never get angry, and you'll always lend a hand with whatever I'm doing. But however sweet you are, no one should tie you down.'

I said nothing.

'You think you're like me, but actually you're just like your dad. Kind, weak, and a sly old lazybones. I don't bear your dad any grudge, you know. Long ago I loved him. But life … life is so long … it made him dull and sucked all the colour out of him. We grew distant, and when that other woman came along, I guess he didn't have the strength to turn her away.'

Mother's eyes were looking right through me, at some distant image of my father. It suddenly occurred to me that maybe the reason she carried on living in this shabby old house, when she could surely afford somewhere better, was because she was still waiting for Dad to come home.

That thought gave me a deep sense of relief. Half the blood in me, the half I thought mother hated, was loved, after all. Come to think of it, I'd always hated myself. And if you can't love yourself, you're not qualified to love somebody else.

'Anyway, it doesn't matter any more. If dressmaking in New York's what you want to do, you must do it.'

She moved to the fireproof safe in the corner of the room and took out a bank deposit book.

'Here, take this.'

The deposit book had my name on it.

'I was saving up for your wedding. But then you went and had that weird wedding that he paid for. I can't see you having a proper wedding any time soon – you'll be married to your work. So I might as well give you the money now. From now on live the way you want to live. Don't worry about me. I'll want you back to bury me, but that won't be for a good many years yet. Just one thing – whatever you do, do it properly, OK?'

✻

In the autumn of that year I entered the design school. When I returned to Japan for the summer vacation the following year, I got a call from Reiko.

'So they finally got Bogey.'

'What?'

'Haven't you heard? It was in all the newspapers. "UNLI-CENCED INVESTMENT CONSULTANCY DEFRAUDED BILLIONS OF YEN IN STOCKS." I'm a housewife, you know, and I read the papers every day. Lulu Kitano got arrested, too, in a separate incident – marijuana possession. Your old friends are in a big mess. I've kept the clippings. I'll send them.'

When the clippings arrived, the first thing I saw was a pair of mug shots: Bogey and Ken-ken.

I felt my chest constrict. Bogey was such a good man, yet the photo made him look like some vile criminal, the way such photos do. No doubt he'd not been in the best of moods when the police photographer clicked the shutter. I could easily picture the scene – sad, but also sort of funny. Bogey had always hated the police.

I showed the clippings to my mother.

'Ma, you've been in Japan all this time. Did you know about this?'

She didn't answer.

'So you knew.'

'As a matter of fact, some detectives came here while you were in New York. I didn't see any need for you to know, but now you do, so that's that.'

'What did they want?'

'They wanted to know if Bogey had passed any money on to you. Funny, eh? A man who's desperate enough to put the squeeze on us for a million yen is hardly likely to have pots of money tucked away.'

Mother was right about that. A guy like Bogey might have plenty of hidden debts, but no way would he have any hidden assets. Bogey always used up all the money he had – he wasn't into saving.

'They asked me "Where did your daughter get the money to go to New York?" I told them the truth – it was money I earned fair and square by working hard for years and years. I told them straight.'

'It's the truth.'

Poor old ma. She hated getting mixed up with the police, yet she'd had to submit to being questioned. And to add insult to injury, the police had even suspected that the money she'd saved up over the years to pay for her daughter's wedding had been obtained by fraud. It occurred to me that I had not been the best of daughters.

'Oh mother, I'm so sorry.'

'Never mind. What's all this apologising? Give me a break.'

'I guess you're right. It's too late for apologies.'

'It certainly is,' she laughed.

Concerned about Bogey, I rang up the girl who used to be his secretary. She'd quit the company long ago and was busy raising a family.

'The police came to our house, too,' she said. 'Because I used to work for the company, they spent eight hours trying to squeeze information out of me. They also asked a lot of questions about you. "You're a friend of hers, right? Where did she get the money to go to New York?" That kind of thing. I told them the truth – you'd told me you saved up the money while living with him.'

'You told the police that I used money I'd saved?'

'Yeah. They were very disappointed.'

'It's not the big money they were looking for, eh?'

Yes, I'd saved a little nest egg while I was with Bogey. That, and the minuscule amount I'd earned, had helped me get to New York. But that money was soon spent – it was easy come, easy go. These days I was a poor, honest student, using money from my mother to pay for my tuition at the design school, and supplementing it with part-time work at a Japanese restaurant in the East Village. Rent was a burden, so I'd taken in a roommate.

'But I'll tell you something,' the former secretary continued. 'The boss showed pretty poor taste, or – how can I put it? – lack of judgment in the last few months before the police came for him. It was outrageous, really.'

'What was?'

She explained that as Bogey had sank deeper into trouble, his sexual conduct had got steadily worse. He'd propositioned every girl he met in bars, and he couldn't keep his hands off his employees. He'd even gone after the girl in the accounts department – the one he used to say was so ugly that when she went into a house you'd have to close the doors of the Buddhist altar to avoid offending the gods.

As well as trying to bed every woman he'd met, Bogey had also borrowed money from anyone who could be persuaded to lend, and, of course, he'd never paid any of it back. Now everyone was angry with him, but I alone understood him. He wasn't a deliberate fraudster, far from it. I am quite sure that right up to the last he really thought he was going to repay all the money he borrowed –

and pay it back ten times over. And as for the women, I'm equally sure he felt genuine, sincere affection for each and every one of them, at least for as long as he was in bed with them.

'He must have been frightened when he realised they were going to put him inside.'

'Who wouldn't be,' said the secretary.

'But whatever happens, you can't hate the guy.'

'Yeah, you're right there.'

Yes, indeed. Whatever happened, the one certain thing you could say about Bogey was that he was not a bad person.

✡

While I was in Tokyo I got a letter from Bogey, written from his cell at the Tokyo Detention House. The letter bore the official seal of the police censor and had been forwarded to me by Uruka, who was acting as Bogey's legal representative while he was in jail. According to the former secretary, Uruka was really generous: she'd abandoned her dreams of a singing career and had devoted herself to nightclub work to make the money she'd need to support Bogey.

It comforted me to know that Bogey was not alone in the world - he was not someone who could survive on his own. And so long as Uruka was looking after him, there would be no need to worry.

The thought that if I'd been as strong as Uruka I could have carried on loving Bogey did not bother me. Like everyone else, I could only be myself. And so long as there was always one person around who could endure being with Bogey, that was fine.

The letter read as follows:

I am ashamed of myself for parting from you in such an awful manner. But I had to make you hate me. In the end, the only thing I could do for you was to cut the tie that bound us. I hope we will meet again in happier circumstances.

'Silly old Bogey,' I said to myself. 'Still living in his own world.'

I don't hate Bogey. Yes, he abused me very badly at times. Yes, our relationship had come down with a crash. But the tears he shed for me, and I for him, were real. They still are. Always will be.

Three years previously, Bogey and I had celebrated our wedding at Nogi Shrine. We were man and wife after that, and I believe we still are today, in a spiritual sense. But in the material world, a marriage such as ours could never survive.

Once a man and woman have parted, they can never 'meet again in happier circumstances'. Meeting an old flame is uncomfortable, because reality gets shoved in your face and the dreams inside you get smashed to little pieces.

The girl I once was – in the days when I was in love with Bogey – was so young, so innocent and so beautiful that she was able to exist in a fantasy world. For a while I really wanted to become Bogey's fantasy. I guess I'll take that feeling and quietly lock it away deep inside my heart.